It's been six weeks since Halloween. Six weeks since Grace stumbled into the ER, almost dead and begging for help. Six weeks since she lost every single memory, including her own name.

Taken in by the mysterious Sisters of the Order of Saint Raphael the Healer, Grace's wounds are dressed and she is assured her memories will return—in time. But does Grace want her memories back? Maybe she's chosen to forget them, maybe there's a reason. The sisters hide things from her. They whisper things about her.

When a demon forces its way into the convent, it declares that Grace is a demon too. Grace demands answers. Answers that may reveal not only who she is, but that the sisters might not be who they say they are, either.

GIVE ME GRACE

Bethany A. Perry

A NineStar Press Publication
www.ninestarpress.com

Give Me Grace

Printed in the USA

ISBN: 978-1-64890-290-1

First Edition, May, 2021

Also available in eBook, ISBN: 978-1-64890-289-5

WARNING:
This book contains sexually explicit content, which may only be suitable for mature readers. Depictions of alcoholism, blood (gore), body horror, child endangerment, child harm, infant death (off-page), death, graphic sex, guns, homophobia (off-page), murder, needles, suicidal images, and violence.

To my fellow screams looking for a mouth (Thanks for that one, Mark).

Prologue

In the Beginning

"Happy Halloween, James, and welcome to the ER's longest night of the year." Anna sat, file in her pale hand, and lowered the medical mask from her mouth. "We halfway yet?"

The resident sat next to her and leaned on the desk. "No."

She groaned.

"Almost." His own mask, a special one for tonight, emblazoned with cartoonish vampire fangs, stretched under his chin. Dark brown cheeks shining, he grinned. "Almost, Doc."

She flopped the file on the desk. "Next up. More Halloween hijinks. Something happened at a party, but it took three nurses to get it out of them." Opening the file, she slid it across the desk to him.

James chuckled. "College students?"

She laughed with him. "You remember those days, don't—"

"Doctor! I need a doctor!"

Anna shot to her feet, adrenaline spiking her blood pressure. Her head swam, but she centered herself and rounded the desk.

The shout echoed up the hall from the ambulance entrance, where the door opened onto the crisp October night and a pallid woman standing there, gripping her own intestines in her palm. She swayed, sunken eyes staring through Anna like she didn't exist.

Other hand pressed against a gaping wound on her head, the skin of her face bubbling with some kind of chemical burn, the woman called again as if she stood alone in the hall. "I need a doctor!"

She collapsed into the floor, her intestines slapping the tile like raw sausage. The sound was not unlike the peculiar sound of smacking your hand against a wet rock, but more visceral.

Barking orders at James and at the four nurses standing gape-jawed in the hallway, Anna rushed toward the woman bleeding on the floor. For a second, she disassociated from her own head. Half of her thought this woman could be dying right here, right now, and the other half insisted it was a particularly gruesome and well-applied costume.

As she dropped down next to the woman, the stench of burned matches threatened to overtake her. But she had more important things to do than wonder where it came from.

On her knees in a growing pool of blood—very real, this blood—she assessed the woman. Her heart beat strong, strong enough to cause visible movement in her throat with each thump. Still, Anna put two fingers over the carotid and let the *beat-beat-beat* help center her. This woman needed surgery, immediately, to get her intestines back where they belonged and close the gaping hole in her midsection. How she'd even survived such a gutting was almost beyond Anna's comprehension.

A piece of the woman's scalp had been ripped away but hadn't torn completely. They would stitch it down later. And though the chemical burn also stank of matches, it wouldn't kill her. First priority was the intestines.

The heart *beat-beat-beat* under her fingers.

THE CONVENT

Chapter One

Grace knelt on the kneeling bar, whatever it was the sisters called it, and folded her hands together behind the pew in front of her. She dropped her voice to a whisper. "Sister Monica."

The novice nun kneeling beside her shook her head a millimeter, her curls almost bursting through her headscarf, and clenched her hands tighter. Her lips moved over a prayer, her eyes squinched closed.

Grace grinned and scooted closer. She did close her eyes, though, making a clumsy sign of the cross over her shoulders. An approximation, at least. Her inability to get it right exasperated the sisters on a damn near hilarious level. "Are we doing your coming-of-age ceremony today?"

Monica's lips stopped moving, and she pressed them together. They didn't disappear into nothingness the way the mother made hers do, but by the time Mon Mother Mary's age, she'd be able to do it better. She leaned, her umber skin mellow in the low light of the sanctuary, and whispered so quiet Grace had to listen with all she had to catch it. "Either shut up and pray or leave and meet me in your room."

Grace swallowed, the blood rushing to her cheeks. "Sorry, Mon. I didn't mean to upset you. I just wanted to take communion with you, if you were going to take your vows."

Mouth dropping open, Monica turned to her. "Why would you want to do that?" Her voice echoed off the vaulted ceiling, the walls, and the windows, including the lone stained-glass window in the sanctuary.

One of the other sisters, Eliana probably, shushed. The shush was so sharp it may have cut the air as it sped across the cavernous room.

Monica stood, stuffing her rosary under her robes, and grabbed Grace above the elbow. She tugged, not unkindly.

Grace held her abs with one hand and stood. The twinge as she did brought back her first memory with force. The *splat-splat-splat* of her own intestines as they hit the floor of the hospital emergency room. Everything before that moment, including how she'd been gutted, was a deep well of nothing.

Her next memory, which was much nicer, was of Monica, sitting next to her hospital bed and assuring her that her full memory would return in time.

As the sanctuary doors closed, the chilly hallway enveloped them. The morning sun hadn't had a chance to penetrate it yet, and the walls radiated last night's cold.

Grace shivered and shook her head to clear it of the slapping sound her guts had made when they hit the tile. For all the good it'd do. "Sorry. I thought you were going to get your habit today and stuff. Take your vows. All that."

Monica shook her head with a frown. "Mother Mary told me I'm not ready yet. I guess I have more study to do." Still walking, she looked Grace up and down. "How're your wounds?"

"Healing."

"You're a fast healer."

"Only because you help me." She rubbed the scar below her stomach. "Glad we finally got the bandages off. How long have I been here again?"

"The Order took you in from the hospital about"—she drew out the *u*, squeezing her eyes closed—"six weeks ago?"

"Weird. I feel like I've known you a lot longer than that."

They turned a corner, bright sun flooding the next hallway—Grace's favorite hallway—dust motes dancing along the shafts, and stopped before the only other stained-glass window in the place.

Raphael the Archangel stood outlined in pinks and blues, gold shining all around his head and shoulders, what the sisters called his halo. His glowing hands rested on the heads of two penitents who knelt before him, their eyes bleeding.

Monica smiled. "The feeling's mutual." Cheeks tinged red, she crossed herself, curtsied to Raphael, and continued down the hall.

Grace cast a glance at the window. Raphael's face wore an out-of-place expression of serenity while blessing two people who cried tears of blood. Despite the eyes, she found peace in the scene.

She caught up to Monica, running her hand through the two inches of hair on her head, the healing scar a line slashed through it. "That library is the darkest room in this convent. You'd think they'd want windows so you could actually see the words in the books."

"The books are old, Grace. They'd react badly to sunlight. We've had this conversation." She stopped, one hand on an enormous door handle. "Did you want to keep me company today?"

"I was serious about the communion, Mon." Grace bit her lip. Six weeks' worth of changing bandages and chatting and following her around the convent made Grace feel close to Sister Monica. Like a real friend. This ceremony was a Big Deal to Mon, and Mon was a Big Deal to Grace. It only seemed right to do it with her, even if she wasn't Catholic.

Monica eased the creaking door open. "I'll speak to Mother Mary." With the hand not holding the door, she brushed her fingertips along Grace's cheek.

Grace's heart tripped a beat. Something about the way her fingers moved like butterfly feet made Grace lose her breath.

"Thank you. You're a good friend. I hope you're still here when I take my vows."

Brows knit, Grace peeked into the library. She lowered her voice. "Where would I go? I don't even remember who I am, much less where home is."

Monica shrugged, her robes shifting with a soft sigh. "If your memory comes back, you'll probably want to leave." She sucked a sharp breath over her teeth. "Not that I don't want you to get your memory back. I just meant—"

"I know. I hope I'm still here too." Grace smiled, lips stretched tight. "If I remember who I am before then, I'll come back just to share your communion. Okay?"

Frowning, Monica lowered her eyes. "I'd like that."

*

"Sister Alexandra," Grace said, leaning into Sister Maria, "my ass might be skinny, but you're gonna have to give me some room."

Squeezing into the bench seat next to her, Alexandra cut her eyes at Grace, deep frown lines going even deeper in the pink skin next to her mouth. "I will thank you not to curse. And I will thank you not to insult my weight."

Cheeks burning, Grace apologized in a small voice. "That's not what I meant, Sister." Suddenly the back of this van had become an inferno.

"Grace," Mother Mary called from the front passenger seat, "have you buckled your seat belt?" She glared over her shoulder, her stern profile outlined in the late-morning sun.

Mary might not have been the eldest, but she was definitely the least fun.

Sandwiched between the sisters, Grace tried to shift. "I'm pretty wedged in, here. I don't think—"

"This van is not leaving the driveway until everyone has buckled their seat belt."

With a sigh, Grace leaned toward Maria. "*Dame el cinturón de seguridad, por favor.*"

Maria nodded. "Yes, you may have the seat belt. Your Spanish is coming along." She pulled the belt free and held it out.

Grace took it and worked to fasten it, leaning her face almost directly into Maria's breasts. "*Gracias,* Sister. You're a good teacher."

"*Bueno.* It was my first language, so I should hope so."

As Monica started the van and put it in gear, Grace tried to inhale. Stuck in the hot backseat, surrounded by the sisters in their robes, she couldn't get a full breath. And like always, everything slid a bit sideways. She just didn't know why.

She fidgeted. "Maria, why aren't you teaching me Latin instead of Spanish? Don't you guys use Latin during Mass and stuff?"

Maria lowered her voice and shrugged, moving Grace's shoulder up and down. "Mother Mary wanted you to learn Spanish. I'm sure she has her reasons."

Grace's stomach shifted as they rounded a corner. On the tip of her tongue sat a question about her amnesia. Like maybe she'd forgotten who she was on purpose, and maybe her life had been so awful she preferred forgetting the whole thing ever happened to living it.

A headache began in the middle of her forehead.

She squeezed her eyes closed, her fingers massaging the spot where an icepick had suddenly sunk handle-deep.

Sister Alexandra cleared her throat. "Grace, what's wrong?"

The van slowed.

Grace opened her eyes and looked at the rearview mirror.

Monica watched her in it, her brow knitted.

"I'm fine," she said, struggling to lift her mouth in a smile. "Just a little headache."

"We're here," Mother Mary said. "Sister Monica, please park in the rear."

The van rolled to a halt. As Monica cut the engine, Maria leaned across Grace and unclipped her seat belt. "Come on, Gracie. Let's get you some air."

Eyes still closed, Grace held her head as Maria helped her from the van. Instead of thinking about her wobbly stomach, she worried whatever caused her to lose her memory had returned to explode her brain from the inside out.

Monica ducked under Grace's arm and clucked her tongue. "Maybe you shouldn't have come."

"Nonsense, Sister Monica," Mother Mary said, her voice no more than six inches away from Grace's face. "You're fine, aren't you, Grace?"

The mother's tone invited nothing but agreeableness. A nice way to say you couldn't say no to her.

Grace nodded, willing her legs to stop shaking. Was this what they called a migraine? Had she gotten those before she ended up at Saint Raphael's? She struggled to open her eyes.

Mother Mary smiled at her, the sun behind her head, framing it. Almost like Raphael in the stained glass. "Just some shopping today. You need things, as do some of us. We can make it through this"—she turned, eyes on the building they'd parked outside—"this mall. Can't we, girls?"

The nuns, most of whom hadn't been girls in decades, agreed.

Sister Joan, reddened cheeks shining, stepped up on her other side. "In a previous life, Mother, I was pretty fond of malls."

"Good. Can you hand me those sunglasses I asked you to get?"

Joan dug into an enormous bag slung over her shoulder. Things inside clanked and bumped. The fact she pulled out an intact pair of sunglasses something of a miracle, she laid them in Mother Mary's outstretched palm.

"Here you are, Grace." Mother Mary's hand glowed in the sun as she slid a pair of large plastic-bodied glasses over Grace's eyes. Her warm fingers swept across Grace's forehead, pausing over the center.

The glasses dark enough to block some sunlight, the headache tried to dissipate. Grace swallowed, gulping cool breaths down her throat. "Thank you, Mother. They help."

Mary's thumb remained on Grace's forehead a moment longer. Caressing, almost. "We have rounds at the hospital tomorrow, ladies. Let's get some supplies." As Grace stared at the pavement, willing her head to not explode, Mary divided their shopping list among them.

"Everyone have their sacrament pouches?"

They answered as a group. "Yes, Mother Superior."

"Sister Monica?"

Grace glanced at her friend. Quick, in case the mother caught her. Mon had repacked the pouch last night as Grace watched and chattered about some foolish thing that'd been on her mind. How they didn't have mirrors in the convent or something.

"Yes, Mother Mary. I packed it as you asked."

"And you have it somewhere easy to access? Close to your rosary, I presume?"

"Yes, Mother."

"Good. We always want to keep them handy."

Grace swallowed, the headache almost convinced it didn't need to blow up her brain, her breathing returning to normal. "Should I have one? What are they for?"

Sister Constance, the quietest of the bunch, squeaked and crossed herself.

A couple of the others did too.

Brows knit, Grace met Monica's eyes. "What did I say wrong?"

Mary gripped her above the elbow and pulled her through the parking lot. Her fingers dug into the muscle and sinew of her lower bicep. "It would be blasphemy to give you one, and I'm afraid explaining what they are goes into centuries more of the Order's history than I care to cover in the parking lot of a mall."

Monica hurried along on her other side. "They're important. We can leave it at that."

"Get the door, Sister."

As they approached the giant glass doors, Grace looked up. Reflected were all seven sisters, Mother Mary stern in her reflection as she led Grace by the elbow. The giant black glasses took up at least half of Grace's pale face.

Grace reached up to remove them.

Mary pushed them back up her nose. "Leave them on, Grace. We don't want your headache to get worse. How's your stomach?"

And as if it heard her, it grumbled. Rolled over itself. "Not so hot, Mother. Now that you ask."

Monica held the door for them all as they passed the threshold.

In the cool depths of the mall, the tinted glass of the doors blocking the sun and heat of the day, footfalls echoed from all directions. People spoke in low murmurs; children screamed on a playground out of sight.

The mother spoke in a hushed tone. "You all have your assignments."

Splitting off in two groups, five of the sisters walked away.

Monica stayed, hands clasped in front of her. "Which of them would you like me to go with, Mother?"

"You're staying with me today, child." She pulled Grace into the mall as Monica tried to cover a gasp.

Scurrying to catch up, Mon walked on Grace's other side. "Is your headache better?"

Grace pressed her lips together, eyes roving over the neon signs. Her stomach turned as she tried not to think about the glowing spot of pain in the center of her forehead. "I think I might be sick, ladies."

Mother Mary guided her to a bench in the middle of the mall. Scanning the people walking by, she sat and leaned into Grace. "Here. Look up. Breathe deep. Don't think about your stomach. Listen to my voice." She continued to speak in an even tone, her voice an unending string of words.

People slid by, not paying attention to them, and Grace relaxed by inches. The mother could be a stern woman, cold sometimes even, but Grace couldn't deny she knew how to comfort. How to heal. When Grace's guts reacted like this, and her head ached, and fear of whatever it was that had almost killed her paralyzed her, the mother fixed it. Every time.

She allowed herself to slide into Mother Mary's calm voice as she would between clean, cool sheets. Monica sat on her other side, holding her hand and whispering prayers.

And just as her legs stopped shaking, and she believed she wouldn't die this time, her stomach lurched. Her eyes popped open and landed on a man crossing in front of them. A man like all the others, a couple shopping bags in his hands. Dad jeans. A polo.

She burped so loud it resounded off the ceiling.

He turned his eyes to her, and before the smile fully formed on his lips, he glanced to either side of her. His expression curdled. He clamped his mouth shut with an audible snap and quickened his steps.

Monica stood, watching after him as he sped through the mall. "Mother," she whispered.

But before Mary responded, Grace spun and puked into a planter.

*

They followed Dad Jeans through the mall past a toy store, a novelties store, something that smelled of sandalwood and lavender, and into a chocolaterie. Rubbing her stomach, Grace inspected their offering of chocolate eggs and figures. Some white chocolate figures were even in the shape of priests. Or bishops. Whoever it was with the funny hats.

Rather than beg some money off Monica or, God forbid, Mother Mary, she begged a sample off the guy behind the counter.

He leaned on the counter, hands folded, and grinned. "Chocolate is a girl's best friend. At least, that's what my girlfriend tells me."

Grace brought the square up to her nose. It smelled like the deepest secrets of the plant it came from. Rich, and dark, and mysterious. "She's not wrong."

It slid past her tongue and coated her throat, the semi-sweet dark chocolate attacking the back of her jaw. She let some melt on her tongue as Mary and Monica roamed the store. She hadn't heard Mary mention chocolate being on the shopping list, but then her head had been screaming at the time.

Dad Jeans clutched his bags, leaning over a glass counter.

Monica leaned onto the counter next to him. She whispered something, something Grace couldn't make out. It was in Latin, but that's about all she could tell.

He shuddered, his backbone twisting. One of his packages fell to the floor.

The man behind the counter left his spot where he'd been watching Grace and sidled close to Dad Jeans. "Sir? Do you need help?"

Dad Jeans growled. Against all reason, the features of his face rippled. Literally rippled. Like someone had cast a stone into the calm water of his face.

Grace's stomach turned again, the chocolate sitting heavy. She inched toward the door to the mall. Coincidentally, closer to Mother Mary.

The mother didn't look at her. But she did pull her phone out of her own cavernous purse and tap a few keys.

With a sniff, she put it away and stepped toward Dad Jeans. "Sir, I must ask that you not be rude to my novice. If you insult her, you insult us all."

He snarled again. "She started it, you bitch."

The shopkeeper gasped and laid a hand on the counter. "Sir. Please don't use that language in here."

Mother Mary smiled, her eyes sparkling as if she was about to take the man down a peg or twenty. God knew Grace had seen her do it to the sisters often enough.

Sister Alexandra, followed quickly by Sisters Maria and Constance, came in and stood inside the door. Mother Mary must have texted them.

Grace swallowed the rest of the chocolate, throat clicking.

Dad Jeans looked over the nuns. His gaze settled on Grace. Eyes wide, he leered at her. "Oh. You. I—"

Mary stepped between them and lowered her voice. "*Dicite nomini tuo.*" She spat it at him.

He shuddered again, falling backward into the glass counter. His packages fell, boxes thumping against one another.

And he and Grace shouted at once.

"Elrasheth!"

"I don't know!" Her head pounded.

Mother Mary glanced over her shoulder. "Grace, go wait by the van."

But Dad Jeans took advantage of her lack of attention. He spun, grabbing the hand of the man behind the counter. With a snarling growl, he plunged the man's hand through the glass counter.

The crash of the glass shattering somehow pleasing, it took up all the space in the small store. It was all Grace could hear.

Oh that, and the man behind the counter screaming. His red, red, red blood splashed all over the chocolate, the little men doused in sprays of it; bishops now turned into cardinals. And he wailed, sliding behind the counter.

Maria leapt in front of Grace, blocking the scene from her. "Don't look, Gracie. You don't have to look."

But Grace did have to.

The shopkeeper's screams weakened as he slid to the ground, blood smearing everywhere like a spilled can of paint.

From the mall, the other sisters came at a dead run. Sister Joan dug in her huge bag.

Mary shouted, "Monica! Get Grace and this man out of here!" She hooked her hands into the shoulders of Dad Jeans and ripped him backward, throwing him against one of the tall, thin display cases in the center of the store. He bounced off of it. Chocolates cascaded from the shelves inside with soft thumps.

Monica leapt over the counter. "Grace, help me," she said, tugging the clerk upright.

From the floor, feet splayed before him, Dad Jeans snapped his hand closed.

The security grates crashed down, a great cacophony of clanging metal. An alarm wailed.

Finally, someone in the mall outside shouted. A guard maybe? A scared kid? Also maybe.

"Grace!"

"Right, right," she mumbled. Pushing the sunglasses up her nose, she stepped around the broken glass and behind the counter, into the no-man's-land where customers weren't allowed.

The pool of blood took her breath away.

Pale, the man behind the counter whimpered. "She's supposed to take her first spelling test today. We studied all week. She has to tell me what she got." He babbled, eyes rolled up in his head.

Monica, stern and calm in a way Grace had never seen her, leaned over him. "Grab his feet, Grace."

She did, lifting legs a lot lighter than they should have been.

"You're not going anywhere, my friend," Dad Jeans said. He rose up and floated a few inches off the ground.

It had to have been stress. The migraine. The puking. The blood. She was seeing things.

Her stomach twinged and her guts knotted.

He snarled. "If you helped me, these bitches would be nothing."

Staring through the dark glasses, Grace turned toward him.

His eyes wide, he locked them onto hers. "You could help me, you know. You *should* help me." His features rippled again. A gale blowing across the surface of a lake.

Monica panted. "We have to get him out of here if he's going to live. Help me." She swung the limp man drooping between them.

And another look at his sad face, the last words on his lips about his little girl's first spelling test, got Grace moving. She broke eye contact with Dad Jeans. "Where do we go?"

Monica hooked her chin. "Out the back."

As they stepped through the door to the store room, the six remaining nuns surrounded Dad Jeans in a circle. Each murmured something, and a couple of them took out their sacrament pouches.

Mother Mary stood over him, pushing him to the ground with her rosary in hand. *"Daemonium liberi eritis,"* she said.

A chill worked its way up Grace's spine as the door closed on the scene. The cool back room overtook them. Her migraine eased, the pulsing spot in the middle of her forehead becoming a pinpoint. "Do we put him down here?"

Monica shook her head. "Let's take him outside. We have to get this bleeding stopped."

They stumbled through the darkened back room, and at least Mr. Behind-the-Counter kept mumbling. He hadn't bled to death. Yet.

Pushing the door out into the daylight, Grace blinked. The glasses helped, but the sun was so bright. Its rays jabbed her in the eyeballs like tiny serrated knives. "What was Mother Mary saying? Was it Latin?"

"Yes. Set him here," Monica said, moving to a dried, brown patch of winter grass. "Press this to his wrist." She pulled a swatch of cloth from inside her own small purse. And she extracted a smaller bag, the sacrament pouch she'd packed up last night.

Grace pressed the cloth to his wrist as tight as she could. "Should we do a tourniquet or whatever? I heard about those somewhere and—"

But Mon wasn't listening. Her lips moved as she laid the pouch on the ground and pulled the string. The square of leather flattened out, and inside were the things she'd packed.

A communion wafer, a tiny ampule of holy water, a vial of wine, a piece of her own robe, a tiny crucifix. What might have been a charred piece of bone.

She broke open the ampule and pressed her finger into the broken glass.

"Careful! What are you doing, Monica?"

"Keep pressing. Don't ask questions."

Grace's hand had floated away from Mr. Behind-the-Counter's wrist. She pressed the cloth tight, both intrigued by Monica's actions and scared of the tone. Almost like the mother's.

Monica prayed, something soft and in Latin. She mixed some holy water with the tiny drop of blood on the pad of her finger and made a cross on the man's forehead. Once she sat the broken ampule back on the square of cloth, she picked up the wafer, kissed it, and placed it on his lips. His pale, pale lips. They had stopped moving.

Grace checked his chest.

Still rising and falling.

Whew.

Mon picked up the crucifix and began a different prayer. A complicated one, one that gushed from her lips like a waterfall. The words spilled all over the man bleeding in the grass.

His breathing eased.

Without looking up, Monica told Grace to stop pressing. "He's going to be okay."

An ambulance came screaming around the corner of the mall.

Mon still didn't glance up. "Go get that ambulance over here."

Grace chased after it. She waved and waved and screamed until they stopped.

After they backed up and the paramedics jumped out and started talking to Monica, Grace sat in a different small patch of grass with poky blades and cried.

Chapter Two

Annoyed, Grace backed into her favorite corner in the convent.

Two days.

Two days had gone by since the scene in the chocolaterie, and none of them had said a word. Not even Monica. Even though Grace had asked. Over and over. Shut down every time.

And so here she was, nothing to do but study her Spanish. Wandering this dusty convent until she found somewhere to go, she dragged her feet around the halls. The library might be a good place, but Monica was sure to be there, and after her odd silence, it was about all Grace could take just to pass her in the hall.

She slid into the tight cubby between a pedestal bearing a statue of a praying woman with a nose ring and the thick archway framing it. She'd meant to ask about the nose-ring woman but kept forgetting.

Plugging an earbud into her ear, she clicked Play on the handheld digital file player Maria had given her.

"*Que hora es?*...What time is it?"

The recording clicked, pausing, a space for the student to repeat the phrase.

Lip poking out, Grace listened and stared up at the nose-ring woman. She squinted. Maybe the woman wasn't wearing traditional nun's robes at all, though she'd taken the long skirt as such and moved on.

"*Cuál es su nombre?*...What is your name?"

The recording clicked again. Pausing.

The click resounded in Grace's head. She pulled the bud from her ear and pressed Stop. *Nombre.* She'd heard a word that sounded like that. A little bit ago. A couple of days. Not that word, but...

She stared at the wall, eyes unfocused. Seemed like there were a lot of memories hiding like this one, waiting to pounce. Why didn't her memory work? Was she going to be a useless lump the rest of her life? Or only until the sisters got tired of her and kicked her out in the street?

As she stared up at the nose-ring woman, it came to her so fast she would have fallen over if she hadn't already been sitting.

"*Dicite nomini tuo.*" Mother Mary's voice echoed inside her head. *Nombre* sounded a lot like *nomini*. And hadn't Dad Jeans shouted a name when she'd said it? Like she'd commanded him?

Grace settled her thumb on the Play button.

The next memory hit her. So hard, she pressed her back further into the wall and might as well have become part of the damn thing.

She'd answered too. Screamed she didn't know.

So much had happened, it'd slipped right from her mind. She couldn't remember thinking about speaking; it had just flown out. Just like that. *"I don't know."*

Why?

She rubbed the tip of her thumb back and forth over the rounded, smooth Play button, centering her thoughts on the rubbing, rubbing, rubbing. As she considered pressing it again, voices echoed down the hall.

"I don't want to bother you about this, Mother."

"Sister Monica, by bringing it up, you already have. We may as well discuss it. You've barely spoken to her in two days. She's taken notice."

She, the one they no doubt meant, pressed further into the wall. There had to have been something she did wrong. There couldn't be any other reason Monica had stopped talking to her.

"I know. I feel bad about bringing her in. I'm not sure it was a wise idea."

Mother Mary opened the door to her office, diagonal from where Grace pressed into the corner. "If you're saying you made a mistake, you're accusing me of making one as well."

Mon stopped in the hall, hands on her hips, back to Grace, almost within spitting distance.

Grace concentrated so hard on being small and unseeable. So hard.

"What do you mean, Mother?"

The mother stood in the doorway, her own arms crossed. Her stern face lined with concern. Or annoyance. Tough to call with her sometimes. "The Order has not grown in some time. You are the future of this Order, Monica, and your ideas about moving us forward are sound." She cleared her throat. "It was the right thing to do. I stand by that."

Monica shuffled her foot, crossed her arms, and wrapped her hands around herself. "I just feel so bad about lying to her."

Mother Mary uncrossed her arms and stepped toward Monica.

For no reason at all, Grace shivered. Her spine almost twisted itself in two, the shiver was so violent.

Hand on Monica's arm, Mary lowered her voice. "It was a choice we all made. If she knew who she was, she couldn't stay here."

From her dark spot behind her, all Grace could see was Mon's head bobbing. Mary's words ran around a hamster wheel in her head. *If she knew who she was, she couldn't stay.*

Stepping back, Mother Mary sniffed. "We will tell her who she is when the time is right. You've done good work, Sister."

Monica spun on a heel and started back the way they'd come.

Grace froze, if freezing more than she was already was possible, and held her breath. Her first foray into eavesdropping on the mother was about to be her last one.

But Monica's eyes floated over the nose-ring woman and Grace's face. They never stopped. She disappeared into the dark hall.

*

When Mass began that evening, Grace covered her stomach with crossed arms and sat in the back. The sisters gathered near the front. Since it was Wednesday, there were even a few members of the scraggly congregation there.

Father Moscone made his regularly scheduled appearance at the head of the congregation, leading them in the stand up, sit down, kneel, stand up, sit down musical chairs. But tonight, his voice dragged, his eyes drooping, and the standing up didn't happen as quick as usual.

Halfway through the third round of it—or the six-hundredth, who could keep track—one of the giant doors behind Grace creaked open. Another of the congregation, late as usual.

And though there were at least fifty empty pews to choose from, they chose Grace's.

Grace lowered her head, pretending to pray.

Rather than sit a hundred feet away as most people did, hoping not to be noticed by the sisters, the priest, and probably God, the person continued until they were well within Grace's church-pew personal bubble. In fact, they settled onto the hard wooden bench not two feet away. Maybe less.

Grace peeked from under her eyelids as everyone knelt.

The woman, dressed in a tank top and cutoff shorts, wore scuffed leather knee-high boots and a heavy jacket. It flopped open and exposed a giant knife in a holster under her arm. Strung around her neck were roughly twelve necklaces, each of them of different lengths, with strange pendants in a variety of shapes that gave Grace the creeps for no good reason. Tucked among them was a rosary not unlike the ones the sisters wore.

When they stood to sit, Grace sat further away. Not only were the woman's wardrobe choices...interesting, but the spikes on her belt had been sharpened, and as Grace looked her over again, she caught the handle of another knife peeking from inside the woman's boot.

And she smelled of the cold winter night. Like fireplace smoke and freezing rain.

When the next invocation began, Grace forgot the words. She itched to leap from her seat and run out the door, into that same winter night the strange woman had come from.

But instead, the woman scooted even closer. The tip of her nose bright red against her pale skin, she grinned. "Is it just me, or does he seem a little uninspired tonight?" Her low, husky voice didn't echo.

Grace shook her head, mumbling the response to Father Moscone's call. Well, a response. She'd lost the rhythm of the whole thing and couldn't remember a single line of the prayer.

The woman spoke again, her voice still low. "I see you're as bad at this whole Catholic thing as I am. My name's Daisy. You?"

If for no other reason than to get her mind off the Mass, Grace smiled. "That's a pretty name. Like the flower?"

Covering her mouth, Daisy tried to keep the guffaw behind her palm. She half succeeded.

Sister Eliana spun, brow cocked, and released her patented shush.

But the laugh had been enough to disturb the mother, who stood and made her way down the center aisle.

Grace's innards cringed. She'd never disturbed Mass quite like this before. Some whispering, sure, but to get the mother out of her seat? Maybe Grace could fit under the pew.

As Mother Mary approached and Daisy spun to face her, Grace considered leaping over the bench. But where would she even run away to?

Mother Mary crept sideways down the row and sat so close to Daisy they may have been sharing the same personal bubble. Her harsh whisper almost didn't make it to Grace's ears. "Daisy. I thought we asked you and your people never to come here."

Scraping a sharpened fingernail against the pew in front of her, Daisy frowned. "Got something to discuss with you, Mom." She made no effort to keep her voice low.

"Ms. Weatherby, you may either call me 'Mary' or 'Mother,' but 'Mom' is inappropriate." She cleared her throat and spoke a touch louder. "Are you going to leave, or will you need to be removed?" Her eyes flashed as they had in the mall.

Grace shrank further into the pew. The hard wood didn't give, but she pushed her feet against the kneeling bar and tried anyway.

"Need to talk to you, *Mother*."

Mary stood. "You don't have to interrupt Mass. If you insist we speak now, join me in the hallway where we can speak in private."

Daisy leaned back, threw both arms over the pew, and crossed her feet over the one in front of her. "Let's talk right here in front of God and everybody." She winked and pointed a finger-gun up front.

Grace glanced at the pulpit.

Father Moscone stood, one hand raised to the cross around his neck, his mouth hanging open. He stared at them. He'd lost the thread of the prayers too.

The few members of the congregation who'd shown up opened their sleepy eyes wide, all watching the mother. Except one of them, whose head bent over the blue glow of their phone.

Expression cold as the stone floor, Mary clenched her hands together and spoke loud enough for her voice to resound in the whole room. "Mass is over. God be with you."

People mumbled "And also with you" as they gathered their coats and scurried toward the door. Even Father Moscone ducked and ran.

As the last of them left and the giant door clanged behind them, except the one still buried in their phone, Mother Mary turned fire-breathing eyes on Daisy. "How dare you interrupt our worship of the Lord."

Daisy scoffed. "Please. You're no more Christian than I am."

The sisters approached, most of them standing in a loose circle around Daisy, Mary, and Grace—who was still trying to push herself into the pew and disappear.

Mother Mary cleared her throat. "What do you want, hunter?"

"That scene at the mall the other day, Ma. The hell were you doing?"

"You know what we were doing there. Saving two lives."

Daisy dropped her feet to the ground. The heels of her boots slammed the stone floor, the thud echoing across the sanctuary. "At the risk of how many others? You know what happens when the cops come?"

"Nothing, as we—"

"They shoot first and ask questions later. It's the goddamned twenty-first century. They think there's a shooter, they kill anyone they see in the wrong place at the wrong time with the wrong color skin." She narrowed her eyes at Sister Constance.

Her mouth tightened, deep brown skin paling slightly, but she stared at the mother and said nothing.

Mary sat. "At least do me the favor of not blaspheming in here."

"Fine. But it was reckless. I don't know when you got so godd—" She slapped the pew.

Grace jumped.

Monica sat on Grace's other side, the wood creaking, and put one cool hand around her bicep, her thumb caressing her upper arm.

Grace's insides calmed.

Daisy went on, "So damned reckless. But it's going to get people killed." She turned to glare at Grace, narrowing her eyes. "Who are you? Why didn't you leave with the congregation?" Her cool gaze skipped to Monica. "Are you protecting her?"

Monica tugged Grace's arm. She leaned into her ear, breath warm. "Come with me."

Grace slid away from Daisy, trying and failing to break eye contact.

But Daisy broke it first, eyes sliding to the right, one finger pointing into the air. "Wait. I've seen you before..." She trailed off, mouth open.

The mother stood again. "Get out, Ms. Weatherby. Please know you are not welcome here."

Monica whispered louder, "Grace. Come on."

Daisy's finger continued to dance in space. "Yeah. Recently. I've seen your face or something." She glared at the single stained-glass window in the room where the moonlight streamed past Uriel the Archangel's smiling face.

Grace slid away, Monica tugging her still.

Daisy snapped her fingers, flinty green eyes lighting up. The snap echoed off the ceiling. "It was a surveillance video! From a convenience store robbery. Were you a hostage, Grace?"

Grace shook her head, a pit forming in her stomach. "I don't know what you're talking about. Robbery?"

"Six people were killed and so was the murderer. But not you. Not you."

Mother Mary gripped Daisy by the back of the neck and pulled her to standing. "That is quite enough. Get out of our church."

A nearby lightbulb popped. It went out with a bright flash.

Clutching Monica, Grace fell out of the pew and landed in the small space between it and the one in front of it. Wedged in, she saw feet approaching the sisters gathered in the aisle.

A shotgun cocked. A male spoke. Must've been the one with the phone. "That's enough. Let her go, Mary."

From down here, Grace couldn't see the mother's face, just the bottom of her chin and the way her grimace took up her whole jaw. Her hand popped off of Daisy's neck, and she backed out of the pew.

Daisy threw a look at Grace. "I know it was you."

Without even knowing what she was doing, Grace shook her head. She pushed away on her heels and the flat of her hands. "I don't know what you're talking about," she repeated.

"Daisy," the man said, "let's go."

The green-eyed hunter gathered her long, wavy, gray-streaked brown hair in one hand and pushed it down the back of her coat. She didn't zip up, but tugged the bottom of her cut-off shorts. Pushing past the mother, her eyes still on Grace, she scowled. "This isn't over, Mother. We can't have you putting innocents in danger just to save some filthy demons."

She spun on a heel, leaving Grace to decipher what the hell she meant by that.

*

Her hand around Grace's bicep, Monica led her through darkened, echoing hallways until they reached Grace's room. Grace's legs were like stilts, her feet so far away she couldn't even feel them. In fact, if Monica hadn't sat next to her on the bed, depressing the mattress enough to roll Grace's leg into hers, she wouldn't have believed any of the walk from the sanctuary to here had happened. She was still back in the cold stone floor of the sanctuary, the word "demon" reflecting off the insides of her skull.

She managed to open her mouth once they sat and unstuck her tongue from the roof of her mouth. But whatever questions she had dried up. She couldn't help but imagine Daisy's flinty green eyes as she narrowed them, seeming to accuse Grace of taking part in robbery and murder.

Did that go any length toward explaining how she'd ended up in that hospital?

Monica twisted her fingers in her rosary. Cleared her throat. Crossed her ankles. Uncrossed them. Recrossed them.

Grace gave her the side-eye. She swallowed the heart in her throat and spit out what she'd been meaning to say since that afternoon. "It's been two days since the mall, and now this. Are you going to talk to me, or should I pack my bags and leave?" She glanced around the room, wondering what she might put in a bag anyway. She owned nothing.

Her eye fell on the giant sunglasses. While Monica sat and twisted her rosary some more, Grace leaned and snatched the glasses from the nightstand.

As she leaned back, Monica rolled into her leg again. "I'm sorry. I don't know what to say. I feel bad you had to witness that scene at the mall."

Grace fidgeted with the glasses. She extended both arms, folded them in on themselves, and extended them again. "What were you guys doing? It seems like you planned it. Like to attack that guy. It seemed like—" She stopped, swallowing.

Monica cleared her throat, again. "Seemed like what?"

"Like he was expecting you. Like as soon as he saw the mother, he knew he was in for a fight."

Monica stood, tugging her headscarf from her hair. She didn't take the bobby pins out, and one of them hung out of her hair sideways as she twisted the cloth between her hands. "I don't know how much I can tell you, Grace. I don't know how much I should."

"Is that because the mother doesn't want you to? Or you don't trust me enough to tell me the truth?" A question that came out a lot harsher than she planned. Whatever.

Monica's chin trembled. "I know it's only been six weeks, but I hope you know I love you. I've felt close to you ever since we met."

"That why you've been lying to me?"

Mon's mouth and eyes popped open, but no sound came out.

Grace scowled. "I overheard you talking to Mary earlier. What have you been lying to me about? Do you know who I was? What happened to me? I mean—" She stopped, clutching the sunglasses, their smooth plastic warming in her hand. "I can't understand what nuns would lie about."

Still twisting the scarf in her fingers, Monica shrugged. "The man in the mall knew who we were as soon as he laid eyes on us. And he should have. He was a bad man, and—"

"Was he a demon? Are demons even real? Or was Daisy lying? Or being poetic or something?"

With a sigh, Monica sat next to her again. Cocking one knee onto the bed, she faced Grace, laid the scarf aside, and pulled out that wonky bobby pin. She took one of Grace's hands and held it.

Grace clutched the sunglasses in her other hand, staring at the glasses instead of Mon. She'd never seen her friend so sincere, and her heart sank to the bottom of her stomach, where it threatened to keep going into her feet. Sweat popped out on her forehead, even in the room's deep chill.

She shivered and considered stuffing the questions back in her mouth.

"Demons are real. That was true." Monica's voice wavered. "The man in the mall was one."

And somehow, it wasn't as much of a shock as Grace thought it would be, hearing the truth aloud. It was more like a warm wave washed over her. The truth released from its cage. "Did a demon do this to me?" She gestured at the scar on her face. The chemical burn. "That's what happened, isn't it? I was attacked by a demon."

"You could say that. Yes." Monica's thumb stroked Grace's palm.

"Why wouldn't you want to tell me?"

Monica scoffed. "Because not everyone wants to hear demons are real. Walking around malls and stuff. And that we—" She broke off, her thumb stopping.

Grace's breath caught. "That you what? Daisy said something about saving?"

Monica pressed her lips together. She shook her head. "Mother Mary might need to fill the rest in. I'm not sure how much I should say. I'm really not, Grace." A tear dropped from one eye, followed by a tear from the other.

"Everything has gotten more complicated than I expected. I don't think this was a good plan."

Grace caught Monica's eyes. "What?"

To her credit, Monica didn't flinch. "Bringing you here. I wanted you to heal. I wanted to help. But—"

"But what?"

An icepick—no, scratch that—a sledgehammer hit Grace in the middle of the forehead. A migraine slammed into her, more massive than the one that'd come on at the mall times ten. Times twenty.

Screaming, she slid from the bed to her knees. Instinctively, she pushed the glasses up her nose and over her eyes and prayed for relief. Whatever God it was these sisters spoke to, she asked for the migraine to stop. Or for him to explode her head. Whichever. As long as it went away.

Monica, her normally dark skin almost white as a sheet, dropped to her knees before Grace. "What's wrong? It's not your head, is it?"

Clutching her forehead in both hands, the pain beating with the rhythm of her heart, she grimaced. "No. Head's fine. No headache here. Just a little hangry." But another wave of pain came over her, her stomach revolted, and she puked her guts onto the floor. Then fell in the puke with a grunt, her cheek slapping the stone. The nose-guard of the glasses dug into the bridge of her nose.

She screamed again as a pickax dug into the center of her brain. She'd never, ever had a migraine like this. Of the half a dozen or so she'd experienced since awakening in this convent, nothing came close.

She wished for death, just for a release from this.

Monica jumped up, shouting Mother Mary's name.

Grace caught her skirt hem. "Don't leave," she whispered. "I feel like I might be dying."

Monica knelt next to her again, her robes in the puke, and swept her cool fingers over Grace's forehead. "You're burning up. My God." She laid her hand on Grace's forehead and spoke in Latin.

But she may as well have lit a fire in her fingertips. It burned. It burned so bad.

Writhing, spreading puke all over her side, Grace begged her to stop.

The door to the room slammed open, a shape in it, outlined in the light from the hall, seeming to glow.

Grace found herself in equal parts awe and relief. Fear and love. Whoever had appeared would either save her, or kill her. She'd never been surer of anything.

*

A multitude of voices swirled around the figure as they approached. The glow came not from behind them, but inside. "Listen to my voice, Grace. Ease your suffering. Listen to my voice. Calm your spirit."

And she did. She couldn't not. What they said entranced her like a spell.

The headache faded, her stomach settling.

The multitude of voices spoke again as the figure knelt next to her. "Listen to my voice. Let your pain fall away."

Glasses digging into her nose, Grace whispered, "I'm okay." She sat up on her elbow, wiping puke off her cheek.

Mother Mary clutched her dry shoulder. "Did this just hit you?"

Glancing past her, Grace sought the figure with the multitude of voices, but the mother stood alone. "Yes. Monica and I were talking, and it slammed into me like a freight train."

Mary leaned into her vision again. "Where, Grace? Where did it come from?"

Grace shook her head. "What do you mean, where? From my head. Like always."

The mother gripped her arm, hard, her fingers like claws. "I need you to focus. Where?"

The rest of the sisters crowded the door. "Mother," Alexandra said, "should we check the seals?"

Mary nodded, still holding Grace's eyes. "Check them. Check them all. Don't forget the—"

The voice of a woman cut through the sisters' chatter, but it came from everywhere as much as the hallway. "Getting careless in your old age, Mother?"

The pain in Grace's head leapt from almost manageable to crushing. Her head might have caved in like a beer can.

Which, for some reason, caused the image of a bar to leap into her mind. An empty bottle lying sideways on it. Grace couldn't see or even think through the pain, yet the image of the beer bottle was incongruously clear. It had been emptied recently. So recently, beads of sweat from the cold beer still crowded the outside of the bottle.

Someone screamed. It might have been Grace. It might have come from inside her head.

But the voice spoke again, from everywhere. The small room echoed with her voice. "Oh, Grace. It's so good to see you." The shadows of the room pulled down from all corners and coalesced into the shape of a person. A short, bent person with fluffy hair, square glasses with a chain not unlike the sisters' rosaries in design, and a shawl draped over her shoulders.

The sisters crowded in the door crossed themselves in near-unison and chanted a prayer together. Something Latin. It buzzed inside Grace's head. It tore at her senses.

The small person waved her hand. "That's quite enough of that, Sisters."

Their mouths kept moving, but the volume of their voices dropped to a low murmur before disappearing entirely.

And the newcomer grinned. Her eyes flashed literal fire, almost like Mother Mary's did from time to time, and she turned to the sisters in the door. Hands raised before her, she walked toward the door.

Monica whimpered. She crouched next to Grace, gripping her arm. Hiding behind her.

The sisters in the door slid backward, most of them fighting against whatever force pushed them, their shoes scraping against the stone floor.

The door closed on their stricken faces.

The newcomer sighed. "That's better. Quiet, at least. Mother, why do you still use Latin? If you're going to annoy the fuck out of us, why not do it in English?"

Mother Mary stood, hands balled into fists. She cursed in Spanish, one of the few words Grace remembered with regularity. "Karithexis, is that you?"

Through the dark glasses, and the screaming head, Grace tried to focus on the newcomer, but the light from her bedside lamp hit her eyes.

She groaned.

Karithexis, whatever kind of name that was, turned toward her. "Oh, my dear." Gripping the shawl around her shoulders, she knelt in front of Grace. "You know, I came like this because you seem to be comfortable with these old ladies and their blue hair. The shape has a few inherent weaknesses, but nothing I can't overcome with enough focus." She followed this with something in a language Grace had never heard. It sounded a lot like growling, but there were words. There were words.

Her breath smelled like rotten meat and spoiled milk. And...onions?

The screaming in Grace's head backed off. Not entirely. Just enough for a moment of quiet.

Stomach bubbling, Grace wobbled to her feet. She towered over Karithexis.

A gnarled hand gripped hers. "It's so good to see you, my friend. When you disappeared after making that deal in the bar, I thought the worst." She snarled. "These nuns are notorious for ruining lives."

Monica stood but backed into the bed. "That's not true! We save lives. We save *souls*."

Karithexis flipped her hand.

Monica flew over the bed and crashed into the wall, arms and legs flailing. A crack echoed in the tiny room. With a grunt, she landed on the bed and bounced, rolling to a stop on her face.

Grace gasped and leapt for her friend.

But the little old lady kept such a grip on her wrist, she couldn't move. Such a small, elderly woman shouldn't be so strong, with a grip like steel bands. Even the mother wasn't so strong.

Mother Mary spoke, her tone foreboding. "Touch another of my sisters, demon, and you'll encounter my full wrath." Her eyes blazed, and light shone all around her the way Raphael's halo surrounded him.

But there was that word again.

Demon.

Grace shivered. Her teeth chattered, her hands tingling. Heartbeat quick and hard inside her chest, she struggled to pull down a breath. As Monica lay on the bed moaning, blood smearing on the clean white duvet, Grace's fingers went numb. There was no way these people were speaking in metaphor. Not when this person had materialized from nothing but shadow.

Again, she tried to back up.

Karithexis smiled in a winning, wide grin. It lit her fuzzy eyes and lifted her whole face. "I have something for you, my dear." She released Grace's arm and dug into the purse hanging limply off her other wrist. "It's in here somewhere."

Someone banged on the door. It shook as they slammed themselves into it.

Karithexis chuckled. "They want in. Should we let them in, Mother?"

Mother Mary growled. Actually growled. "I command you, in the name of Jesus Christ, to leave this place."

"What, Mother, not going to try and save poor little old me?" Karithexis clucked her tongue. "What would Raphael think of that?"

The door swung open, and the sisters in the hall began to chant again, the Latin buzzing in Grace's head like a swarm of bees.

Sweat popped up on her forehead, something about the chant making her skin crawl.

Chuckling, Karithexis pulled a hand mirror from the bag and dropped the bag to the ground. "Here we are. Grace, if you would."

A large incorporeal hand gripped Grace around the neck. She moved through the air, toes scraping along the ground, pulled, inexorable, toward what had to be a demon. There was no other explanation. A literal demon.

She gritted her teeth and fought against that invisible hand. With her feet, her arms flailing, but also in her mind, despite the return of the pounding, blinding migraine.

Her forward motion stopped. She didn't go backward, but she didn't go forward.

"Dammit," the demon cursed. "Stop the fucking spell. I can't concentrate." Switching hands with the mirror, she held it out toward Grace and flipped the other hand toward the gaggle of sisters in the door.

Sister Maria detached from the group and floated into the room.

The demon snarled. "You should be teaching our friend Grace Latin, bitch. That way she could understand you're trying to kill her and me and every demon within a hundred miles. Here you're supposed to be saving us or whatever high and mighty shit you do, and you throw it out the window as soon as you're backed into a corner."

Maria shook her head. "That's not true, you're—" She gagged, hands flying to her neck.

"Shut up." The demon turned to Grace. "They're your enemy. I know you've forgotten who, and what, you are. But if there's one thing I'm not lying about—"

The mother found her tongue again. "She is lying, Grace. It's a liar! All demons lie." She growled again, pulling the sacrament pouch from inside her robes.

Karithexis clucked. "You don't have her best interests at heart. Oh, speaking of hearts."

The mirror flashed in Grace's face. Below the giant sunglasses, her mouth hung open like her jaw had become unhinged.

As Grace stood, entranced by her reflection, the demon leapt for Maria. This little old lady, sweater over her shoulders, for God's sake, sank her hand into Maria's chest before Grace had the chance to even inhale.

Maria couldn't catch her breath. She tried. Gurgling, she tried.

The room stank of copper as her blood pooled beneath her feet. It splattered hot and wet onto the stone. It leaked from between Maria's lips as she continued to chant in silence. Her lips matched the words of the other sisters.

"I've tried to master the whole beating heart thing like in Indiana Jones," the demon said, winking at Grace over her shoulder. "You know the one, right? We love that one. Anyway." She yanked her hand free, covered almost up to the elbow in blood, dripping viscera in her clenched fist. "Ugh. No dice."

Maria slumped to the floor. Her lips didn't move anymore.

Karithexis slurped some of the bloody slop in her hands. Sucked it up like spaghetti. "Well, shit. Let's try again."

Sister Constance, the next one in the door, slid into the room.

Grace's gut screamed. She shouted, "What do you want with me? Stop it!"

The demon turned to her again, blood smeared over her teeth when she smiled, her waxy red lipstick mixed in with it. "Come here. Let me show you something."

Grace took a step toward her.

Mother Mary glowed, chanting with the sisters. She stepped closer, the pouch raised.

"Don't take another step, lying bitch." The demon snarled, dragging Constance through the air. "Or I'll turn another of your precious sisters into lunch meat."

Mary stopped. Still glowing, still chanting, sacrament pouch still raised above her head. But she stopped.

Stepping closer to Grace, Karithexis spoke. Everything around them quieted, like they were in a bubble together. "Look at us here, finally. Two peas in a pod. It's been a while, Grace. Hurts you'd forget me." She pinched Grace's chin between her fingers. "We had some pretty fun times together."

Grace flinched away. "I'm sorry. I didn't mean to." Nonsense, but it was all she could come up with. And the screaming in her head scratched against the sides, increasing again.

The demon stepped closer, the blood drying on her chin. Some flaked off; some got caught in her wrinkles as she spoke again. "I suppose I could let bygones be bygones. Forgive and forget, that kind of thing. Did the sisters teach you that?" She spun the hand mirror around and twirled to stand next to Grace. Both of them popped up in the mirror, an angry red smear of blood under Grace's pale chin and huge black sunglasses over her eyes.

She shifted her gaze to the demon's face in the mirror.

Her face was normal, except for Maria's blood painted across it. But her eyes. Her eyes were like deep holes, sucking all the light out of the air around them, the edges ragged.

The demon smirked. "Oh, let's take those glasses off, shall we?"

Grace twitched, trying to get her hand up.

But Karithexis ripped the glasses from her face and threw them to the floor. She stepped on them, the plastic popping and crunching under her heel. "Oh, that's better. Look at those pretty faces."

She gripped Grace under the chin again and forced her to stare into the mirror.

Grace's eyes looked just like the demon's. Black holes. The depths of nothing. Edges ragged, no light within them.

The hair on top of her head crawled away from her scalp. Her teeth chattered again. Though she felt her eyes widen, the mirror only showed her two unmoving black holes. Hell, staring back at her.

Mother Mary came from nowhere, smashing her sacrament pouch right into the demon's head. Holy water and wine and whatever else she had in the pouch splashed everywhere. Some of it onto Grace.

And oh God, it burned. The smell of charred skin filled her nose, acrid and sweet at the same time. Followed by something that stank of burnt matches.

Karithexis laughed and burst into shadows.

The mirror clattered to the floor.

The sisters fell silent.

Grace sank to the floor and cried.

Chapter Three

Candles lit every corner of the room and the corpse in the middle. The fire flickered on the walls, leaving the ceiling in shadow.

Grace rolled her eyes and tried to forget what she'd seen in the mirror. The twin black holes in her face that just looked like eyes to everyone else. "Isn't a wake kind of senseless? She's got a giant hole in her chest. Pretty sure she's dead."

Monica, on her knees next to the table where Maria had been laid out in clean clothes with clean skin and no heart, didn't answer.

"Don't your knees hurt?"

Again, Monica said nothing. Grace had to assume her eyes were closed and she was praying. Or asking her God for guidance. Or wondering what she was supposed to say to someone who she said was her friend but told nothing but lies.

Nothing.

Grace exhaled through her teeth. "Talk to me."

Monica's shoulders raised. "What do you want me to say?"

"You could tell me what the fuck is going on. Start with 'You're a demon, Grace.' Or something."

"Don't curse so loud. The mother will hear you."

Grace blew out one of the candles without looking at Maria's face. They'd closed her eyes and smoothed her brow, but they'd left her hair up, like she always wore it.

How did that little old lady reach clear into her chest? Demon or no, how did she even have the strength?

And Grace was, what? Like that?

She knocked over the blown-out candle.

Monica sighed. "Stop it." Replacing the candle on the table, she blew a stray hair out of her eye. "What would you have done if you woke up in that hospital with me sitting next to your bed and I told you, 'Hey, stranger, I'm a nun and you're a demon'? You think that—"

"You're not a nun. They won't let you into their club." She clenched her teeth.

Mon stood, using another candle to light the one Grace had blown out. "You don't have to be rude."

"Why not?" Heat flared in the center of Grace's forehead. Every candle in the room flickered. "Six weeks, Mon. Six weeks you lied to my face. Every single day. Why?"

"I didn't know how to tell you." Monica's cheek twitched. She twisted her fingers in her rosary.

"That's a piss-poor excuse. You sat there and changed my bandages for weeks and we talked and laughed like friends, but you were just..." Grace stared at the wall, fists clenched and throat aching. They really had felt like friends.

Monica shifted on her feet. "What?"

Grace covered her black eyes. What a nightmare. "How did this happen to me?" She peeked through her fingers. "How did I end up in that hospital?"

Monica shook her head. "You got into trouble somewhere. It's kind of what demons do."

Something tickled Grace's mind, but she couldn't catch it, so she switched topics. Something else had been bugging the hell out of her. "Mother Mary said demons lie. When Karithexis told me all that stuff about you, Mary said the demon was lying. But I think you're lying. I think you're all bigger liars than anything that demon said."

Arms crossed, Monica spun. "Look, Grace. You don't have to. It's just—" She huffed.

"I don't have to what? Blame you for lying to me? For pretending to be my friend while you did what? What were you doing with me?" Her chest tight, Grace balled her fists and shoved them into her elbows. Her palms started sweating, but she tried to ignore it.

"I wanted to tell you, okay? I wanted to. But it was going so well. You're..." Monica shuffled her feet.

Grace's chest didn't loosen. If anything, it got tighter. But she couldn't push any more words out.

Monica went on. "You're different. I've met a few demons. Not as many as the mother"—she chewed her lip—"but a few. And you're not like them." Eyes wet, she glanced at Grace and met her eyes for a moment.

Fists clenched so tight her fingernails dug into her palms, Grace inhaled. "Different. From the others. That's the best you've got? I'm gonna ask you one more time, Monica. What. Were. You. Doing."

Mon exhaled, eyes drifting over the body. She bit her lip again.

"Fine. I'm leaving." Barely breathing, Grace spun.

Monica grabbed her arm. "You know when you get those headaches?"

"Yes." She breathed it out, no louder than a sigh.

"You get them when another demon is near."

The rest of Grace's breath fell out all at once. "That's what you were doing? What, using me as some kind of demon dowsing rod or something?"

Monica nodded, hair bouncing into her face. "We've saved like half a dozen demons because of you."

The candles flickered over the dead nun's face. Grace swallowed. "Saved?"

"It's what we do. We release demons from the hold of their master. Or hell. Or something."

"You're not sure?"

"It's unclear. But the texts say demons are held to their earthly bounds. We have an ancient exorcism that—"

"Ancient? How long have you been doing this?"

"Me?"

Grace dropped her arms and rolled her eyes. "No, Mon. The Order."

She shook her head. "I don't know if I should tell you."

"Who can?" The good news was Grace's chest had loosened. The bad? Her heart flew along at a hundred miles a minute.

"I think it should be Mother Mary. I don't know how much she wants me to tell you."

An image of the mother flitted through Grace's mind. Her stern brow. Looking down her nose, severe frown crossing her lips.

Shoulders falling, Grace exhaled and tightened her arms. Her breath came halfway down, got bound up around her crossed arms, and flew back out, burning both ways. "She won't tell me anything. I'm just going to go." She crossed to the door in two large steps and extricated one hand. The doorknob cold and slippery in her sweaty palm, she tugged the door open.

Monica sniffled, but she didn't say anything. She didn't try to stop her again. She didn't try to exorcise her. She didn't do anything but stand there and cry.

"Sorry, Monica. I can't stay with you people. All you do is lie. You're as bad as that demon." She waited, her throat working. Was Monica even going to try one more time? Or was she done?

Just more sniffling.

Grace shook her head, staring into the dark hallway. "I'll stay until after the funeral. I owe it to Maria. But once that's done, so are we."

The door creaked closed behind her. Cold hallway engulfing her, she stared at the wall. What now?

*

Father Moscone stood at the front of the sanctuary, coffin beneath the pulpit. Draped in flowers as it was, if Grace sat right, all she could see were the flowers as the father delivered a listless sermon in the midst of Mass. The rosary went on forever, and Grace was ready to leave through the big doors and never look back.

But there was still internment left. Something inside her wanted to see Maria sunk deep into a hole in the ground and covered with dirt. Some part of her longed for the smell of wet earth and tears.

So she waited out the damn Mass, sitting alone.

More of the scraggly congregation turned up than usual. They'd come on the promise of free food after the funeral. Stomachs rumbled throughout the cavernous room almost louder than Father Moscone spoke.

In the midst of all the standing and kneeling and shit, Mother Mary slipped out one of the side doors.

Grace glanced around. Everyone had their eyes squeezed shut. Apparently, it was rude to have your eyes open during prayer.

Like during sex.

Eyes wide, Grace shot to her feet. Who'd said that? And how had the voice come from inside her head?

Luckily, everyone else stood at the same time, and no one noticed her breathing hard.

On silent feet, she edged out of the pew, then slinked to the rear of the sanctuary and around to the door Mother Mary had escaped through. One of the wan-faced congregation looked up as she opened the door, but she frowned at them and slipped out anyway.

Not knowing where Mary had gone, she let her feet take her toward her favorite hallway.

And of course, she found the mother there, standing before the stained glass of Saint Raphael. Their patron saint, the archangel. Her head bowed, Mother Mary clutched her rosary and held it against her pinched lips.

Grace crept toward the praying nun. Holding her breath, she edged down the hall until she stood in the sun falling through the window. The light hit her feet as the sun rose higher, closer to the middle of the shortest day of the year.

Taking in Raphael's calm expression, Grace let the scene wash over her. His hands glowed, not unlike she'd imagined Mother Mary's doing from time to time. But that must have been a trick of the light. Raphael was an angel with, if this scene were true at all, some kind of powers. Maybe the opposite of the deadly power Karithexis had demonstrated when she'd reached straight through Maria's breastbone.

She hadn't bled from her eyes like these poor souls, but blood had sprayed from her mouth and all over everything in front of her.

Grace had washed blood from her hair until the water ran ice-cold.

"I suppose the solstice is ruined this year." Mother Mary sighed. "Perhaps it's for the best."

Before she had room for any other thoughts, Grace's mouth went on without her. "All that's happened, and *that's* what you have to say? The solstice is ruined?" Mouth open, she stepped back. Heat baked up her throat and into her cheeks.

Mary lowered the rosary, still staring at the window. "I don't have to explain anything to you."

Grace's forehead tightened. "Oh, that's it." She backed up a step. "I was going to wait until you buried

Maria. Thought I owed her something. Like her death was my fault, I guess. But you. This. Fuck you," she said, raising her voice so it echoed through the hall, "and fuck this, and fuck him." She jabbed a pointed finger at the window.

It got the reaction she hoped for. Mary turned, eyes ablaze, mouth open.

But Grace cut her off, "And you give me any more of your high and mighty bullshit, it better be the goddamned truth. At least. You owe me that, you—" She stopped short of calling the mother a bitch, but damn, it was close. She crossed her arms and finished, almost under her breath. "It better be the truth."

Shifting on her feet to face her, Mother Mary smiled. The pink sunlight coming through the stained glass crept impossibly upwards, encircling her. Engulfing her.

Entranced, Grace couldn't turn away.

"Grace."

The multitude of voices from the night Karithexis had appeared spoke.

And they were coming from the mother.

"Let me show you, before you leave, who we are. Who we really are."

Mother Mary's hands lifted from her sides, glowing as Raphael's did.

That same sense of peace Grace got from looking at the stained glass flowed through her, down to her molecules, as the glowing hands touched either side of her head. The hallway in front of her faded.

Chapter Four

"One more time, explain to me why we're crouching in the mud on the side of the road in the middle of winter?"

I grinned under the scarf covering my mouth. My arthritic joints didn't like it any more than Millicent did. I wasn't about to admit that aloud, though her crankiness always made me smile.

And she knew it. Her elbow crammed itself between two of my ribs, almost missing my strapped-down breast. "If they don't come soon, I am going home. I have better things to do."

"Oh yes, like Gerard?"

She scoffed and adjusted her leather breastplate, the Order's crest emblazoned on the front.

I waited, the *clop, clop* of horse hooves and squeaking of wagon wheels reaching my ears in a whisper. I'd done something like this fifteen times on this same road, yet with the Inquisition out there wreaking havoc on the entire continent, acid crawled up my throat like each time before it.

Swallowing it down, I glanced at Millie.

"Yes, maybe." The smile was apparent in her voice.

With a snort, I stood. "Yes, and I've got ale to brew, but some things are more important than men and ale." I shifted my eyes. "They're coming. Ready?"

She whistled through her teeth, a signal to everyone else.

The woods moved in a subtle way, as though a group of people started holding their breaths. The wind sighed, and the leaves rustled, giving me a sense of peace, even as the carriage approached. Adjusting the sword in my hand, I hefted my shield.

The daggers in my boots weren't visible, but as always, their steel pressed against my skin, warmed from hours inside the boots as we waited. My right foot tingled, the pins and needles close to unbearable.

I tried to shake it without stomping.

The carriage rolled into our stretch of road, silent but for the clinking of the tack and the wheels crunching through half-frozen mud.

Peering through the brush, I waited for the others to step in behind the carriage.

A bird called. In the midst of winter, an unusual noise.

My sign.

I stepped into the road, my shield extended and sword held at my waist.

Strong and young and solidly-built, Millicent grabbed the lead horse's bridle and pulled. It bent to her will and pulled the entire team to her side.

The burly, suntanned driver tugged the reins. His wrinkled face pinched. "Whoa, whoa. What's this then?"

Rolling to a halt, the carriage creaked. Someone banged the floor from inside.

I angled my sword at the door. "If you would, Fina."

A woman with skin almost as dark as the rich walnut-colored carriage approached the door, sheathing her sword and pulling a dagger.

Climbing to his feet, the driver shouted. "Here, you can't go in there. We've got places to be. You don't understand who's in there."

I yanked the scarf down from my mouth and let him see my toothy grin. "Yes, we know. This is the Grand Inquisitor's coach."

The carriage rocked as Fina disappeared inside. A man cried out. First, with an indignant "What is this?"

His next cry was the wail of an injured fawn.

Preceded by Fina, the bishop and his bushy eyebrows stepped from the carriage. Black and white robes swirling around him, he clutched a satchel to his chest.

Showing him my teeth as well, I lowered the shield. "Ah, dear Bishop Savaric. How pleasant to see you in this position once again."

"You'll pay for this, witch. I know who your family is. Who all the people you care about are." He glanced at Fina, rabbit eyes moving quickly back and forth, bushy brows high on his forehead. He stepped forward and lowered his voice. "The Inquisition with see them burned, as will you be. I'll even let you hear their screams before you die. A little favor." His cheek twitched like he attempted a smile.

The acid crept up my throat again. I may have never had children—likely why I'd gotten so old in the first place—but I had more nieces and nephews and cousins than I could count.

Over the bishop's shoulder, a black plume of smoke rose into the midday sky. Day in and day out, the drumbeat of "witchcraft, burn them" echoed. The ash of burned bodies fell in a constant rain over the roofs of every village for miles.

I scowled. "Your lies have no bounds. The records." The tip of my sword hovered toward his midsection. Taking a step, I poked the tip into his satchel. "Please."

He clutched it closer. "This is the only proof I have of your villainy. And that of your family, witch."

The warmth of my itinerant companion rode down from the crown of my head to my toes. I looked down at my pale hand as it gripped the sword.

My skin glowed from inside, radiating soft light. I spoke to it, the glow or the being causing it, within the bounds of my mind.

You come now. Why?

I cannot allow you to be burned at the stake. So many of your sisters have already fallen. Take his records, burn them, and find out who did this to you.

Tempted to ask more questions, I was cut short as a demon flew over the horses. Thankfully my companion had already flooded its essence deep into my sword arm.

The horses stomped, their eyes rolling and teeth gnashing. Only the driver kept them from bolting as he jerked the reins.

The demon went straight for Millie.

With a shout, she released the horses and drew her sword. She murmured a few words, and the spell etched into the sword's face glowed. She slashed at the demon.

It jumped back, but too late. The sword sliced through it, and thick green smoke poured from what should have been a gaping wound. But the spell prevented damage to the body and attacked only the demon within.

Yet another leapt onto the carriage. Before I had a chance to shout the spell that would immobilize it, it dug its teeth into the neck of the driver. Ripping and tearing, ligaments and blood vessels popping no louder than the crackling of a fire, the demon seethed.

Blood sprayed the driver before he fell, unable to scream, to the bench. Bubbling and groaning, he leaned back, his head coming to rest on the top of the carriage. Other than the blood squirting from his neck—less now, already—he might have been sleeping.

Fina bared her teeth. "Face me, demon. I will show you what a real fight is."

The bishop backed into the carriage, satchel clutched to his chest.

Before I got distracted by the demons fighting my girls behind the carriage, and surely there were half a dozen back there, I sheathed my sword and snatched the records from the bishop. My companion coursed through my every nerve, and heat concentrated in my hand. I'd not known the love of a man in decades, but this feeling neared that.

As the flame erupted from my hand and burned the records, satchel and all, to a crisp, the feeling surpassed it.

Engulfed by heat, nerve endings tingling from head to toe, I grinned.

My companion and the voice of every Head of the Order before me spoke as I did. "Thank you for your cooperation, Grand Inquisitor. Until we meet again."

I spun to leave, my insides abuzz.

One of the demons dropped from a tree onto my head.

Although my companion's strength exploded through me, the inside of my skin on fire as though I was the one tied to a burning stake, I swallowed the power creeping up my throat like bile and cooled the top of my head even as it begged to split from my body with a tearing not unlike the poor driver's throat.

I pressed cool fingertips to the demon's forehead as it writhed atop my shoulders. The power coursed through me, but I kept it cool. Not burning. Not this time.

The feeling as the demon slid from my shoulders to the ground did not rival the love of a man. It surpassed it in every way imaginable. It engulfed every sense of being I'd ever had. It showed me the universe, laid bare, its secrets mine for the asking.

What did I do with that power?

I turned to the demon on the ground and freed it from its mortal cage, its suffering, its guilt. From the life it once knew and the lives it ruined with its misdeeds.

Where did it go as it left the body? On that score, my companion was silent.

The secrets of the universe folded in on themselves and slipped from my fingers. The great deep blue seeped from my eyes and back into the sky.

My companion withdrew, leaving my insides cold, and I turned to the bishop.

Demons knelt on either side of him, gripping his legs in their hooked fingers. His robes under their claws were damp, though from blood, sweat, or piss, I could not tell.

He trembled. "Help me. Please, Mary."

My girls had defeated each of their attackers, holding them at bay while Millicent drew a circle around them all. Carriage, horses, everything. Without my companion, the exorcism would have to be spoken as a spell.

Something this man would burn me at the stake for.

I stepped toward him, drawing my sword again and menacing. "These demons are one thing, but you, Bishop, are true evil." I spat at his feet. "You murder innocents to further your own position."

His eyes darted back and forth, the sweat on his forehead dripping into his bushy eyebrows. "Those accused of the crime of witchcraft can—"

"Ladies of the Order, release these demons. Our business here is done. Let them do as they will with Grand Inquisitor Savaric." I grinned, a real smile this time. "He deserves to be left to his own devices."

As I spun to leave, the bishop's small voice, almost a whisper, came to me.

"Wait."

The hungry demons to either side of him crawled toward his head. Soon, they would devour his body as a bear would its prey; alive, and screaming.

I knelt outside the circle.

Millie stood ready, the parchment containing the exorcism spell unrolled in her hands.

"Bishop," I said, "leave me and my family and these women alone. Forever. What you see here today stays with us, and you stop accusing us of witchcraft. For if we save your life, you will owe us that debt." The hard dirt and gravel of the cold road pressed into my knee. Though the joint screamed, I stayed there, staring up at the bishop from under my brow.

"I can't, I can't." He shook his head, clutching the cross hanging around his neck, his eyes closed as one of the demons licked his ear.

"Then I cannot help you. May your God be with you."

He screeched. "Wait!" Panting, he tried to back further into the carriage behind him. It leaned but did not give. "Wait. Join me. Us. The church. Do what you did to that demon. Help us with these creatures. And I promise you will die of old age and not the inferno."

I laughed. I laughed so loud it hurt my throat.

Clutching his cross, he whimpered, "And I will tell you who betrayed you. Whose fault it is your name was even in that book."

My companion returned with the force of a gale. Overwhelmed, I almost lost my footing. Lucky I'd already been on my knees. My strained joints and the hard road receded.

You must take his offer.

It's ridiculous. I cannot take the offer. Work for his church? The very people who burned over half the Order on their stakes for ridding their world of evil?

You must. You've been betrayed. They will kill all of you. And the evil will win.

THEY ARE THE EVIL.

Then show them the way.

And damned if my companion didn't have a point. Could we, from the inside out, make something of a difference? Save ourselves, save others, and continue to hunt the demonic forces of the world? Anyone with a gift or desire to help could be enfolded into our ranks in safety. Avoid the stake, and join us.

It could work.

Chapter Five

Mother Mary's hands still glowed as she pulled them away from Grace's head. Her skin translucent, the blood flowing through her veins remained visible until the light faded.

Mary knelt in the floor, next to where Grace had sunk to her knees. "A secret branch sanctioned by the Vatican, we joined with the church to escape the Inquisition. Since then, our Order has taken on many women, still outcasts for the most part, people with a desire to help and a gift to do so. In addition to some women of God, who believe they are doing his work."

Grace's mouth flopped open and closed like a fish lying on a sandy bank. Tears tracked down her face.

She wiped the tears from her cheeks, but when she pulled her fingers away, it hit her that it wasn't tears.

It was blood. She'd been crying blood.

Gazing up at Raphael, she whispered, "What did you do to me?"

"I'm sorry, Grace. It happens sometimes."

"The woman you showed me. Her name was Mary too. She had some kind of companion. Is that..."

"We've come to call the being Raphael. His history is throughout more than one religion. He's traveled across millennia, healing those who are what can be called demons."

Grace sighed, still gazing up at the haloed figure. "Like me."

"Like you."

Brow furrowed, Grace finished wiping her face, probably smearing blood all over instead. Her breath caught in her throat as she processed the vision. "Can you do what that Mary did? Can you heal me?" Clutching the base of her neck with one hand, she covered her black eyes with the other. "Can you free me?"

The multitude of voices whispered next to her. "Is that what you want?"

Swallowing around the lump in her throat, Grace squeezed her neck. What did she want?

Mary, just Mother Mary, spoke again. "You're not sure what you want. I can see that. In addition," she said, standing, "Raphael chooses, not I. Let me take you to your room where you can pack your things."

As Mary hefted her to her feet, Grace's slow brain tried to catch up. "Pack? My things?"

They glided down the hall. "You said you were leaving."

Grace gave her an absent nod and watched the floor disappear beneath her feet. The emotions from the vision flooded over her. She'd been helping people. She'd been hunting and freeing demons, consumed with the knowledge and warmed by the feeling that she could help so many, heal so many. Change the world, even.

She swallowed, stepping into her room. They'd washed the floor, but it smelled like bleach still and the stones had been left with a tinge of rusty red in an uneven splat. "If I'm like Karithexis," she said, lowering to the bed with the mother, "can I even be forgiven? What horrible things have I done?"

The image of Karithexis's arm buried in Maria's chest blazed through her mind's eye.

As though reading her thoughts—and who knew, maybe she could—the mother spoke. "I haven't got a list of your misdeeds, but surely they've been great. Demons are not nice creatures. They create chaos, destroy lives, and murder. They seem to—" She stopped, swallowing.

Grace crammed a fist into her diaphragm. "Seem to what?"

"Enjoy it."

Fighting to swallow, Grace fell sideways, losing air and the will to take in more. Smearing flaky blood on the thin blanket, she turned her face to the mattress, drew her knees into her chest, and wrapped her arms around them.

The darkness didn't overtake her. It came from inside.

The springs squeaked as Mother Mary stood. "Soon, the bell will toll. I hope you'll join us for Sister Maria's funeral."

*

The tolling bell brought Grace out of unconsciousness.

Drool covered her cheek, and she rubbed her face on the blanket to dry it.

During the excitement of Karithexis's exit and getting Maria to the useless infirmary, the mirror Karithexis produced had been shuffled under the bed.

Now Grace dropped to her knees and crawled beneath the bed to retrieve it from the shadows.

It'd shattered, one jagged piece lying separate from the frame.

She clutched the piece in one hand until it hurt and used her toes to back out from under the bed. The pain in her hand was no more than she deserved, and she squeezed so tight she drew blood.

Leaning against the bed, she used the sliver of mirror to check her cheeks. It being so small, only her cheeks fit in the reflection. She didn't have to look at her eyes—or lack thereof. Small favors.

The drool had washed off her blood tears on one side. The other side was a flaky trail from her cheek to her jaw. She scratched with a nail until it disappeared.

Shoving the mirror piece into her pocket, she grabbed her sunglasses and wandered to the cemetery.

Behind the church, down a grassy, rolling hill, a dirt path led to the massive cemetery full of dead bodies. Several curved walls, what the nuns called a columbarium, ringed it. Small plaques listed the owners of the ashes inside tiny compartments. All that was left of them.

Through the glasses, Grace squinted at the sun. Sunset would creep up faster than necessary and bring the longest night of the year with it.

A long night Grace wasn't sure she'd survive. If she brought herself to ask Raphael to free her, would the angel do it?

But if she did that, she'd never find out who she was or if what Karithexis had said was true. And there was more, questions she hadn't formed in her head or answers she was afraid of. She couldn't go into oblivion without at least attempting to get those answers.

Down at the bottom of the hill, the nuns stood in a circle. Some of the congregation had shown up too. They were too far away to see well, but they stood around something sticking up from the ground that wasn't shaped like the coffin Maria had been in a couple hours ago.

Voices murmured behind Grace as she shuffled her way down the hill.

She glanced over her shoulder.

The mysterious Daisy, her face set in a frown, followed Grace down the hill. A handful of men and women flanked her, walking behind her, and talked amongst themselves.

Daisy made eye contact with Grace.

Heart in her throat, Grace spun back around and sped down the hill. Though the grade was gentle, she almost lost her footing a few times in her hurry to escape Daisy.

She approached the graveside and frowned.

Long logs, each about four feet tall and spiked on the ends, stood upright in an oval. Tied together, they supported a wooden litter made of smaller branches. Atop the litter, a shrouded body covered, head to toe, in a piece of fine linen that'd been tied around the ankles, waist, and neck.

"Hm. A proper funeral," Daisy said.

Grace faced her, the need to puke washing over her, her stomach cramped and mouth tingling. "What do you mean?"

"You may not know this," she said, clutching a tuxedo jacket around her waist, her necklaces and charms stuffed beneath it, "but there are people in this world who can use a dead body to their advantage. Powerful spellcaster like Maria, could do a lot of damage if the right necromancer got their hands on her. Best to torch the body." She brushed her black twill pants, cut off above the knee in what wanted to be a straight line but didn't quite make it. Her knee-high black leather boots made it so only about four inches of skin, her knees, were exposed to the winter air. And her knives were still evident inside them.

Eyes roving over the rest of what must have been Daisy's band of hunters, Grace leaned closer. "You know they're witches?"

Daisy shrugged, her hair falling over one shoulder. "Nobody could turn a spell like Sister Maria. No one I ever met." She hooked her elbow. "Only seemed right to bury the hatchet for one day and pay my respects."

Without thinking, Grace took her arm and let Daisy lead her to the pyre. Her stomach did gymnastics inside her, but the feeling of needing to puke passed. Mostly.

Monica frowned at the approaching hunters and bit her lip.

Daisy angled right to her. She stopped, standing between Mon and Grace.

Daisy released Grace. "Hey, newbie," she said, leaning into Monica. "How're they treating you? Let you in on all the grand secrets yet?"

Monica stared forward like she was drilling holes in the body with her eyes.

"Yeah." Daisy grinned. "Didn't think so. Couldn't have you knowing enough to work on your own. You might leave them without your young, strong hands." She leaned closer to Monica and lowered her voice.

Grace copied her lean to listen.

"I mean, you know that's why they keep you around. To do the heavy lifting. The grunt work. That, and your pretty young face makes a great PR campaign. You know—" Daisy cleared her throat. "—you join us, and I'll show you everything on the first day. We could use you. I mean *really* use. Not whatever it is the sisters are doing with you."

Monica folded her hands inside her novice robes and stepped away. She shook her head, the perfectly placed headscarf rippling.

Daisy snorted and, with another look at Grace, walked around Monica and stood at Maria's head. Her group of hunters followed her in silence, including the man from the other night, who'd pretended to have his face buried in his phone until Daisy needed backup. He winked a bright blue eye at Grace as he passed.

Grace sidled next to Monica. Without any preamble, she leaned into her friend. "I'm sorry."

Monica laid her head on her shoulder. "Me too."

Grace breathed deep. She shoved one hand in her pocket and fingered the shard of glass there. The other she threw around Monica's shoulders.

When the mother lit what Grace could only describe as a torch, she closed her eyes. It didn't happen right away, but as the greedy flame burned the linen covering the body and started on the hair and skin, the acrid scent of burning hair making a home in Grace's brain, the tears fell again. In her head, she was Grace, and she was also that long-ago Mary. The woman who had put everything at risk to avoid the stake, the smell of her sisters burning alive still fresh in her mind. Imprinted on her heart.

Grace cried and didn't care if the tears were blood or water.

Chapter Six

"Grace."

One foot inside the van, Grace stopped and peered over her shoulder at the mother.

"Sit up front with Sister Monica," Mary said.

Mouth open, Grace glanced in the van.

Both of Eliana's thin eyebrows rode high on her forehead. The other sisters froze. You could have heard a pin drop.

Grace swallowed and pulled her foot from the van. "You got it, Mother." She tried to ignore the commotion in the back of the van as the sisters tried to rearrange and let Mother Mary have the seat closest to the door.

Monica grinned sideways as Grace slid into the passenger seat and yanked the door closed.

"What?"

Grinning wider, Monica shook her head and started the van. "Where should we take them? Tijuana?"

Grace giggled. "Does me being up here mean we're in charge?"

With a chuckle of her own, Monica rolled her eyes.

Mother Mary yanked the door closed and sat to fasten her seat belt. "Grace. Buckle up please. Sister Monica, you know where we're going today."

Mon nodded, Grace buckled, and the van left the convent.

Grace hadn't realized there was even a working stereo in the van. She and Monica flipped channels till they settled on pop rock from the previous decade. The rest of the sisters rode in silence, but up front, Grace and Monica rode in their own bubble, staring out the front window with the world unrolling in front of them. The convent sat on the edge of town, and it didn't take long to start riding past pastures filled with dairy cows.

Monica leaned sideways. "Hey, Grace."

"Yeah."

"What do you call a cow with no legs?"

Brow furrowed, Grace turned from the window. "Uh."

"Ground beef." She snickered.

Suppressing a laugh, Grace shook her head and kept her face straight. "Hilarious."

"What do you call a cow with two legs on one side?"

But Grace's head covered the punch line in red pain. She spoke but couldn't hear anything beyond the cotton in her ears. "I don't know where we're going," she said, clapping a hand to her forehead, "but I think we're here."

The van slowed and turned a corner.

Grace kept her eyes squeezed closed and tried to breathe through the pain. She wanted to ask Mary to fix it, but having seen what Raphael had done to that demon in the vision, she also wanted to stay as far away as possible from those glowing hands. So she threw all her concentration into getting through the pain and took no notice of the number of turns they took.

When Monica turned off the van and squeezed her knee, she cracked one eye.

They'd parked on a dirt road deep in the woods with giant stands of trees all around. It curved off ahead of them and behind them, with nothing on either side.

Brow wrinkled, she covered her eyes with her hand. "Where are we?"

Mother Mary opened her door. "We've been researching this demon for some time. We'd found an approximate location, and you have now pinpointed it."

Grace slid out of the van onto boneless legs. Her stomach revolted, but she swallowed and kept it down.

Monica leaned against the van next to her as the rest of the sisters got out their giant bags. Equipment clinked and clanked. Sacrament pouches were checked and secured. "Are you okay? You don't look so great."

Before she spoke, Mary stepped to the front of the van.

"I've seen demons disregard life for the many decades I've been with the Order. But this one is something special. It enjoys killing on an entirely different level. The wake of destruction behind this demon is wider than almost any I've seen before. And any I suspect I'll see in the future."

Even with her head pounding, Grace caught the hitch in Mary's voice. "Almost any?"

"Your friend Karithexis and the Order have something of a history. That demon has been on our radar for its ruthlessness for longer than I've been a nun."

"Well," Grace said, walking past the mother and deeper into the woods, "we should…" She trailed off, hand falling away from her head.

Monica joined her. "What is it?"

"What about me? You seem to know these demons by name. Do you know about me?"

The sisters went silent around her, like they were all holding their breath.

A gunshot from up ahead saved them from having to answer. A gunshot—followed by a scream so loud and long it might never stop climbing or taper off.

And it didn't. Instead, it was cut short.

Mary held her arm out, stopping them. "Everyone remember what we spoke of before we left. Grace, what did I tell you?"

Grace shook her head. "Before or after you told me to sit in the front?"

Stern frown crossing her lips, the mother shook her head. "I told you to keep your senses peeled for something, anything, you think we don't notice. We will be wholly involved in this, but you may be able to see things we cannot. I don't know. Just pay attention."

Without a good idea of what the mother meant, Grace shrugged.

On silent feet, the nuns crept up the road.

"Grace," Monica whispered, "stay behind me. In fact"—she leaned toward her—"take these." She dug in her pocket.

Grace's stomach took a trip to her toes and back. "You didn't bring me all this way to have me stay in back. Let me help. Let me do something. I feel like—" She gripped her jittering stomach. "I feel like I owe you at least that."

Monica held out her closed hand, palm down. "You don't owe us anything. Here." She shook her fist. When Grace opened her hand beneath it, she dropped two small orange floofs into it.

"What's this?" Grace pinched one between two fingers and squeezed. It squished into almost nothing.

"Earplugs," Monica said. "When I tell you, stuff them in your ears as far as they'll go. And stay behind me."

Eliana huffed. "Ladies." She crept behind the mother, some kind of metal contraption shaped almost like a gun in her hands.

The other sisters drew knives and guns Grace had never seen, and, if she wasn't mistaken, the outline of a long sword hid beneath Mary's robes.

Swallowing, Grace hopped a step to match her footsteps with Monica's, earplugs squeezed in her hand so tight her nails dug into her sweaty palm. She stuffed the earplugs in her front pocket and exhaled through her teeth.

As they rounded the last bend, the van far behind and out of sight now, and the house came into view, Monica reached out with her free hand and grasped Grace's.

Sweaty palms and all, Grace gripped her back.

The house squatted in a small clearing where trees loomed over it. Hemmed it in. Even in winter, skeletal as they were, they blotted out almost all the light coming from sunset. Red and orange light bled through, falling in thin streaks on the roof of the ramshackle wood cabin like fingers.

Grace shivered. A moan came from inside the cabin, and she hoped it was the same person who'd screamed earlier. At least it would mean they were still alive. She clutched Monica's fingers even tighter.

Monica squeezed back and lifted a crucifix in her other hand.

Without words, the nuns formed an upside-down half circle. Almost like a flock of geese in their V-shape, with the mother in the lead, but rounded. Like a shield.

They started whispering in Latin.

The addition of bees in Grace's head along with the migraine and her fuzzy stomach wasn't what she hoped would happen, yet here she was, with bees in her head.

But the buzzing subsided as a light surrounded Mother Mary. It grew, a thin, white film in the air, and tendrils expanded from one sister to the other until it made an almost physical wall between them. A sheen in the air that, if Grace leaned one way or the other, disappeared in an iridescent flash. Like a heat illusion.

A memory that didn't belong to her hit her with such force she lost her footing.

Rising from a flat blacktop, heat waves rippled. Her feet burned. She clutched a small satchel in one hand, and squeezed a piece of glass in the other so tightly it brought blood.

And like the image of the beer bottle, it left as quickly as it'd come.

She stumbled.

The sisters walked forward as one, the air shimmering between them.

Someone inside screamed, but as it tapered off, it became laughter, rising and falling into hysterical, bubbling giggles.

Grace shuddered, her head breaking open in the middle as if it had a seam. At least, that's how it felt. She clapped a hand to each side, fighting to hold it together, to keep it from flying apart.

Mother Mary stopped and stood tall. Sisters Joan and Alexandra broke off from the sides and dumped a line of salt on the leaves and dead, dry ground surrounding the cabin. They disappeared behind it, still dumping salt in a wide swath.

The laughter inside ended in abrupt choking and gurgling.

Jaw clenched, Grace waited for the sisters to reappear.

They did, having crossed each other's paths, and still dumping salt. Enough for an army for months. Years. And it sparkled in the thin sunlight, bouncing light into Grace's eyes.

Meeting back up with the others, Joan and Alexandra returned to their former places at the ends of the V and took up the chant again.

Still standing tall, Mother Mary called out.

"Demon Jalithesh, in the name of Raphael the Healer, the Archangel, we command you to meet us and accept we have come to free you."

A low chuckle came from inside. All the sisters flinched as the door flung wide.

A bloody man, well over six feet tall and almost as broad as the door frame, stepped onto the porch. Covered in blood from head to toe, he wiped his tanned face and hands with a dirty rag. He flung it aside. "Ah, the Order has finally come. Took you long enough." He bared his teeth.

"Let's party."

*

As one, the sisters stopped whispering. The shifting curtain of white energy coalesced with a moment of such bright iridescence, Grace closed her eyes.

Which gave her headache time to make itself known again.

She concentrated on the headache, letting the sisters and the laughing demon fade into the background, and found she could grip it with both hands and squeeze until it receded.

Imaginary fingers crushed the life out of it. She'd have to remember that trick for later.

The demon screeched.

Grace's eyes popped open, and she backed up as he bore down on the sisters, flying about two inches off the ground. She tripped over a root and fell on her ass.

Monica fell on top of her. Her elbow landed in Grace's gut, digging into the healing scar.

Stomach a mess of knots, healing injury burning, she steeled herself, waiting for the demon to land on one of them. Waiting for him to try to reach inside their chests like Karithexis had done to poor Maria.

Jalithesh stopped in midair as he hit the salt line. He seethed through his teeth. "What is this? Can't be regular salt, bitches. You know that won't stop a thing like me."

Mary chuckled. "Maybe you think too much of yourself." She started chanting in Latin, pulling the sacrament pouch from under her robes. She extracted her ampule of holy water, broke it open, and tossed droplets at the demon.

They sizzled as they hit.

The strong scent of burned matches floated through the air with the wispy smoke coming off the laughing demon's skin.

Taking her eyes off him, Grace knelt and helped Monica to her feet. "Sorry. I'll try to stay out of the way."

Monica grimaced and pulled her own sacrament pouch from under her robes. "Remember what Mother Mary told you."

Biting both lips between her teeth, Grace stepped behind Monica again.

The demon chuckled, face inches from Mother Mary's. "Let me guess," he said, pausing when she threw holy water in his face. He wiped it, his hand burning, and smiled. "You're using your nonlethal bullshit to try and save this vessel, huh? Why don't we go on ahead and make that impossible?" His hand disappeared behind his back.

Grace narrowed her eyes. Vessel? What did that mean?

Brow lowered, mouth stretched impossibly wide, he yanked a knife from his belt and wrapped both hands around the haft. Blade pointed inward, he stretched his arms to their limit.

As he plunged it toward his stomach, Monica screamed and leapt inside the salt circle. She strained against the knife arm, deflecting it.

He knocked her to the side.

Blood flew from her face. Or her neck. Grace couldn't tell.

Grace took off after her friend. At the speed of light, her insides went from painful to gone. Disappeared.

One of the sisters shouted, and someone's fingers slid off Grace's arm, but none of it stopped her. She slammed into the salt line.

A wall exploded in front of her, fire engulfing her. Hot flames surrounded her, burning not only her skin but within her head and inside all her organs.

Suspended in the burning wall, she writhed and screamed. A high-pitched wail that echoed off the naked trees. The pain was more than she'd ever known, even on Halloween night when she'd stumbled into the ER, insides on the outside.

The demon growled. "You would dare use another demon to attack me? *Me*?" He picked Monica up by the neck.

Through the flames, the pain screaming from the inside out, Grace couldn't see much except a limp Monica, suspended several feet in the air. Blood dripped from somewhere above Jalithesh's hand and oozed from between his fingers. In the moment before Mother Mary broke the circle, Grace knew that's what they'd have to do to both free her from its grasp and save Monica.

As Mary scraped her foot through the salt, Monica lifted her sacrament pouch over Jalithesh's head with a weak arm.

Grace flopped to the ground. Boneless.

Monica broke the bag over Jalithesh's head. The tiny ampules inside shattered. The stench of a thousand burnt matches flooded the clearing.

Hair on top of his head literally on fire, the demon tossed Monica like a rag doll.

She crashed into the side of the cabin and slid down the wall, coming to rest half on and half off the porch. Still. Silent.

Before Grace could think to work her muscles and stand, Jalithesh picked her up much as he'd done Monica. "One of my own, huh?" He pressed his forehead to hers, vacuuming massive amounts of air into his wide nostrils. He chuckled. "You can help me whether you like it or not."

Something—Grace didn't know what, but something like a string of energy—flowed away from her. It pulled out of her forehead as he squeezed her throat closed with his hand.

She tried to ignore both and instead slipped her jacket off.

He chuckled, and energy flowed back into Grace from him, red and sick.

Everything within her revolted. She wanted to puke her own guts out onto him, a steaming pile of offal. Anything to get rid of the feeling coming from him.

She threw her jacket over his head.

It smothered the flames, broke the connection, and cut off his laughter. He tossed Grace blindly.

She flew, her stomach somewhere near her mouth, and landed between the sisters and the demon, twisting her ankle and falling on her ass.

She grunted and clutched at her ankle as the sisters advanced on the demon.

As the iridescent shield they'd built between them passed over Grace, she shuddered. It tugged at her, every molecule of her, trying to rip her apart piece by piece. She left her body as it tugged, rising a few inches from the ground and staring down at the stunned woman below her, eyes wide and wet.

Someone stared back. Someone else inside her body.

And then the sisters were past. She blasted back into her body, her teeth clashing together over her tongue. The metallic taste of blood filled her mouth.

The sisters advanced on Jalithesh, and he chuckled, pulling the jacket off his face with slow precision. He laughed, glowing with red light around the edges of his skin, and glanced down at Grace. "Thanks for the boost, friend."

Breathing heavy, willing her body to cool from the inside out, Grace clenched her teeth and swallowed the blood. Now that the sisters and their shield were past, she couldn't take her eyes off Mon's still form on the porch.

Her worry almost covered the whispering in her head.

Grace had no way to know if Jalithesh heard her too, but as she concentrated, the whispering became clear. She'd tuned into a radio station hooked directly to his brain.

Aloud, he continued to taunt the sisters with insults as they closed a circle around him. But in his head, there was a secret voice. Plotting.

Easing toward the cabin, she tried to concentrate on what the words inside his head were, but the chanting from the sisters swelled, overtaking everything.

Teeth clenched, she tiptoed onto the porch and crouched behind Monica, who still laid half off the side, her body wracked with shivers. With ginger care, she lifted Mon all the way onto the porch and wrapped her arms around her.

The whispering in her head and the chanting of the sisters fell away. Even the way Jalithesh laughed, loud enough for it to be heard from miles away, disappeared as she examined Monica's wound.

With the knife, the demon had opened a red gash across her face from below her jaw to her forehead. It went through her right eye.

Blood glued it shut.

Holding her breath, Grace put her arms around Monica. She tried to share her own body heat with Mon. A gentle warming, nothing like the warmth of the fire from the salt ring. Eyes closed, she imagined wrapping Monica in a shield like the one between the nuns, glowing and iridescent.

As she focused, Monica's shivering stopped. The blood *drip-drip-dripping* onto the porch slowed.

But the whispering crept back in, words becoming clear. It wasn't a language Grace recognized. Not with her ears.

She concentrated on the message. What he was saying beneath the words themselves.

And the fire I shall rain shall be to the glory of you, oh child of Mara. They will cower before me and know that you are more powerful than any they have ever seen. More powerful than their angel. All-consuming with your anger, your hatred. They will eat their own spirits, if you will join me in this fight.

COME TO ME NOW, RAGA. IT IS TIME TO JOIN ME.

Sweat drenching her forehead, Grace bolted to her feet. She shouted across the clearing. "Mother! He's calling another demon!"

Mother Mary glowed brighter, the iridescent sheen between the sisters encasing Jalithesh. It became firm and opaque. Grace couldn't see in anymore.

Monica whispered from the porch where she lay, "Grace. Earplugs."

Grace knelt next to her, eyes still glued to the light cocoon encasing the sisters and the demon within. What would come out of it? A butterfly? Or something worse entirely?

Monica wheezed. "Earplugs."

It hit her what Mon was saying.

Shaking, she dug the orange floofs out of her pocket and shoved one in her right ear.

The other squirted through her sweaty fingers and disappeared between the wide slats of the wooden porch.

"Shit!"

Monica held out a limp hand, squinting through one eye. "Come here."

The chanting from inside the cocoon grew louder. The demon screamed, and the words in his head were incoherent, now. Only the buzzing of the spell remained.

Monica gripped Grace's head and hugged her close, pressing her left ear into her breast.

Arms wrapped around her, Grace buried her face in Monica's chest and listened to the voices in her head, the chant of the sisters. It was like listening to the other end of someone's phone conversation from across the room.

Daemonium erit liberum

Remittetur tu errata

A te levavi, ira tua

Auferetur ex tu tristitia

Et non desperandum

Dare nobis tu timorus

Damus diligitis

Libera ab hac vita

Relinquere integrum pellis indumentis

Onera portarent liberati tu

Liberum a es in iniquitate tua

Daemonium es liberum

The clearing fell silent.

Grace lifted her head.

The white light surrounding the sisters faded like an afterimage, leaving them standing in a circle around a moaning man lying on the ground.

Above them, the air had substance. It sighed, pulsed, and faded. The shape there hadn't been apparent until it was gone. Like smoke drifting away on the wind.

The man slumped to the ground.

*

The ride to the hospital was a red blur.

Monica's eye leaked watery pink blood from under the lid, droplets of it caught in the lashes, the blood around the gash clotting.

Hugging a semiconscious Monica in her lap, Grace cried the whole way, and the rest of the sisters attended the man in the floorboard. A body Jalithesh had inexplicably called his "vessel."

Grace considered the shimmering air above the sisters as it left the body. It shivered before breaking apart like dissipating fog. She desperately wanted to know where it'd gone, but all the sisters were far too busy to tell her. So, she held on to her friend and asked her God to help.

At the hospital, the same one she'd wandered into on that cold Halloween night, the nurses took one look at Jalithesh's vessel and Monica and ushered them all into the ER. They whisked Monica off before Grace even had a chance to ask where she was going.

She flopped into a chair in the waiting room and closed her eyes.

"You look a lot better than the last time I saw you."

Grace started, head falling off her hand where she'd rested it and fallen asleep.

A man with deep brown skin and even deeper brown eyes sat next to her, smiling. A surgical mask stretched under his chin.

"I'm sorry?"

He smiled wider and stuck out a hand, connected to a well-muscled arm. "Dr. Adams."

She took his hand and shook. Cold air hit her skin where she'd drooled down her arm. Snatching her hand away, she wiped her wrist on her pants leg. "Doctor?"

"I treated you a couple months ago. Wasn't it Halloween?"

Nodding, she narrowed her eyes and studied him again. The guts she'd injured that night twisted, wondering exactly what he thought of a woman who stumbled into the ER the way she had, alone. What must he have thought about how she got that way? "Did you? I don't remember much."

"You're healing well." He looked her over with a gentle, relaxed expression, his eyes soft. "It's good to see you recovering so well. Did you come in with the sisters of Saint Raphael?"

"Yeah, yeah. I stay with them."

His eyebrows lifted. "Do you?"

She swallowed. His open face invited her to spill everything. Not only why she stayed with them, but who she was, who they were, and what had happened. She slid her tongue between her teeth and bit down.

The pain centered her. She rubbed the scar crossing her head. "I don't remember who I am, so they let me stay. How is Monica?"

Brows coming together, he shook his head. "You still don't remember? They didn't take you home? Let you see where you lived?"

Her breath stopped. "What do you mean?"

He leaned in, glancing around the waiting room. "Anna, I mean, Dr. Byles, couldn't stop thinking about you. She discovered you'd been reported missing, so she found your name and address and emailed it to the sisters about three weeks ago."

"I didn't see that." But she was beginning to suspect her body belonged to this missing woman, and not Grace herself.

With another quick look around the room, he stood. "I'll show it to you if you want."

She copied his search around the room. Sisters Joan and Constance sat in the corner, Styrofoam cups in their hands, eyes on the news blaring from the TV. None of the others were anywhere to be seen.

Ducking her head, she followed him through the double doors to the ER. She peeked into each room they passed, looking for Mon. She didn't see her, but she did see the injured man they brought here.

Hooked up to an IV and a bunch of machines, he lay in a darkened room, eyes closed. Bandages covered most of his exposed skin. If he was still alive after they'd freed the demon, that had to mean the demon had hijacked his body—possessed it.

Eyes sliding past him, she followed the doctor into an office about halfway down the ward. A nurse sat, feet up on a footstool, eyes half open. "Hey, Doc. Who's your friend?"

"Funny, she had the same question." He winked at Grace and sat at a computer. Wiggling the mouse, he narrowed his eyes at the screen and punched a few keys. "Have a seat. What are you going by?"

"Grace." She pulled a wheeled chair from under the desk. The scraping of the wheels across the linoleum floor put her teeth on edge. Everything was too shiny. It smelled like blood and pine cleaner, like the night she'd woken here.

Her stomach churned while the circle on the screen spun, booting up after the doctor logged in.

He brought up a file folder and clicked it open.

Someone screamed in the hallway.

Heart in her throat, Grace bolted to her feet. Had the demon returned? She rushed to the door and peeked out.

"Daniel!" A woman, three children hanging off her arms like satellites, hurried down the hall. Her eyes wide, skin pale and pasty, she shouted again. "Daniel!"

The man who'd been taken over by the demon answered in a croak. "In here."

Grace couldn't see their reunion, but the kids crying and laughing, and the woman's relieved sobbing, was unmistakable.

She turned back to the doctor.

On his screen, a copy of a driver's license floated in the blue.

The face she'd seen in the mirror, minus the black eyes, stared out at her.

"Grace, meet Natalie," he said, angling the screen toward her.

Breath caught in her throat again, her lungs tight, Grace crept toward the screen. And on it, a street address listed right there, right under the name "Natalie Bauman."

She tried to smile. Her lip lifted. "Could you print a copy of that for me please?"

*

In a chair outside Monica's hospital room, Grace flipped the folded paper over and over in her hands. The sharp points on the edges dug into the pads of her fingers as she spun it. Inside the folded paper?

Natalie Bauman.

Her address, hundreds of miles away.

Grace unfolded the paper, eavesdropping on Mother Mary and Monica's conversation.

"I know, Mother. But he was about to kill that man."

"You had no right to put yourself into that position. You could have gotten us all killed, child."

Monica sniffed and said nothing.

The mother continued, "I see now I was right to postpone your induction into the Order. You're not ready, despite all the good you've done and everything you've learned."

Grace stared at the paper and the face there; her light brown eyes, lighter brown hair hanging next to a pale, happy face with scant makeup. Her smile radiated from the picture with its own light, like it was the best day of her life.

Eyes skipping to the issue date, Grace tried to ask that voice in her head, the one who must be the real owner of this body, what the date meant.

But she was silent.

Mother Mary approached the open door. "Get some rest, Monica. We'll have to leave you here overnight, but you should be able to come home tomorrow."

Embarrassed to be seen eavesdropping and entirely unready to speak to the mother, Grace folded the paper in her hands and concentrated—hard—on not being seen. As hard as she had in the hallway alcove, the day she'd overheard Mary and Monica talking about her.

Mary's eyes skipped over Grace much like Monica's had on that day. She walked toward the door to the elevator a few steps and stopped.

Turning around, brow furrowed, she glared at Monica's door. And she looked right at Grace, but she didn't make eye contact and her eyes never stopped.

Shaking her head, she spun again and left the ward.

Grace considered what had happened. Had she actually made herself disappear, or something? The mother had stopped for a moment, but then grazed over her as if the chair sat empty.

Huh.

Standing, Grace refolded the paper, digging the corners into the pads of her fingers again and twirling it between her hands. Though her heart tried to beat out of her chest, she slid around the doorjamb and sidled into Monica's room.

Mon lay in the bed, an IV stuck in her arm and surrounded by beeping machines. A smaller bag also hung from the IV pole.

Grace squinted at it.

"Painkillers," Monica croaked, her face turned away. Bandages wrapped her head several times, coming down onto her forehead.

Sitting on the chair next to the bed, perching on the end of it, Grace turned the paper over again. "I have to ask you a question, Mon."

Monica turned toward her.

Grace tried not to gasp, but she couldn't help it. Gauze and medical tape covered half Monica's face, a thick pad over her eye.

Mon gave her half a smile. "I guess I could get an eye patch and go into pirating, since this nun thing isn't working out so well."

"Shit, Monica. Your eye."

The other half of her mouth lifted. But her chin trembled, and she turned away again.

Grace cleared her throat and spun the paper again, wearing the sharp corners down. How to begin? Would Monica tell her the truth? "The doctor told me who I am. He said I was reported missing, and the doctors sent an email to the sisters with my—her—identity three weeks ago."

Mon watched her through the one slitted eye. "What's your question?"

She cleared her throat again. "Does this body—Does it—Did I steal this body from someone?"

Leaning on the pillow, Mon nodded. "Maybe. We tend to call the bodies vessels. Often, they're stolen, but also, sometimes people make deals with demons. For money, power, all kinds of things."

Grace sat back, smacking into the chair and huffing all her air out. "So this isn't even my body? It belongs to this, this Natalie Bauman person?"

Mon leaned up to look at the folded paper. "What's that?"

"Her license. Her address. Someone reported her missing."

The scene in the hallway, the woman and her children screaming for their dad, hit her. There might be someone out there looking for Natalie. Someone who would be happy to see her.

If Grace gave her back to those people, would that fix this hole in her center?

"I'm going there, Mon. I'm going to find this woman's home."

Voice thick with tears, Mon glanced at the window. "When?"

"Now, I think."

Monica pressed her full lips together. A tear slipped down her cheek.

And Grace couldn't leave her like that. Not after everything. She scooted up in the chair again and laid her chin on the bed railing. "I overheard what Mary said to you. About postponing your vows. I'm sorry. Was that my fault?"

Monica shook her head, and a tear snuck from her eye. "None of this is your fault, Grace. It's mine. This whole thing about being a nun has been an experiment in failure. I'm terrible at it, and everything that's happened to you is my fault. So much of it was my idea." She cupped

Grace's chin with cold fingers. "I'm sorry. It was wrong to keep you in the dark."

Grace laid her hand over Monica's and leaned into them both. "Monica. I have to go."

Lashes wet, Monica stared at the ceiling with the one eye she had left. IV tubing stretched across the bed, she put her other hand over Grace's. "I'm coming with you."

THE VESSEL

Chapter Seven

"You should have stayed in the hospital longer," Grace said, limping down the side of the road with Monica hanging on her shoulder.

"If I stayed until morning, the sisters would've come back. Do you think they'd let you leave?"

Chewing her lip, Grace shook her head. It socked her in the gut, thinking of the sisters as her jailers. But that's what they were, weren't they? They'd held her there, in the convent, not telling her she was a demon. Not telling her she was living in someone else's body. Not telling her anything. Just feeding her and taking her on demon hunts.

She sighed and stopped, glancing at Monica's bandages. "Thanks for coming with me. What would I do without you?"

"Not get so many weird looks from these cars driving by, I think." She gestured at her face. "I should work on covering this up."

Grace started to walk again but paused. "Mon, do you have any money?"

With a chuckle, she shook her head. "I've got a couple bucks and my license. The gas card for the convent."

"We probably shouldn't use that."

"Is our road trip going to be to the end of the block?"

The sun had set hours ago, and the chill of winter worked into Grace's bones. They needed a car. Or at least somewhere warm. How would they get either of those without money? Grace sighed. "You thirsty?" She angled toward the gas station on the corner, its bright LED lights screaming into the sky and sending spikes directly into Grace's brain.

They crossed the parking lot, only one car parked on the side of the store and none at the pumps. The bell dinged with a tired rasp when Grace pushed the door open and pulled Monica through with her.

The guy behind the counter looked up.

Dragging Monica, Grace dipped down an aisle. She grabbed two waters, clutching the necks of them both in one hand, and considered what she might say to the man up front to get them out of here with free water.

But on the way up front, an image assaulted her.

A convenience store.

Like Daisy had mentioned.

She came around the chips and beef jerky, peering through the snack cakes. She'd always enjoyed getting these humans to do things. It made them so happy to knock things over and break them, and some of them even liked to kill. Got some kind of rush from it. It was easy enough to convince those to do things like the one nearing the counter was doing now.

He'd killed a woman with a coffee pot, but before he had, she'd kicked him in the knee hard enough to make him stagger. He might have torn a ligament, but before he had a chance to give in to the pain, Grace propelled him forward with a simple command.

Dragging one bloody foot, he stalked to the front, seething through his teeth and bleeding from wounds that might have killed someone else—someone not under a demon's suggestion.

The man behind the counter screamed into the phone. He'd called nine-one-one. They'd never get here in time, even if they were in the parking lot. The killer was on a roll now, and so was Grace.

She grinned from behind the snack cakes. "Eyes," she whispered.

She liked to keep the commands simple. It was fun to see what the humans came up with on their own. They were so creative sometimes.

The killer laughed, clutching what was left of the coffee pot handle.

The clerk screamed and backed away from the counter.

Grace smiled and licked her teeth.

Her human puppet leapt over the counter, snagging the clerk by the collar. He brought up the coffee pot handle, jagged pieces of glass hanging out of it, and smacked the clerk in the eyes with it. How he did that with his stomach hanging over the counter and the tiny bit of leverage he had impressed her.

Phone slipping from his limp fingers, the clerk lifted his hands to his eyes.

With no more instruction than she'd already given him, the killer dropped the coffee pot handle, swatted the clerk's hands away, and grabbed the short pencils lying on the counter that people used for their lottery tickets.

As the doomed clerk screamed like a teakettle, her beautiful killer jabbed a white pencil into each of his eyes.

Grace stopped in the middle of the aisle, sweat popping out on her forehead. Her stomach rolled.

Monica whispered. "You okay?"

She swallowed the bile in her throat. "I know what Daisy was talking about." She started toward the checkout again.

"What? About what?"

"Hi," she said to the clerk.

He bobbed his head at them. "You ladies look like you've had a rough night." Brow furrowed, he took in Monica in her robes, eventually meeting her eye.

Grace released her and leaned on the counter, setting the bottles down. "We have." Her eyes skipped to his name tag. "Josh. We'd like to take these drinks to go."

He reached for one.

She laid her hand over his and stopped it in midair. Swallowing, she tried to call up the feeling from her memory, or vision, or whatever that was. "We're just going to take them, Josh."

"Yeah. Let me ring them up." But his hand didn't move.

She concentrated harder, feeling the voice inside her head, trying to remember her vision and the voice deep, deep inside. How she'd used that inside voice, telling the killer what to do. She'd been warm, like she'd sat in front of a fire that baked her insides instead of her skin. "No. We're not paying for them."

His eyes glazed over. "You're not paying for them. You're right." He glanced at Monica again. "I—" He paused and swallowed, lowering his hand. But it didn't hit the counter; it continued to hang in space about an inch above it. "I have an old Halloween mask here; it came with an eye patch. Do you want it?"

Line between her brows, Mon shrugged at Grace.

Grace returned the shrug.

Monica held out her hand for the eye patch the man brought from behind the counter.

His chin trembled as he dropped it in her palm, and his eyes skipped back to Grace.

"We'll take the money in the register," she said.

The register bell dinged. He laid all the money out flat on the counter.

Eyes on his, Grace scooped it up.

A single drop of blood oozed from the clerk's nose. His chin trembled again.

Monica grabbed the waters with one hand and gripped Grace's arm with the other. "Grace. I think we're done."

But Grace held on tight to the connection, drilling it into his brain. "And your car. We need your car."

Without a word, he dug his keys from his pocket and laid them on the counter. A tear tracked down his cheek, meeting more blood from his nose under his chin. They mingled together, a pale, watery drop of blood splashing onto the counter.

"Grace."

She swallowed, snagging the keys. Backing away from the counter, she stuffed the money in her pockets and grabbed one of the waters from Monica. She held it in the crook of her arm and gripped Mon's hand.

Holding hands, they backed out of the store, the clerk staring off into space.

A slow trickle of blood dripped from his chin.

*

Hundreds of miles and several hours of rest later, they sat across the street from the address on Natalie's license. When Monica prodded Grace about how she'd done what she had in the gas station, Grace tried to pretend it hadn't happened. What kind of damage had she done to that man's mind? Why had he been bleeding out of his nose? Too many questions.

Natalie's house sat across the street. A breeze rippled the row of hedges in front of the neat blue townhouse. The white trim sparkled.

Grace exhaled through her teeth. "Do you think anyone else lives there?"

Monica shrugged. "Someone reported her missing." She opened the door to the gas station clerk's little coupe.

Hopefully there'd be someone home. The car was too cramped to camp in.

She helped Monica up the stairs, limping on her own sore ankle. All the driving had not helped it, especially considering the coupe was a stick.

She took the paper with the license on it out of her pocket and checked the address again. Holding her finger up to the doorbell, Grace paused. Her heart beat so loud she couldn't hear the traffic going by on the street behind her.

Monica put her own hand over Grace's and pushed the doorbell with the tip of her finger.

Wooden floors creaked inside.

"Thanks," Grace whispered out the side of her mouth.

Monica pressed her lips together, adjusted the cheap costume eye patch over her bandaged eye, and waited.

The shining white door swung open. "The sign says no solicito—" Standing in the door, a woman with reddish-brown hair hanging over the frames of her blue glasses, pale skin covered in several layers of well-applied contoured makeup, ran out of words. Her hands flew to her mouth. A huge, sparkling diamond ring on her left hand almost blinded Grace. She whispered from behind her fingers, "Nat?"

Grace shuffled her feet. What should she say? Yes? No? I don't know?

The woman in the door continued, "We thought you were dead. Where have you...You cut your hair?"

Her hand reaching up to follow the track of the healing scar on her scalp, Grace wobbled on her feet again. The short hair stuck up just enough to slide between her fingers.

Monica's eye flew between them both. When neither of them spoke for at least thirty seconds, both of them frozen in place, Mon stepped forward and stuck out a hand. "Sister Monica. I'm with the Order of Saint Raphael the Healer. Grace, um, Natalie, has been staying with us these past couple months."

"What? Why? You're a nun? Is this some kind of program?"

"Program?"

The woman in the door lowered her hands. "Like the halfway house you bailed on, Nat. You know the one, right? Where you left all your stuff and disappeared? We thought you were dead."

Monica kept talking. "She got into some kind of accident. When she woke up in the hospital, she had amnesia. We took her in until we could sort out her identity."

"Amnesia?" The woman swiped at her eye, smudging the perfect lines of her eye makeup.

Offering her hand again, Monica took a small step forward. "What's your name?"

Absently, the woman shook her hand, her eyes still on Grace. "Sorry, where are my manners, Sister? Shanna Bauman. You called her Grace?"

Grace started. Feeling slammed into her gut where it'd gone missing while Monica spoke. Bauman. The same as Natalie's last name. So she did have a family. She lifted the paper halfway up. "Are you, uh, are you related? Are you Natalie's sister?"

Shanna's face crumpled. She pulled her hand from Monica's and covered her mouth again. Tears streamed down her face, running tracks through the top layer of foundation, and she glanced at the paper. "You're my wife. That license picture was from our wedding day. You"—she sobbed into her hand—"you don't remember me?"

Gut-punched, Grace pulled down a breath but couldn't let it out. She'd casually broken this woman's heart while standing on her porch on a sunny afternoon. And there was no way to take that back.

Monica cleared her throat. "Could we maybe talk inside?"

As if on cue, a voice called out. "Shan? Who is it?"

Before Shanna answered, a small, wrinkled hand wrapped around the door and pulled it open wider.

A withered old woman wearing huge square glasses with an old-fashioned glasses chain not unlike the sisters' rosaries stepped around the door. She pulled her sweater tighter over her shoulders.

All the air left Grace's lungs. All of it. Like she'd stepped out into the vacuum of space. Her hands tingled and her mind blanked. She reached for Monica. Grasping her arm, she almost backed off the porch.

Shanna's hands fell to her side. "Mom came to help with the kids, Nat. Since you were gone."

The old woman smiled, and all Grace could think about was blood smeared all over her teeth. About her slurping up Maria's guts through them, her arm covered in blood.

"Natalie, dear," Karithexis said, "what's wrong?"

Monica tried, but her voice had no force behind it. "She—" Stopping, she swallowed, a click in her throat loud enough for Grace to hear. She backed up a step. "She has amnesia, um."

Karithexis's grin rolled her cheeks up like a paper blower. The corners of her mouth pointed at her ears. "Amnesia? You mean to say you don't remember your own mother?" She stepped forward, hand outstretched, fingers hooked into claws.

Grace jumped back so violently she fell down the stairs and into the railing. She scrabbled at it, trying to catch it, but went ass over teakettle instead and into the bushy shrubs in front of the porch. They scratched her back and arms as she fell, sharp limbs drawing blood, and a shout ripped from her throat.

Stuttering through an apology, Monica rushed down the stairs and helped Grace out of the bushes. Hand wrapped around her bicep, she clutched Grace and stood so close she vibrated against her.

Shanna witnessed the whole production in silence. Arms recrossed, her frown sank deeper and deeper, and when Grace finally stood again, small lines appeared next to her mouth, her frown so severe it looked painful. "You know what, Nat? I cannot do this with you right now. Why don't you call me when you think you can stay sober for longer than five minutes?"

She followed the grinning demon into the house and slammed the door.

*

"Grace."

Hands wrapped around the wheel so tight her knuckles had gone white, Grace clenched her teeth and whipped past a slow-moving semi. She cut in front of it so fast the driver flashed his brights in her eyes and left them on. Even in the daytime, she got the message.

Stomach an empty hole in her center, she squeezed the gas harder and sped away from the pissed-off truck.

Monica's own hands clenched the door handle and the oh-shit bar above her. "Grace."

But the angry bumblebees in Grace's head wouldn't stop buzzing. She drove faster to escape them, to leave them behind with Karithexis hanging over Natalie's family like a thunderhead.

"You're driving a stolen car with no license and going over a hundred miles an hour on a crowded freeway. Grace," Monica said, laying her hand on the wheel, "slow the fuck down."

The curse caught Grace's attention. Monica cursed from time to time, but it was always light curses like "damn" or "hell." She let her foot off the gas and hit the turn signal.

Tires thumping as they went over the rumble strips on the side of the road, the car came to rest on the shoulder. Grace pulled the wheels all the way to the dirt and turned the car off.

The truck passed, blowing its horn the whole way. Once the sound faded into the distance, Grace peeled her hands from the wheel. Her knuckles ached.

She sighed, stretching her fingers out. "That demon is going to kill them. She's already possessed Natalie's mom. She's going to kill them and eat their guts for breakfast."

Mon squeezed her knee. "Not if we stop her."

Grace exhaled a laugh, staring down at her lap. "I don't know if you remember, but last time we met Karithexis, you ended up bleeding all over my bed and she reduced me to a crying puddle in the floor." She swallowed, her throat tight. "And Maria," she began. She couldn't finish. "It's not like we can run back to the convent with our tails between our legs. I don't even know if they'd help us."

Hand still on her knee, Monica pulled a slow breath through her nose. "I know. But we can't let Karithexis hurt these people. It's not their fault this is all happening."

"I think this Natalie made a deal or something."

Mon's thumb caressed Grace's knee. "What makes you think that?"

Grace shook her head, trying not to think about the last time she saw Karithexis and failing. "When she killed—When, um—" She stopped and inhaled deeply. "Last time, that demon said something about a deal in a bar. And I saw a vision of a beer bottle. I think—I think Natalie made a deal with me."

Exhaling through her nose, Mon narrowed her eyes. "Do you know what it was?"

Shaking her head from side to side, Grace leaned until her forehead rested on the steering wheel. "What are we going to do?"

Traffic flew by on the left side, rocking the car. Some cars blew their horns.

Someone tapped on the driver's-side window.

Grace started, heart in her throat. A quick glance in the rearview mirror showed her a flashing red light. A male torso walked up beside Monica's window. He wore a uniform, with several weapons hanging off his belt. A policeman.

Looking out her own window, Grace found the torso of a woman in the same type of uniform.

The woman rapped her knuckles on the window again, and the window muffled her voice. "Roll it down."

Turning the keys a click with one hand, Grace pushed the window button with the other. She hit the auto-open by accident, and the window rolled all the way down. Chilly winter air and exhaust poured through it.

A woman with flashing green eyes and gray-streaked brown hair rolled into a bun on the back of her head leaned into the window. She chuckled.

"I really should have seen this coming," Daisy said.

*

Steam drifted off the coffee in Daisy's cup. She stood, cutting her eyes at the man sliding into the booth. They'd both removed their equipment and badges, and when Daisy sat back down, her hair cascaded over her shoulder, almost hanging in her coffee.

She swallowed a mouthful, a line between her brows. "Took you long enough."

"Sorry, Daze." He swept his hand through spiky brown hair, standing it on end, and flashed his bright blue eyes out the window next to the booth. "I can't park her just anywhere."

With a chuckle, she shook her head and looked at Grace and Monica where they huddled in the booth across from her and the man she'd introduced as Gareth. "You and that car." She swallowed another gulp. "So. What were you doing there?"

Grace cleared her throat, staring at her own cup of cooling coffee. She couldn't even sip it until it was almost tepid and had no idea how Daisy downed almost half a cup while the steam still billowed from the top.

Daisy chuckled. Her necklaces clinked against the table as she leaned forward. "Fine. We'll come back to that." She angled her chin at Monica. "What happened to you?"

Monica's fingers grazed the eye patch. "Demon."

Gareth snorted. "No shit. She means what happened with the demon. What demon?" He didn't make eye contact, but instead unscrewed the cap of the salt shaker. The lid sprayed a mist of salt all over the table. Some of it got in his coffee. He started dumping it in a fine line around his cup.

Grace glanced at Monica.

She stared down at the coffee, the steam floating up into the eye patch.

Under the table, Grace squeezed her knee.

Monica took a sip of the coffee. "Its name was Jalithesh. I stopped him from destroying his vessel, but it was— I was impulsive. I jumped in too quick." She swallowed, her jaw bunched. "I was foolish."

"You were heroic," Grace said. "You saved that man's life. I saw his family when they got to the hospital. You gave them that. That joy."

The salt shaker hit the table, three-quarters empty. Gareth started the process of sweeping all the stray salt crystals into a line surrounding his coffee.

Entranced, Grace watched him neaten the salt into a tight circle.

But Daisy leaned over her cup further, her strange pendants clanking against the table again. "You did, did you? Pretty brave. Good work." She gave Monica half a smile.

Monica swallowed but said nothing else.

Grace wanted to hold her. Instead, she turned to Daisy, one hand around her coffee cup, and pointed at the necklaces. "What are those anyway?"

Daisy grinned again and leaned back, throwing one arm over the booth behind Gareth. "Who are you, Grace? Seeing you in that video, then with the sisters. You're not a novice. You don't smell like one." She cut her eyes at Mon, a smirk playing across her lips, but Monica didn't so much as twitch. "What do you owe them? Have they got something on you? Are you like a gofer or something?"

Her eyebrows drew together, and Grace pictured a small, furry rodent. "A gopher? What's—"

"Not a woodland creature," Gareth growled. He lifted his coffee cup from the carefully constructed salt circle and swallowed a sip. "A go-fer." He enunciated each syllable with precision. "You go for stuff. Get them things. Help them out with stuff maybe they can't get themselves." He side-eyed Daisy and shook his head.

Daisy smiled and pulled one leg up into the booth. She leaned on her knee.

The waitress appeared. "Can I get you guys anything else? Did anyone want some food? Something sweet to go with the coffee?"

One elbow on the table, Daisy poked Gareth in the shoulder. "He's watching his weight. Me, I'll have something. What do ya got?"

As the waitress ran through the dessert choices, Grace leaned closer to Mon. "You okay?"

She shrugged. "I think it's too much."

"What do you mean?"

But before Mon answered, Daisy kicked Grace's shin under the table. "Get you something. Her too. On us."

Before she said no, Grace's stomach grumbled. They hadn't eaten anything since the road last night, when she'd used some of the stolen money to buy them a gas station sandwich to share. Still, she didn't want to owe the hunters anything. She shook her head.

Gareth snorted, sending the salt in front of his cup flying.

The waitress stared at it with tired eyes.

He shook his head and swept the salt back toward the cup with the flat of his hand. "I heard your stomach from over here."

"They'll both have the breakfast home run or whatever you people call it," Daisy said. She'd lowered her leg again and leaned against the booth, toying with one of her odd-shaped pendants.

The shape of it alone set Grace's teeth on edge.

Daisy's green eyes sparkled as they landed on Grace again. "And bring them that brownie thing you're bringing me. Chocolate's good for the soul."

Without writing anything down, the waitress left after one more sidelong glare at the mess Gareth had made.

"Tell you what," Daisy said, after two minutes passed in silence. "The dinner is a freebie. But if you tell me at least one thing about what you were doing at that house, you guys can come with us, and we'll give you a bed too. Look like you could use one."

Monica whispered into her cup. If Grace's own coffee was any way to tell, hers was almost cold. She spun the full cup in her hands. "What makes you think we don't have our own place to go?"

Gareth lifted his cup to his lips, tilting it so far his exposed Adam's apple strained. He sat it down outside the salt ring. "You ain't working for the sisters on this case, are you?"

Before Monica answered with what would have been a way smarter answer, Grace let the words fall out of her mouth. "You can't prove that."

With a snort, Daisy grinned. "We know now, don't we?" She glanced over her shoulder, and when she looked back at them, her eyes hardened. "If you were, you'd have tried to call them already. Made up some dumbass excuse to go to the bathroom and run outside instead. I rode with you all the way here. Didn't even hear a cell phone buzz. You don't have one to share between you, do you? Don't even have a pot to piss in. And it's too cold to sleep in that car. You'll both die of hypothermia."

Monica forced a laugh out her nose. "Like you care."

Daisy's shoulder moved up and down in an exaggerated shrug. "Maybe I do. Maybe I care about getting that demon out of that old woman. It's been on my list for a while, if it's who I think it is. That one and its friend." She frowned, her brow dipping so sharp it might have been able to cut paper. "Been on my list for a while."

A million things flew through Grace's head. Daisy knew who Karithexis was? What had the demon done to her? And who was the friend she was looking for? What if it was Grace, herself?

She blurted an answer before she got any further down the thought tracks. "That demon murdered Sister Maria."

The waitress brought Grace and Monica heaping plates of food. Scrambled eggs, bacon, toast, potatoes, jam, and a side of pancakes. For both of them.

In front of Daisy, she sat a mounded monstrosity of chocolate. A comically huge brownie topped with chocolate ice cream and so much fudge it ran over the sides of the bowl.

Daisy showed the waitress all her teeth and thanked her. She flapped her hand. "Scoot."

After the waitress had gone, Daisy dug a spoon into the chocolate heap with such force some of the fudge splattered into Gareth's salt circle. "That demon is a fucking menace. You two come stay with us. We'll exorcise or kill that thing if it takes all we got and then some."

"Thought you hated working with the Order," Monica said, fork picking at the potatoes.

"You ain't with the Order. We already established that." She shoveled a spoonful of chocolate in her mouth and spoke around it, her voice as sticky as the fudge. "Consider it a one-time thing. After we're done, you get the fuck out. Deal?"

Mon took a tentative bite of bacon and chewed, turning her eye on Grace.

And though Grace's stomach said this was an awful idea, and Daisy was as likely to kill her as not when she figured out what Grace was, getting Karithexis out of Natalie's mom was the least she could do for the woman she inhabited. It was, at the very least, the first step in giving Natalie her life back.

So, she nodded. "Deal."

Chapter Eight

Daisy slammed the door of the little coupe and stepped back, hands on her hips. "Where'd you get this?" Her necklaces clanked against her belt. She'd strapped the weapons on after they left the diner and gave Grace directions while reclined in the backseat, all seemingly without looking out the windows.

Grace cleared her throat. The memory of the blood dripping from the clerk's nose hit her with the force of a truck. She stumbled and glanced across the roof at Monica, who was nice enough to answer for her. "It was a donation."

Daisy snorted. "Get it under the five-finger discount, then? Yeah. I know that coupon." Shaking her head, she led them toward the apartment complex. "We're going to have to dump it. If it really was a donation, we don't need the Order tracing it. If it was stolen, we don't need the cops asking questions." She opened a gate to a courtyard in the center of the single-story, U-shaped apartment building ringing it. "We've got some on the payroll though. Cars and bodies hide easy. If you let me, I'll call my salvage guy. They'll have it down to parts in a couple hours."

The man standing behind the counter bleeding, watching them back out of the convenience store, floated to the top of Grace's mind again. She swallowed, the guilt threatening to pull her knees from under her. He needed his car. But had he reported it stolen?

A more important question needled her. What had Grace done to his brain, crawling around in there? The kind of power she'd exerted over him couldn't come without a price. It couldn't.

"Do it," Monica said.

Daisy grinned.

A door squealed open.

Grace turned in time to see Gareth disappear into one of the apartments. He peeked over his shoulder, gave her half a wave, and closed the door. Grace would have bet on him laying a salt line right behind it.

Another door squeaked.

"Daze!" an excited voice screeched across the empty courtyard.

Daisy angled her head. Arms crossed, she led them toward the screecher. "Alice, honey," she said, tucking the necklaces into her jacket, "how are you today?"

A youngish redhead pulled her door closed. Freckles splashed across her nose and down her cheeks, a mole sat over her right eye, and her expressive brows raised together and widened her blue eyes. She smiled, and Grace swore she caught the ghost of braces on her front teeth. She spoke in a breathless rush. "You and Gareth are back early today, which is great, because I have so many things I wanted to—"

"Alice, honey." Daisy grabbed her waving hand. "Something's come up." She gestured to Monica and Grace. "We have a room for these two to share?" She looked at Mon with half a grin. "Maybe some clothes too?"

The girl stuck out her hand. "Alice."

Grace and Monica shook, introducing themselves. Alice's calloused palms rubbed against Grace's, the exact opposite of what Grace expected from her demeanor and expression. She looked like a bookworm, someone Monica would get along with, but the rough skin of her hands announced her as a worker.

"We've got a room, Daisy. Needs new sheets and stuff, but yeah. Only one bed though."

"Good. You guys go with Alice. I'll see you at the meeting." She spun on the heel of her black leather boot.

"Daze, wait," Alice said, walking after her. "About the spells..."

Grace strained, but she couldn't hear the rest. She leaned closer to Mon. "I can't hear what they're saying."

Monica grunted. "Rude to eavesdrop, Grace."

Grace frowned, a stone settling on top of the huge meal Daisy had given them, including that giant brownie. "Are you okay? You hardly ate anything, and you like—I don't know. You're—Are you okay?"

Arms folded over her chest, Monica shuffled her feet. "I'm sorry. I didn't mean to be short with you." She tried on a smile that failed.

Grace took her in. "I think we should see if any of these people can help with your bandages. They need to be changed."

That got her at least half the smile she wanted. "You're pretty good at it. You helped me with your own enough times to just about be qualified for nursing school. You have a healer's touch."

The man with the blood dripping from his nose made another appearance.

Followed in quick succession by the bodies she left behind her in the other convenience store. The spreading pool of blood on the floor.

Alice walked back over. "I'll show you where the sheets and towels and shit is."

Grace shoved the blood and murder and guilt as far away as it would go. "Can you get us some bandages for her eye too?"

*

Grace sat on the bed, the small studio apartment crowding in on her, and tried not to peek at the half-open bathroom door. "Do the clothes fit?"

Mon pushed the door open and stepped into the dim room. She'd found a pair of jeans that fit and was wearing her bra on top with no shirt. "Haven't worn jeans in so long. It's weird." Crossing the room, she smiled. It wasn't a whole smile; there was something sad at the edges of it. She flopped on the bed and lay back. "My God, Grace, I'm so tired." She closed her eye.

Joining her on the bed, Grace rubbed her leg. "You can't go to sleep yet. I need to change your bandages. Then there's some meeting or whatever Daisy wanted us to go to, remember?"

Mon sighed and sat up on her elbows. "That sounds so fun. Can't wait."

Grace chuckled and stuck her hand out.

Mon took it and sat up, scooting close. "Did they bring you some aspirin or something? I'd be a liar if I said this didn't hurt." She gestured at her injured eye.

Grace sat a plastic bag between them and rooted through it. "I see something called aceto-...uh, acetomen-something. And also this one." She picked up another bottle. "Uh, morphine in this one."

"Hand me the first one."

She did.

Mon tapped out two pills and dry-swallowed them, her throat working to get them down. She capped the bottle and handed it back. "Thanks."

Dropping it in the bag, Grace rooted through the rest of the supplies. All things she'd seen before, when Mon had changed her bandages for all those weeks. Gauze, tape, scissors, some smelly ointment, some saline for cleaning. They'd even thrown in a new eye patch that was much nicer than the one Monica was wearing. She laid it all on the bed next to her. Leaning over the bag, she started to take off Mon's eye patch. Her back twinged, abs constricting. She straightened. "Hang on."

Mon smiled and watched her as she moved the bag and scooted closer.

She still wasn't close enough to not strain. "Here," she said, bending her left leg. She scooted, picked up Monica's left leg, and laid it over her right, her own leg immediately warmer. Pushing with her foot, she scooted as close as she could. "Better. Better?"

Flushed, Mon nodded and removed the eye patch, unfolding her other leg and laying it on the bed next to Grace.

Removing the old bandages with ginger care, Grace tried to think about something to say. She normally didn't have that trouble with Monica, but her friend was being unusually quiet. She cast about, but the only thing she thought of was that clerk whose car they'd ordered demolished.

"I don't know if I ever want to go back to them," Mon said. It was so low Grace almost missed it.

Her stomach sank. "Why not?"

"When I joined them, Mother Mary told me I could be what my family wouldn't let me. Complete. Whole." She sniffed and held her hair out of the way while Grace cleaned the wound. "You know my family ran me off. Called me sinful. But Mary said they could teach me a purpose so great that the reasons my family hated me would become unimportant." Her lip trembled, and she licked it, biting the corner.

Grace tried to clean the wound and watch her face at the same time. "Did it?"

"For a while." She met Grace's eye for a second. "For a while."

"Is that why you don't want to go back? Because whatever it is didn't go away?"

She lifted her hand and flopped it down. It landed on Grace's leg, and she sat, staring into Grace's eyes, her own remaining eye wet. "I don't know. You heard what Mary said. I can't cut it."

Pausing in folding a new bandage for her eye, Grace laid her hand over Mon's. "That's not true, and we both know it. And that's not what she said. But if you want to give it some time, some thought, you know I'll support you. Whatever you need." She squeezed her hand.

Mon bit the corner of her lip again and held eye contact. She let go of her hair, and it fell in her face, partially covering her wounded eye.

Grace brushed the hair away from it, trying to keep it from getting in the ointment she'd already put there. Also, it seemed like the thing to do. She smiled. "You know. Losing this eye has given you a certain something. Like you're rugged and tough but beautiful. I don't know." She leaned back. "It suits you."

Dropping her eye, Mon ran her thumb along the back of Grace's hand. "Grace. There's something I think I need to tell you."

"Anything." She went back to work with the bandages.

"I—"

Someone knocked on the door and spoke through it. "Meeting time. Let's go."

Grace picked up the tape. "You wanna tell me real quick before we head out there?"

Mon shook her head. "Finish the bandage. Maybe later."

*

Firelight flickered over the gathered group of about twenty hunters.

Grace sat in a lounge chair, wrapped in a thick jacket Alice had given her. The embers from the fire baked heat, the deep crimson beneath the flames wavering in the heat mirage. Whatever wood they burned had a mellow, almost nutty smell. Maybe oak, definitely comforting in some mysterious way.

What wasn't comforting was the way one of the hunters tossed a few sticks into the fire and stood. He leaned so far over the flames Grace worried his short beard might catch fire.

"So what you're telling us is these strangers from the next state over are coming on the hunt we've spent *months* putting together? Just like that?"

One leg draped over the arm of her chair, Daisy fingered her necklaces and stared up at him without moving. The firelight flickered in her eyes. "Yeah, Jim. Just like that."

The Black woman next to him smiled, a large, expressive grin that was hard not to smile with. She tugged his belt. "Sit down. We could always use the extra hands."

Jim, pale skin between his beard and eyes flushed, narrowed his eyes at Grace and Monica.

Grace tried to shrink inside the jacket.

"Only if they know what the hell they're doing, Lindsey. They look soft to me. Look like they're gonna get more than one of us killed. You're good, Daisy. I trust you." He turned back to her. "But I don't trust them." His finger jabbed in Grace's direction.

Monica flinched.

Some of the people around the fire murmured. It spread through the group like a cresting wave.

Daisy lowered her foot from the chair. Her toe touched the ground.

Lindsey tugged on his belt again and Jim sat, still staring at Grace.

And Grace turned to watch Daisy. With the fire flickering on her lowered face, she looked almost as menacing as Karithexis had, standing on Shanna's porch and grinning at them like some kind of underfed circus lion.

"You don't trust them, Jim. I get that. But you trust me. And I know they're good in a fight. Besides. They've got a personal stake in this, much as we do." She eyed them, and her face softened. But maybe that was a shadow from the fire. "I don't think I could stop them if I wanted to, short of cuffing or killing them. You want to do that?"

He grunted. The fire popped, and the mellow smoke wafted into Grace's face again.

A blonde woman on his other side spoke up. "The last time I saw you, you were wearing nun's robes."

Monica crossed her arms. "When was that?"

"At the funeral."

Some of the assembled group mumbled again. Someone whispered Maria's name.

The blonde went on, "I had to pay my respects. She was my favorite of the Order."

Jim snorted and ran his hand over his balding head. "Only because she saved your life, Samantha."

Lindsey laughed, flashing that magnetic smile again. "You act like that's not a perfectly good reason to like someone best. It's why you like Daisy."

Several people chuckled. It rippled around the group like the wave of murmuring had.

The tide turned, ever so slightly.

Daisy laughed too. Low, under her breath, barely audible. But it was there. She flipped her hair over the chair. "That, and my sparkling personality."

The mood broke. Several people guffawed, and Jim almost fell from his chair.

"Breathe, Jim," Samantha said, rubbing his back.

"I don't know what's so funny." Daisy turned toward Grace with a slow twist, her eyes still on Jim. "I'm a joy to be around."

As one, the group laughed again and broke up.

In the dying firelight, Daisy threw a wink at Grace and followed them.

Monica leaned into Grace's ear. "I'm glad Daisy got them to avoid talking about why I'm not wearing the robes now."

A voice came from Grace's other side. "So, can you guys help me with some supplies in the morning?"

Her insides in a twist, Grace jumped. "Dammit, Alice. Don't sneak up on me like that."

Alice grinned, her cheeks shining, and took the empty seat next to her. "So? Help me out?"

Grace glanced at Monica.

She'd gone quiet again, staring into the dying embers of the fire. Maybe thinking about whatever it was she wanted to tell Grace.

"Grace?"

"Sorry." She blinked and turned to Alice again. "Yeah. Sounds great. What time?"

"I'll be outside your door bef—" She yawned, losing the rest of the word in a bunch of vowels. "Sorry. Before sunrise."

"Before what now?"

"We have to dig up some roots that are more potent before sunrise and gather up some mushrooms that only grow in the morning. We need them for some spells. You in?"

"I guess?"

Alice chuckled, tucked a red hair behind her ear, and stood. "It was nice to meet you. See you in the morning."

As she left, Grace scoffed. "Do I even know what before sunrise looks like?"

Monica chuckled. "I know I do. We should go to bed."

They left the warm circle of fire, the other hunters' eyes boring into the back of Grace's head. Daisy tipped a small salute to them as they left, flinty eyes narrowed.

*

Hand draped over the wheel, Daisy glanced over. "Your friend Monica seems to have a lot to say."

Grace spun and stared through the back window at the car behind them. Daisy's tiny car only had two seats, and nothing Grace had said would get her out of riding with her. She'd almost tried to get them to leave her with Alice and the others by telling them she wasn't qualified and knew her way around a hole in the ground better than a spell. But Daisy had insisted, and she was as difficult to deny as the mother.

Daisy snorted. "So do you."

"Sorry." Grace turned around, and telling Daisy she didn't know what was wrong with Mon was on the tip of her tongue. She reconsidered. Monica was her only friend. She barely knew Daisy, and what she did know was Daisy would murder her in seconds if she found out what Grace really was. "I guess I'm just nervous."

"Tell me about the convenience store."

Two images overlaid themselves.

The clerk, Josh, giving them his keys. Bleeding from the nose.

And the murderer, pushing the broken coffee pot handle through his own neck with slow precision.

But with it came the warmth that had coursed through her when she'd told them to do it. The wave of power-like adrenaline, like the tingling feeling she'd get when she and Monica sat giggling at some silly joke, laughing until they couldn't breathe. Only a thousand times more.

"What—" Her throat closed around the words. She cleared it. "What convenience store?"

"I told you I saw you on a tape. I watched it again last night. It was you." She turned, that hand still draped over the wheel. "What were you doing?"

Shoving one hand under her leg, the leather seat sticking to her palm, she clenched her teeth. "I don't remember."

"Bullshit."

It wasn't like Daisy pulled a gun, but she implied the threat in the set of her teeth. The hand draped over the wheel didn't clench, and nothing she did was overt.

Instead, the atmosphere in the tiny car filled with intention. Like the promise to do her harm was a solid thing, something that ballooned out and seeped into every nook and cranny in the tiny space. Something that prevented Grace from breathing, pressing on her chest, encasing it like a corset.

Grace tried to swallow, but her tongue seemed to swell to twice its normal size. What she wouldn't give to roll the window all the way down, stick her head right out into the winter air, and gulp it down like water. But she was stuck in here, with that simple word hanging in the thick air. *Bullshit.*

She cleared her throat again. "It happened before I was injured. Before I met the sisters. I don't remember anything from before I walked into the hospital. No more than—" She stopped.

Daisy spoke in the vacuum. "No more than what?"

Grace had to go on, had to say something. She had to break the tension before it killed her. "No more than bits and pieces. It's like when I try to catch the memories of my life from before, they squirt away like—uh." She stopped again, unable to pull a single simple metaphor from the ether.

"Like smoke."

"Yeah. I don't remember any of it. Just waking up to Monica telling me I could come with them while I healed."

Turn signal clicking in the tiny cabin, taking up almost all the space for sound, Daisy turned the car into an alley and shut it off. She stared in the rearview as the others pulled in behind her. "Look. I don't need to say this, but I will because the Order has a hard time listening and who knows which of their bad habits you picked up. If you're lying to me," she said, leaning toward Grace, "if I find out you're trying to hurt any of my people on purpose, or if this all turns out to be some kind of elaborate plan you've put together with the sisters to get me out of the way or something, I'll end you so fast you won't have time to watch your own head spin."

Again, Grace tried to swallow, but her throat had gone dry. She settled for nodding. She'd never heard a tone as threatening as Daisy's. But around her unique green eyes and the small crow's feet surrounding them was a hint of softness, a kindness she hid under all that bravado. Grace had seen it the night they met, when Daisy joked about being a bad Catholic.

Grace caught Daisy's eyes. "It's not a lie. We want to get this demon away from that family as much as you do."

Daisy got out. "Yeah, why is that, anyway? You know these people or something?"

She spat the word too quick, without thinking. "No."

The rest of the team approached, and Monica stopped next to Grace, her hands clenched together. "I don't have my sacrament pouch. I feel like something awful is going to happen."

"What, you mean those little hex bags the sisters carry? Come here, darlin'. Got something better for you." Daisy motioned to the trunk. Which, in her tiny car, was in the front. She lifted the lid.

Grace looked in and her eyes widened. Air wheezed through her lips from far, far away.

The trunk itself had been outfitted like some kind of large tackle box. There were steps and levels. There was a bookshelf with four books on it. Large, leather-bound tomes nestled quietly amongst the guns, grenades, and so many other things all strapped into place. Grace's head spun.

"Here, take this," Daisy said, holding up a satchel to Monica. "What kind of salt do the sisters use?"

"Usually it has diamond dust."

Daisy exhaled through her nose. "That's that Vatican money. Diamond dust. Ridiculous."

Grace fell into the alley wall. No wonder she'd been so firmly held in that transparent wall of agony. It wasn't just a salt line, and even though she didn't know exactly what diamond dust would do, it was clear it made the line more powerful.

"Love to get my hands on some of that fancy salt," Gareth said, leaning against the wall next to her. "Those sisters have some of the best toys."

Grace glanced up at him, and in the darkened alley, his blue eyes turned a shade of gunmetal grey. "There's some pretty fancy toys there in Daisy's trunk. I don't think I've ever seen such a stash."

He grinned. "Gotta keep it on wheels somehow. And hers is the fastest; plus, she never gets pulled over. Can't have us all carrying that kind of stuff when the friendly cops can only do so much."

Daisy showed Monica the books. She pointed out the spell they'd helped Alice gather materials for at the crack of dawn and asked Monica how many times she'd gone over it.

"About five or six."

"Yeah, that's good enough, I think. You want to help cast? It's tricky work."

Monica flushed. "I'd be honored, Daisy. But don't you think some of your people would be better suited?"

"What did I tell you?" She closed the trunk. "You come join us, I'll show you the real stuff. No better time to get your feet wet." She elbowed Grace. "Need a weapon?"

Without thinking, Grace shook her head. But Gareth tapped her on the shoulder.

"Here. Take this." He held out a sawed-off, crucifix engraved in the barrel. "You need it, this'll slow 'em down long enough to get that spell going."

"Won't it hurt the vessel?"

"Not our concern, Grace. Our concern is the living. The ones not infected by a demon. That woman and those kids, they're our concern. The old lady is as good as dead anyway. This demon is not nice."

The pain in Grace's head came on at the same time a voice spoke from the shadows. "I think that's a bit of an understatement. Don't you?"

*

Eyes squeezed shut, Grace stumbled and ran into the wall. As her back hit, her eyes popped open.

All the hunters jumped at once, Daisy in front of them. "Where did you come from, demon?" She held some kind of metal thing in front of her she'd taken from the trunk. It was inscribed with all kinds of strange symbols and shaped a bit like a set of deer's antlers. She spoke a few words in a language Grace didn't recognize.

A glow came from the antlers.

Grace squeezed her headache like before, and it receded. Able to breathe again, she stepped forward with the sawed-off.

Karithexis grinned. "Let's say I've got an early warning system." Two humans stepped out from behind her, each menacing with good, old-fashioned guns. They aimed at the hunters, but Karithexis held up her hands. "I'm just here to talk."

"Don't need to do no talking with you," Gareth said. He brandished a gun, eyes flicking to Daisy.

It took all she had to concentrate, but Grace caught Monica speaking under her breath the way the sisters would chant, almost in silence. She wanted to go stand between her and the demon. Getting her feet to move was a different story.

Karithexis chuckled. "If you leave us alone, I'll leave your precious family alive. That's what you want, right? You'd kill this vessel as soon as look at me, but you want those children alive, don't you?"

That did it. Grace's feet moved, shuffling toward Karithexis. She sighted down the short barrel. She tried to speak, to confirm their interest in the family, and maybe to threaten the demon a bit, but her voice had flown.

Even though she hadn't spoken, Karithexis turned to her. The smile, the one like a paper blower, curled her lips again, working its way slow and steady up her cheeks to end in severe points. She must've been stretching the skin beyond its limits to make such a wide leer, and it traveled down Grace's spine like goose feet over a grave.

"So nice to see you again. I mean it." Karithexis flipped her hand.

The hunters flew, leaving Grace standing alone. Even Monica flew back, but her whispering didn't stop. Out of the side of her eye, Grace caught her hands beginning to move in some kind of figure-eight.

She got the feeling Karithexis shouldn't see what Mon was doing, so, much as her bladder didn't want her to step closer, she did, her hands slick on the stock of the shotgun. She wiped one on her pants. "Let her go."

The demon chuckled, eyes twinkling. A light breeze swept up bits of paper and blew them past along with the pungent scent of trash rotting in dumpsters. Her curly white hair shifted in the breeze, the chain on her glasses swaying. "Why don't you come with me? There's so much you don't know. So much those nuns didn't tell you. They lied to you for months and months. You know that, don't you?"

Grace wanted to shake her head. Take a step back. But it's not like the demon was lying.

Not this time.

Monica spoke louder. "Bound by my hand, you will not move." Light flashed, rushing around Grace in a warm wave.

Karithexis froze with her mouth open, her features as immobile as a marble statue.

The men on either side of her jumped toward Monica.

Without thinking about it, Grace aimed the shotgun at one and glanced at the other. From inside her head, she sent her voice, as she'd done in the vision. As she'd done in the convenience store. *You will stop.* The voice flowed through her, warming her.

She tingled. It felt damn good.

The man stopped moving and the other paused, staring down the barrel of her shotgun.

She adjusted her grip. "I don't want to shoot you, but I will."

His head twitched. Like a shiver but much more violent. It swayed so far Grace thought for a wild moment his neck was about to break of its own will. He stepped forward.

Grace cocked the shotgun, her pounding heart pressing down on her bladder, if that was possible. "Stop moving. Please."

He didn't. He stepped forward again.

The breath that charged in and out of Grace's open mouth barely made it to her lungs. Her head swam.

A shot cracked in the tight alley, and the man fell, clutching his knee.

Jim stepped up next to Grace and gave her a slight grin, cocking his gun again.

Karithexis hissed through her open mouth. She gurgled, but the spell held her. Her expression didn't change.

The man on the ground squealed and howled. Sounded like her hold over him had broken.

Grace backed up to Mon again, who was chanting once more.

Grace wanted to ask if she was holding the demon there or if she was preparing a new spell, but something told her Mon wouldn't be able to answer without breaking her concentration. Instead of asking, she stood between Karithexis and Monica.

The hunters advanced on the men and the demon, Gareth with a gallon milk jug full of salt in each hand. He started pouring around Karithexis.

The demon laughed. Through her open mouth, she laughed loud enough for it to echo off the buildings surrounding them.

Wincing, her ears ringing, Grace backed up and lost her concentration holding the other man. He advanced again.

Karithexis abruptly stopped laughing. Her mouth snapped closed. "Well, that was fun, Sister, but I think we're done playing with that spell. Afraid I can't let you finish the circle, Gareth." She snapped her head toward him, turning it to an unnatural angle. Her clawed fingers closed into a fist, blood spraying from it.

Gareth stopped, the salt left in his jug spilling into a pile. He screamed, gripping his wrist and yanking. "No! Not the salt! Daisy!"

"It's funny to me you think a little salt will stop me anyway, G. You should know by now. Remember what happened last time?" Her head snapped back around with an audible pop. She waved her hand.

Gareth flew, his solid frame smacking into the wall. He slid to the ground, still clutching the empty jug and bleeding. Grace couldn't tell from where, but slick blood soaked his hair.

"You know, demon, I think you'll find us full of surprises today," Daisy said, advancing. The antler-like contraption she carried glowed brighter.

If Grace hadn't been looking at her, she wouldn't have believed it, but the demon flinched. Karithexis squinted against the glow and backed up. But before she touched the salt, she regained her footing and glared at Grace. "Grace, my dear. I'm glad you've changed sides, really. Those nuns are nothing but bad news. Do you know they were the ones responsible—"

Monica shouted, "No! You *lie*! I bind you!" The light shot past Grace again, cooler this time. And it was rigid, like solid fog.

As it went around and through her, Grace's lungs constricted like they were made of stone.

Thankfully, it passed before she had a chance to freak out about not being able to breathe, but sweat popped out on her brow to join her slick hands.

The spell hit Karithexis again. She froze, her wide eyes fixed to Grace.

Samantha stepped up next to Grace. She brandished a giant wooden crucifix, knuckles white.

"Are you religious, Samantha?"

Sam grinned, just enough to wrinkle the edge of her eye. "We can have a theological discussion some other time, yeah?" She stepped forward, and Monica flanked Grace. The three of them joined Daisy as she approached Karithexis with the antlers held out.

The silver metal gleamed, even in the low light. It rippled, distorting all their faces in the shiny finish.

Like a bad acid trip.

Grace jumped like she'd been goosed. That voice, it had to be Natalie. If only there was a way to talk with her. Grace could use the help.

Karithexis started laughing again. "You people are so slow. Are you ever going to—"

Daisy murmured, and the antlers flashed bright silver.

Grace covered her eyes, dropping the shotgun. It clattered to the ground, and she tripped over it.

Monica tried to catch her, but instead they both ended up on their asses on the damp pavement.

Teeth clashing over her tongue, Grace tasted blood. She was lucky she hadn't bit her tongue clean off in the last few days.

Snarling, the demon advanced on Daisy. Before Daisy backed up, Karithexis grabbed her around the neck and squeezed.

Daisy gagged, her gray-streaked hair flying behind her and her necklaces clanging together. One vibrated so loudly Grace almost made out words coming from it.

Samantha and the other hunters surrounded the demon.

The one man still standing next to Karithexis pointed his gun everywhere.

And the demon laughed, squeezing Daisy's neck. Blood started to run between her fingers, and Daisy sagged. Karithexis waved her other hand, and some kind of tornado surrounded her.

The salt blew away. So did all the people.

As they all crashed into walls, cars, dumpsters, and one another, groaning and wailing, Karithexis laughed. Maneuvering around the antler thing Daisy still held, she licked the blood oozing over her fingers.

Monica clutched Grace, her fingers digging into Grace's arm in five spots of pain. "I can't do the spell again, Grace. There isn't time."

Eyes wide, Grace looked around them. Everyone else lay on the ground, gripping wounds or trying to work their way to their knees. Gareth's face covered in blood, he moaned and rolled from side to side, hands wrapped around his ribs.

Grace stood, taking in both of the men flanking Karithexis. She spoke to them at once, with the everything she could muster.

ARMS.

As though an electric current ran through them both, they froze where they were. The one on the ground stopped holding his shot knee and stood like the wound didn't exist. The other turned toward Karithexis, dropping his gun on the ground with a clatter. Blood flowed from their noses in a steady stream.

They grabbed her and pulled.

Screaming, she released Daisy and fell back a step.

Daisy fell to the ground, coughing, her hair caught in the blood on her neck.

Teeth grinding together, Grace concentrated on the men. She ran to Daisy.

Though she wanted to help her up, her hands recoiled from the antlers. Something deep inside kept her from touching them, almost like when you tried to force two magnets with the same poles together. So instead, she gripped Daisy under the armpits and hauled her to her feet.

The men held Karithexis, who screamed and wailed.

Still coughing, Daisy advanced on her again. She pressed the largest point into the demon's chest and spoke a few words in some tongue that was neither Latin nor anything inspired by it.

The glow almost blinded Grace.

Karithexis wailed, her little old lady vocal cords straining under the force of it.

"Go back to hell, demon," Daisy said, pressing the antler into her skin. It pushed through, but slowly, as if Daisy were forcing it into brick. "Never come back."

But before she finished impaling the demon, Karithexis started laughing again. She ripped her arms free of the two men on either side of her.

They stumbled, and the breaking connection tore at Grace's mind. The headache from the absence of it was immediate and more engulfing than anything she'd ever known. She dropped to her knees so hard she was sure both kneecaps shattered.

Karithexis backed away from Daisy, wheezing. "Takes me a while to get my strength up in this old vessel." She put her hands on her knees and wheezed again, exhaling through tight lips. She leered at Daisy. "That's a neat toy you have. Let me see it." She waved her hand again, and the antler device flew from Daisy's outstretched hands.

Daisy collapsed to her knees. "No! You can't!"

A weak, hoarse laugh echoed from inside Karithexis's throat. "You have no idea who you're fucking with, do you?" She gripped the antlers, and their glow faded.

She snapped them in two.

Daisy wailed, what sounded like mourning and anger all rolled into one. She pounded the wet alley with a fist.

Still backing up, Karithexis turned to Grace again. "I wouldn't trust these ones any further than I can throw them." She stopped with a chuckle and eyed the hunters lying around her. "Figuratively. But at least they didn't put you in the hospital. Your Catholic friends can't say the same thing, now can they?"

And it was as though she rammed her fist into Grace's heart, the way she'd done Maria's. With only the air left in her throat, she squeaked out two words. "They did?"

Karithexis's laugh echoed in the alley long after she blew into shadows and disappeared.

Chapter Nine

Daisy shut the door behind her and wrapped her arms around herself. She'd removed all the necklaces, somehow naked without them. Not to mention her pale, wet face.

In the courtyard, Grace sat in a chair. "How is he?"

"Gareth's tough. He'll be all right." She wiped her nose, but her attempt at eye contact failed.

Monica shuffled her feet where she leaned against a pole. "Can we see him?"

With a sigh, Daisy moved away from the door. "He's sleeping. You shouldn't, but—" She stopped and shrugged before continuing. "Probably wouldn't hurt anything. Big idiot." Still avoiding eye contact, she walked into the courtyard and stood, staring into space.

"Come on, Grace." Monica angled her head at Gareth's door.

Grace couldn't take her eyes off Daisy. Not that she'd known the woman for long, but she didn't seem the type to shrug and sigh. From the first moment she'd met her, it was clear—Daisy was a woman of action. This silence put her off.

The door creaked as Mon opened it. She grabbed Grace's hand, breaking the salt line with one shuffling foot.

Grace followed her in and closed the door.

In here, with the shades drawn, one small light on the desk gave them a touch of illumination. The apartments were all shaped the same, though some of them had the bed on an opposite wall and flip-flopped bathrooms. Gareth lay curled up around his ribs, shivering under the covers.

Looking around, Grace found his room a lot more pleasant than she'd imagined it'd be. With his obsession with salt lines, she'd expected a lot more occult symbols, chairs she couldn't sit in maybe, random mirrors that might burn her with a single touch. Maps with lines drawn using yarn. Stuff like that.

Instead, a sixty-inch TV hung on one wall, facing a spacious and comfy-looking recliner. A computer in the corner gave them the only other light in the room, LEDs inside its clear case shifting red, green, and soft blue over Gareth's sweating face and the art on his walls—paintings showing alien landscapes and dreamy vistas of outer space. His room wore the distinct feel of a man who liked to spend his off-time relaxing.

He moaned.

Monica sat down on the bed next to him and laid her palm across his forehead. She closed her eye and pressed her lips together. "He's not doing too well. I think he might die. The head injury is more serious than Daisy let on, and he's got eight broken ribs."

Perched on the edge of his recliner, Grace sighed through her nose. Her breath came out hot on her upper lip. "Why didn't they take him to a hospital?"

In the dim light, Monica shook her head. What Grace couldn't see laid heavy in her voice. "What's a hospital going to do for him? Put him on a machine? Daisy laid some kind of spell over him that's helping him breathe. That's all they'd do for him there too."

Grace leaned, almost out of the chair. "She did? How can you tell?"

"I can feel the spell work. Come here."

Grace didn't move. She couldn't see anything of Gareth's face except a sweaty sheen.

"Grace."

She shifted to the bed without standing, scooting her hips over while still bent, and sank down next to Monica. She rolled into her leg.

Mon took one of her hands and laid it on his forehead. "Can you feel his energy? It's like—" She broke off, rubbing the fingers of her other hand together and moving her lips up and down like she was tasting the air. "It's like the way air feels when it's wet. The way a flame feels when it's calm. How a rainbow looks in the harsh light of sunrise." She smiled. "The way purple tastes."

As hard as it was to keep up with Monica's words, Grace tried to catch the meaning. And as she stared down at Gareth, there *was* something. Not like the things Mon said, but something that radiated all on its own. She whispered, "I think so."

"Good. Now, do you feel the thing rubbing it? With the grain, not against it. Flowing into it."

And as soon as Monica put a feeling to it, it sprang up in front of Grace. It was like a dovetail. Or a smoothly flowing stream dumping into a larger one, with eddy currents off to the side, like it spilled over a bit. She told Monica what she saw in a whisper almost too low to hear.

Mon nodded. "Yeah, I can feel that too. The whole spell doesn't catch; some of it sloughs off. His energy is drained; it can't hardly keep up with the spell."

"Is it all that's keeping him alive right now?" Grace leaned in, trying to feel the heat coming from him. But he was cold, so cold.

Peeling her hand from his forehead, Monica grimaced. "I think it is."

Grace sat back. She exhaled through her teeth. "Then what are we doing in here? Are we here to say goodbye or something?"

"I think you can help him."

Her brain struggled to catch up to her ears and to what her heart already knew. It started galloping. Her stomach turned over, but not in a good way. Like she was going to puke, that way. "What did you say? My ears are ringing."

Monica gripped her shoulder. "You can help him. Just do what I tell you." She sighed. "Do you think doing the Jedi mind trick on people is all the power you have?"

Grace cleared her throat. "I hadn't—I hadn't really thought about it."

"Lay one hand on his forehead, and one on his heart."

"I can't reach it. His arms are in the way."

Monica took her hand and, with a gentle touch, slid it between Gareth's arms and his chest.

Beneath Grace's hand, his heart beat. Slow, but steady. Steady, but weak. She laid her other hand on his pasty forehead.

His face slack, his eyes rolled behind his lids. But he didn't stir or show any signs of waking. He continued to shiver, his body growing colder even as Grace sat there with her hands on him.

"Okay, Grace. Concentrate. I'm not sure how you do this; I only know how I do it. You might have different powers or a different way to use them. Go with what feels natural to you and listen to my voice."

She closed her eyes to listen to the delicate tone of Monica's voice. A balm to her spirit from the moment she'd woken up in the hospital.

Her mind wanted to get sidetracked. To think about how the sisters had put her in it and then lied about it. And if Monica had been in on it.

But there'd be time for that later. Right now, if she could save Gareth, she had to try. Yeah, the hunters planned on taking on Karithexis anyway. That didn't matter; the guilt over their injuries still laid on Grace's shoulders like a winter cloak.

"Feel the energy. His energy. The flowing river. Think about the green trees hanging over it, the light of the sun bouncing off the trickling water. The gurgling as it flows over rocks, rushing past tiny waterfalls and continuing on. Flow with the water; feel it trickle over your fingers."

As she spoke, Grace sought the feeling of his energy again. Even with his weak heartbeat, his fragile state of mind, the energy flowed strong in the river as Monica described. The water eroded away the dirt on the banks as it flowed, pulling rocks and pebbles along in its wake. He had strong energy.

"Do you feel it?"

She nodded, eyes still closed, mind's eye still on the stream.

"This is the tricky part. You've got to build a dam. Slow the flow of it, bind it up, create a pool of energy."

"Why?"

"Focus. A dam."

Grace focused on the dam and blocked the water. It began to pool.

Gareth started to shiver. Hard. Harder than before, almost like a seizure.

"Monica." Her voice shook.

"He's okay. Focus. Can you see the dam? Is the water pooled?"

"If we kill him, Daisy's going to kill us."

"Grace. Focus."

Squeezing her eyes tight, she focused again. The water pooled deep enough to swim in. Her dam was good; it didn't leak at all.

Gareth continued to shake, the covers falling off of him and half into the floor. He moaned.

"Now, listen to my voice, just my voice. Scoop up the water in your hands and imagine infusing it with light."

"Scoop it?" The pool in her mind rippled.

Gareth continued to shake and kept moaning softly, in the back of his throat, almost like a whimper.

"With both hands. Reach into the pool and bring out as much as you can in your hands."

She did, listening to Monica repeat her instructions in a soft, low monotone. But something about it wasn't right, scooping up a handful. It didn't seem like it would work. More of a stopgap, like Daisy's spell, something that would have to be redone, over and over, in the hope he'd overcome his injuries.

"Concentrate. We're losing him."

And they were. He shook so hard, the entire bed shook with him. Grace's ass slid closer and closer to the edge of the bed, the cover falling completely in the floor with a flat *thwump*.

But she couldn't shake the feeling it was wrong to do it Monica's way.

As Gareth stiffened, every muscle in his body contracting at once, her mind slipped sideways. She remembered Monica telling her when they'd first started this—an eternity ago—she didn't have to do it Monica's way and to go with what felt natural.

So she did what felt natural.

She plunged both hands into the pool. Bright light, blinding and engulfing, filled the entire scene in her head. It swept across the trees hanging over the banks, infused the burbling river, and sank below the surface. Solid beams shot out from the water, magnified as though they were coming through glass. The round pool lit up, as bright as the sun, and as beams broke the surface, Gareth's body relaxed.

He was either dead, or she was doing it. He was healing.

She kept the bright scene in her head, held it there like an eggshell, and when the light wanted to overtake the entire thing, she let it. It filled every bit of the vision from edge to edge.

Monica exhaled so softly Grace almost missed it.

She opened her eyes.

The room was bathed in the same bright light, the tears on Monica's cheeks shimmering, her eye half closed against its brilliance. Her full lips fell open, and she stared at Gareth.

Grace turned to the man on the bed.

He floated about six inches off the sheets, and he *was* the light. He hadn't been bathed in it, sheathed in it. He had *become* it.

The door burst open, and the sunlight streaming in paled in comparison. Outlined in it, Daisy stood with one hand on the doorknob and the other on her holstered gun. Her hair blew away from her face in the breeze blowing through the room and out the door.

Monica whispered, "That's enough, Grace. I think that's enough."

Grace let the light fade from the scene by the river. She released the dam. A great torrent of glowing water pushed through, destroying the rest of the sticks and twigs blocking it and sweeping them away in a wave of shining water. The babbling of the brook lowered to more of a hum. A singing voice, lighter than the tweeting of a bird.

Gareth sank onto the bed, breathing easy. As the light faded from the skin of his face, he opened his eyes and sat up.

He glanced at Daisy and smiled at Grace. "Did we win?"

*

Daisy sat on the sidewalk outside Gareth's door, head in her hands. "You gonna tell me your story now, or do I have to drag it out of one of you?"

She used that same gruff tone Grace had come to expect of her, but the way her hair cascaded over her shoulders and in front of her face made her vulnerable, somehow. Like a child.

But she wasn't a child. Right now, she was high explosives with a huge "handle with care" sign stamped on the side.

Grace sat next to her, keeping about six inches between them. "I've never done that before, I can tell you that." She glanced up at Monica, and the feeling hit in the back of her throat. What she wouldn't give to get into their room and cry. Her eyes stung.

Monica sat next to her. "We haven't been entirely up-front about Grace and her origins."

Daisy chuffed. "No shit."

Chest tight, Grace waited to see what Monica was going to say. Was she about to tell Daisy she was a demon? After what had just happened? Maybe it was for the best, but then again, Daisy might take her head off her shoulders before Mon was even done talking.

"We were doing rounds in the hospital one day, you know, praying for people, looking for signs of demonic injuries or curses, and there she was. I knew she was a witch from the moment I saw her, but she's got amnesia. She doesn't even remember her own name."

Grace bit her lip. Hard.

Karithexis had told her the nuns put her in the hospital in the first place. If Daisy weren't here, now would be a great time to point out Monica hadn't just "found" her in the hospital. She'd known she was there from the second they walked in.

But Daisy was shaking her head. "A witch. That's what you're going with?"

"You saw the spell she did."

Hands covering her face, Daisy spoke through them. "She healed him so well, I think he's going to outlive us all, now." She dropped her hands, and her eyes bounced between the two of them. "What did you really do to him? How did you do that?"

Locking her fears about the sisters in a box and dropping them into the "for later" pile, Grace shrugged. She opened both hands and stared at her palms. "Monica told me how; I did what she said." A grin surfaced without asking. "It was a lot easier than I thought it would be."

"I've never seen a witch do that," Daisy said, leaning onto her knees, "not even Maria. Never."

Grace shrugged again and spoke so low she wasn't even sure she spoke. "I just did what she told me." Even though that was a bigger lie than the witch thing.

Gathering her hair in one hand, Daisy reached inside her jacket.

Grace clenched her teeth, sure Daisy was about to pull out one of her many guns or knives and kill them both.

She tugged a hair tie out of her pocket and wrapped it around her hair. "Come with me."

Without waiting, she stood and walked down the sidewalk, the poles holding the awning up casting shadows over her every time she walked between one of them and the setting sun.

Monica stood and held a hand out for Grace.

Slipping her fingers inside Mon's cool grasp, she stood, and they followed Daisy to the end of the U-shaped row of apartments. Daisy entered the last one, and Grace let her feet slow. Surely she had something to whisper to Monica before they went in there. Doubt about what was going to happen inside, or maybe about how the nuns had put her in the hospital.

Daisy called out from inside, her voice echoing. "Stop taking all day, ladies."

Grace followed Monica into the room, still clutching her hand.

Standing in the kitchen with her arms crossed, Daisy spoke low. "We still have to hit this demon. I don't know how, but she broke the *Geweih*. I worked on getting that weapon for months." She slapped the table in her kitchenette and rounded it. "Months."

Grace took in the map on the wall with threads crisscrossing it, the whiteboard with scribbles lying over one another, the haphazard spell materials and weapons sprawled on every surface. And books stacked on a cinder block bookshelf. So many, the boards bowed in the middle.

She stuffed the smile that wanted to come up and faced Daisy. "What's a *Geweih*?"

"The weapon that demon snapped in half like a twig. I can't tell you how much magic was imbued in that thing.

How much effort went into making it, the power of the spells inside it." Daisy flopped into one of the two chairs at the table. "I could tell you, but it's not worth even getting into. Or the spell books. Very special. Secret. I've never even laid eyes on them."

"Wow."

Daisy waved her hand. "Come in, shut the door. Have a seat. We need to talk about the next strike."

Monica fell onto the bed. "The next strike? She almost killed all of us. If it weren't for Grace, Gareth would already be dead."

Daisy pointed at Grace where she stood in the door. "I owe you for that. Name your price."

"I—" Grace shut the door and sank down next to Monica. "I don't have a price."

With a grimace, Daisy opened the book in front of her and put her feet up on the other chair. "I don't know what we can possibly arm ourselves with for the next strike, but I'll find something. That's where you two come in." She flipped a few pages. "I need new ideas, and obviously you two are full of new ideas and skills. We have to have a new game plan. Something that won't get us all killed. Maybe only half of us."

*

Monica stirred massive amounts of cream and sugar into her coffee. "Are you sure about this?"

"No." Grace's black coffee scalded her tongue. Outside, the sidewalk bustled with people, the inside just as crowded. "But if she comes alone, it's worth a shot."

"If she doesn't?"

"We probably won't make it out of this coffee shop alive."

Mon snorted. "This is a great plan. I'm glad we came up with it."

Even without additions to her coffee, Grace stirred it with restless hands. She scanned the faces outside, hoping she'd see who she was looking for and also not. She cleared her throat half a dozen times.

"Ask me." Mon stared into her coffee and kept stirring. What a pair they must have made, staring into their coffees and avoiding eye contact.

Before she thought about it any more and backed away from the question, Grace spat it out. "Did you know? Did you help them put me in the hospital?"

"You have to understand. You were...Um. We, uh."

"I'm a demon. You were trying to kill me."

"No." Her voice too loud, the simple negative echoed off the glass. Monica ducked her head and turned toward Grace. "No. We don't kill people."

"What about demons?"

"Demons, for the most part, used to be people. We don't kill people." She laid her hand over Grace's and squeezed.

Grace turned one eye toward her. "What were you doing?"

Someone spoke from Grace's other side. "I can come back, if you're busy."

Grace jumped, and Monica removed her hand. "No, Shanna. I'm glad you came." She glanced around her.

Tucking one strand of hair behind her ear, Shanna sat across from her at the round table and set her purse on it. "Just me. Like you asked. Mom is with the kids."

Nausea rolled through Grace from toes to crown. That demon alone with Nat and Shanna's children? Great. Maybe she hadn't thought this thing through.

Shanna looked between them both, green eyes half-open. "Sister Monica. Nice to see you again, I guess. You're not wearing your robes?"

Mon shifted. "Let me get you a coffee."

Grace's voice came out of her mouth before she had time to think. "Chai. She doesn't like coffee."

A flush crawled up Shanna's cheeks. "So you do remember."

Monica paused, ass half out of her seat, mouth open.

With one tiny shake of her head, Grace made eye contact with Shanna. "Go get the chai, please, Mon."

She did, leaving Grace and Shanna staring at each other over a shiny metal table.

Grace looked down into her coffee again. "I'm sorry, Shanna. I don't remember. I don't know where that came from; it just did."

"You sounded almost like yourself for a second there. But you're all weird again." Shanna sighed. "I believe you."

With an exhale hard enough to ripple her coffee, Grace glanced up. "Thank you. That means a lot to me." She swallowed the lump in her throat. This moment of naked honesty from Shanna, her heavily painted eyes wide and open, was the perfect time to ask her for what they needed. But Grace's heart pounded, and all she could think about was the kids being watched over by Karithexis. Instead of asking what she'd practiced a thousand times on the way here, she blurted, "Can I come see the kids?"

Shanna's head started shaking before she even spoke. "I don't think so, Nat. Or uh, what did she say you're going by?"

She whispered it at the table, half wishing Natalie would show up again. "Grace."

"Grace. I don't know if that's a great idea. They're doing really good, you know. They had a hard time the last year or so after. Ya know." She waved her hand and scanned the room, biting her lip.

Grace crossed her arms and leaned on the table, pressing her elbows into the hard surface to help center her. Her head swam. "I don't know. I'm sorry."

Shanna glared at the table and rubbed a dull spot in the shiny metal. "Well, the org went under and you started drinking more, and it was one thing after the other." She made eye contact. "After you stole Conor's piggy bank, you, uh. You ended up in the halfway house eventually."

"The halfway house. You mentioned that."

Monica interrupted, setting a chai in front of Shanna and another coffee in front of Grace. She sat with her own and sipped. "Sorry."

Grace's roiling stomach and twisted brain soothed by Mon sitting there, she spun her cup. "The halfway house. That's where I disappeared from?"

Shanna sniffed, her bangs falling over her glasses again. She swiped at them and cleared about half. "That one. Yeah. Anyways, it was a tough year for all of us, and the kids are finally doing better."

"Even though they haven't seen me since, since when?"

Shanna shrugged. "June? May, maybe. You disappeared from the halfway house in August."

August. The Order had found her in the hospital on All Saints Day.

No.

They'd put her in the hospital on Halloween.

What had she been doing between August and October?

Would Karithexis know?

"They actually are getting their homework done again. Deandre quit wetting the bed. Again."

Grace knocked back the rest of her tepid coffee and took a sip of the hot one, scalding off another layer of tongue. "I feel like if I saw them, I'd be able to remember more. You saw how seeing you helped me remember a couple things."

Monica chimed in, "A doctor at the hospital told us if we saw where she lived and her family, it might jog her memory."

Shanna sipped the chai and gave the cup half a grin. "You did remember the chai. You used to make me chai in the mornings. Some mornings, you wouldn't even have time for your own coffee, but you always made sure I had my chai. Until. Well." She shrugged again and made eye contact for a bit longer.

Grace caught her breath with an unbidden smile. The woman's eyes mesmerized her, framed as they were in paint and sparkle, the green within deep as a pool.

She was my girl from the moment I laid eyes on her. She has to know, even when I was fucking up, I still loved her. With all I had to give.

"Which wasn't much, was it?"

Shanna's brow furrowed. "What?"

Grace shook her head. Nat's voice came and went, like all the other times, without asking either way. And she was alone in her head again, no more sweaty palms or clenched stomach.

Shifting in her seat, Mon cleared her throat. "Shanna, we hate to ask, but we think this will help all of you."

With another sip of the chai, Shanna nodded. "You can come home. But not when the kids are there."

Grace opened her mouth.

Shanna fixed her with a stare, mouth drawn into a thin line. "Not yet."

*

Awake and staring at the ceiling until Monica's breathing deepened was no way to spend the night, but Grace didn't know how else to do it. Lying next to her, her skin warm against Grace's when she shifted under the covers, Grace kept going over the few words Monica had spoken about the hospital, needing to know more but terrified to ask, and convinced, at this point, there was a lot Monica wasn't telling her.

What was her purpose in keeping it from her? Shame? Or was Monica with her, still, because she was reporting back to the Order? Still on their side, still keeping an eye on Grace for them?

The deeper question, the one begging to be asked, Grace had to ask herself. Why was she so scared to find out?

As the sun crept over the horizon, she opened her eyes, without any real idea of when they'd slipped shut. She sat up and rubbed them.

Though the room held a morning chill, Monica slept half under the covers. They'd fallen askew, and her borrowed shorts and tank top didn't fit exactly. Most of her thigh peeped from under the cover. Her chest moved up and down in a regular, hypnotizing rhythm, and something stirred inside Grace—in her head, and in her gut. Warmth. Longing. A need to reach over and feel her smooth skin, to wake her and beg to be held. She couldn't stand thinking Mon had something to hide from her, and her desire for Monica to pull her close and tell her everything would be all right built in her chest until it almost spilled from the edges.

Instead, she leapt off the bed and dressed in silence. Whatever was happening to her had to be Natalie's influence. She'd been attracted to women, after all, and Grace didn't even know what it was like to be attracted to someone. She wasn't sure she wanted to be and couldn't remember the last time she had been.

After scarfing down a breakfast in the communal kitchen, about half the group of hunters bustling about and bumping into one another, she took a plate of eggs and bacon for Mon, along with a giant coffee packed with as much cream and sugar as coffee.

On the way to the room, she hoped Monica would still be asleep. She'd put the plate and cup down and slip between the sheets with her. She'd run her hand along her smooth waist, feeling that rich, coppery-brown skin warm under her fingers.

She snapped out of her reverie when the door opened in her face. Some of the coffee sloshed over her hand.

"Shit, Grace. Let me get that." Mon took the coffee from her and opened the door wider. She spoke over her shoulder as she walked back into their apartment. "Are you okay? You look a little flushed."

*

When Gareth knocked on their door at nine, they met him outside. "Daisy told me what we're doing today. You ready?"

They nodded.

"I hate to send you in alone. You're sure one of us can't go with you? Alice could come. She's nonthreatening."

Grace hopped in the back of his loud muscle car. "I think you outside in this should be enough. Kari—um. The demon isn't supposed to be there."

Mon glanced over her shoulder from the front. "What if she is?"

Grace stared out the window, the highway sliding by. If she was, they'd likely never leave the house.

When they rolled to a stop across the street, only one car sat in the driveway. Not that Grace knew whose car it was, but she hoped it was Shanna's and that Karithexis was away like she was supposed to be.

Stomach in her throat, blocking her from breathing, Grace stepped out onto the sidewalk.

Monica followed. She'd never put her headscarf back on, but she'd snapped her curls into place at the nape of her neck and her eye patch lay flush against her skin now that the bandages had come off.

She grinned. "What?"

"You still look like a pirate."

Lips pressed together, she checked for traffic. "Thanks, Grace. Way to compliment me."

"If it helps," Grace said, leaning close, "you're a sexy pirate."

Foot halfway off the sidewalk, Monica stumbled and almost fell in the street.

Grace grabbed her, her thoughts from the morning intruding again, and helped her steady before she fell into oncoming traffic.

Gareth leaned out the window. "You ladies okay?"

"We're fine."

He tapped the side of the car. "I'm on your speed dial. Daisy programmed me and her in those phones she gave you. Call me at the first sign of trouble."

Spotting a break in the traffic, Grace tugged Monica. "We will."

They crossed the street and hurried up Shanna's stairs. After ringing the bell, Grace stepped back. Butterflies replaced whatever had been happening in her stomach. One hand on her heart, she waited with wide eyes.

When the door opened onto Shanna, alone, Grace's memory doubled. Some of the same feelings from the morning resurfaced, and she remembered Monica standing in the apartment door, beautiful and inviting.

What was happening to her?

Shanna shuffled her feet, eyes cast down, and invited them in.

They followed her to the kitchen, and Grace peeked in every room they passed. The townhouse was longer than it was wide, and stairs disappeared up into the dark second floor.

Shanna took them all the way to the kitchen in the back and leaned against the counter. "So? Anything?"

Grace shook her head.

But that's not what they'd come for, was it?

"Excuse me, sorry," Monica said, right on cue.

Shanna lifted her sculpted eyebrows. "Yes, Sister?"

"It was a long drive in, and I had a lot of coffee. Could I use your restroom?"

Shanna pointed. "There's a powder room at the top of the stairs. We wanted to put one in down here, but Natalie didn't want to lose the kitchen space." Her eyes flitted to Grace. "So it's upstairs. First door on the right."

"Thanks." Monica disappeared around the door and into the hallway.

Grace sat at the table. "I don't remember anything. Looking at my picture on the license was the first time I even really considered my life before the hospital." She crossed her arms. "I wondered who I was, but I was afraid to find out."

Shanna slid the chair across from her out with a soft squeak. "What were you afraid of?"

"This?" Grace looked around. "Coming home to a place I didn't recognize to be told I was a terrible person anyway."

"You're not a terrible person, Nat. Sorry. Grace." Shanna leaned across the table and took Grace's hand off her arm, her fingers cold. "You fucked up. A lot. The org was your life."

Grace blinked. "You mentioned that before. What's the org?"

With a chuckle, Shanna withdrew her hand. "Wow. You really do have amnesia. The org, you called it Helping Hands of Grace…"

Grace's turn to chuckle, she shook her head. "Yeah, maybe I remember more than I thought."

"Ha. Yeah. Anyway." Shanna flushed, red creeping up her cheeks even with the coat of makeup laying over them. "It was a charity you built yourself. You did all kinds of things, from helping build clubs for underprivileged kids to planting community gardens."

"But it failed, as all things do," a voice said behind Grace.

Ice froze her teeth together. She turned, her neck creaking, her breath bottled in her mouth. She couldn't move it up or down.

Karithexis stood in the door, hands covered in red, red, red blood. "When you put too many dreams and not enough realism in a thing, it has a tendency to fall apart." She wiped her hands on the apron hanging at her waist, smearing it with bloody, finger-shaped streaks. "You always were ambitious. Grace."

Chapter Ten

Grace popped out of her chair. She growled through her teeth. "The fuck are you doing here?"

Shanna gasped. "Natalie!"

The wince began inside and ended outside. She'd cursed at what Shanna thought was Natalie's mother.

Beaming, every tooth showing, Karithexis held up her hands. Her red, red hands. "Sorry. Need to wash up."

As she breezed past Grace, the smell of old lady almost overpowering a deeper odor beneath, something like ashes and flame, Grace's stomach clenched. What had she done to Monica?

Well, it was up to Grace now. She had no choice. She had to kill the demon, or these people were all going to die. Today.

She reached in her pocket for the only weapon she carried. A good, old-fashioned gun.

Grace couldn't carry so many of their weapons. No salt, none of those weird symbols Daisy wore, no holy water. She couldn't even load this gun; the bullets were made of silver, and the powder inside them had been blessed by a priest. Daisy had even gotten a rabbi to do an extra blessing, "just in case."

Either way, Grace's bulky winter jacket covered the gun in her pocket, and she wrapped her hand around the grip, finger not yet on the trigger.

Hunched over the sink with her back to them, Karithexis clucked her tongue. "Shanna, why is she still wearing that coat? Please take it from her and hang it in the foyer. You know how I feel about coats in the house."

"Sorry, Mom." Shanna stood and held out her hand. "Grace, please."

Eyes wide and dry, Grace stared at the hallway. Monica had to come around the corner. She had to.

She let her finger slip around the trigger, the metal already warm from her hand.

The demon dried her hands on a towel and peeked over her shoulder. "Let her take your jacket, and I'll show you what I was working on. Shanna, please."

Before Grace could squeeze the trigger and shoot the damned demon through the back, Shanna tugged the coat off.

Her hand slipped off the gun, and it went with the coat, with Shanna, down the hall and out of sight.

Turning around, Karithexis grinned, some of her hair streaked with blood. As she spoke, Grace fixated on it. "Follow me. I'll give you the tour. Maybe that'll jog your memory." She gave Grace a grotesque smile, wide and mocking, and elbowed her in the ribs hard enough to fracture them.

Grace's stomach wound itched. She rubbed the scar on her head, the fading chemical burn on her face. Even in the midst of her worry for Monica, she couldn't shake the fear that she'd likely participated in giving Grace those scars, and then lied to her about it. For months.

"I know what you're thinking," Karithexis said, walking down the hall.

Grace followed, unclenching her teeth. "Oh? What's that?"

"You're realizing you feel different in this house. More..."

Frowning, Grace tilted her head. She did feel different. No headache, for one thing. Neither time she'd seen Karithexis here. "More what?"

The demon wiggled her head back and forth. "Human, I guess. I put a little bubble in place. In this house, we're cut off. From the outside and from our powers. Level playing field." She winked, glasses chain swinging like the pendulum of a clock.

"If you can't use your powers, what have you done with Monica?" She leaned close. "Did you kill her with some kind of weapon instead of your bare hands?"

Karithexis chuckled and led Grace into one of the rooms off the main hallway.

A Christmas tree stood in the front window, its presents long gone. Karithexis led her past it and to a corner, behind the couch and beside a bookshelf, where an easel sat. A canvas leaned on it, and paint—blue, green, and so much red—slashed across the canvas, still sticky and shining.

The relief that flowed through Grace was almost enough to knock her to the floor. Her knees buckled.

"Whoa, whoa, Grace." Karithexis caught her under the armpits before she fell. "Sit down." Without her power, Karithexis's grip was only as tight as an octogenarian could make it. She trembled under Grace's weight but still helped her to the couch.

Grace sat with a poof. She exhaled, tears threatening, and gazed up at the demon. "Where is Monica?"

"Still in the bathroom. You think she's okay?"

Throat tight, Grace swallowed. She had to give Mon time to do what they'd come here for. "I thought you weren't going to be here."

"I couldn't resist the chance to see you." Karithexis sat next to her, close enough for their knees to touch.

Shuddering, Grace slid away and leaned on the arm of the couch.

"Those nuns were using you," she said.

"I know."

"They put you in the hospital. It was a spell; I don't know exactly what. I don't know if they meant to give you amnesia, but here you are. What about your vessel?" She glanced around the room. "Can she remember anything?"

"I don't know. I can't get her to talk to me."

Her voice rose, sharp and piercing. "You what?" She turned. "What do you mean, you can't talk to her?"

Grace sighed. "I don't even know where to start."

"Sometimes I wish that would happen. Some of these people, like this little old lady, they won't shut the fuck up. She keeps on chattering; I have to threaten her to get her to shut up. She's babbling about you, about her Natalie, right now."

"What's she saying?"

"She's pissed at you. At Natalie. She fucked everything up."

"She always thought the org was a bad idea." Grace covered her mouth and spoke from behind her hands. "I don't know where that came from."

Karithexis smiled, showing all those teeth again. They were too white and straight. Were they dentures? Was a demon wearing dentures?

"So that was Natalie; she is in there." The demon leaned close and stared into Grace's eyes. "When you want to talk to her, call out. She's there. And she remembers."

Grace wanted to back away. Being near the demon made her skin crawl. And yet.

"I don't have to remind you that we're cut from the same cloth, Grace. What you did to the man in the convenience store was a thing of beauty."

Her memory doubled. "Which one?"

The laugh came from somewhere inside Karithexis's chest and bubbled out her throat. She coughed, still laughing. "After you broke out of the hospital. Why? Was there another store clerk?"

Grace gave her head a fervent shake.

"Not long after you left, I came in and found him bleeding to death in his brain. He was sprawled on the floor behind the counter, blood coming out of his nose. You turned his brain to mush. But you got what you needed, didn't you?"

And it had felt good. Like the men in the alley, the power flowed through her with warmth.

So similar to the warmth curling in her gut that morning while she'd watched Monica sleep. So similar.

She whispered, "How do I talk to Natalie?"

"I find with the less talkative ones if you can make them comfortable, they're more likely to talk. Look around. See what Natalie's life was like, and use what you learn to draw her out. We're going to need her help if we're going to finally complete our plan. That's why we recruited her, after all."

Standing, Grace wiped her wet palms on her jeans. She walked to the bookshelf, looking over the titles. Brightly colored plastic toys took up the front of most of the shelves at knee level and below. Pictures also sat on most of the shelves, and Grace leaned close to look at one.

Shanna and Natalie, posing in front of a tree with their kids. One young boy who was the spitting image of Shanna, even down to the reddish-brown hair hanging over his eyebrows, and the other boy who couldn't be any more than two in this picture, his brown skin shining in the sun and his small afro curled around his head.

While Grace looked, a slight smile lifting her lips, what Karithexis had said hit her. She spoke with her back still to the demon. "What plan?"

The floor creaked as she approached. The demon stopped next to her and peered at the picture, her whisper bouncing off the glass. "Freedom."

*

Daisy sat with her feet up on her kitchen table, leafing through a book scrawled with some language that hardly looked like one. "You got what we needed?"

Mon dug in her pocket. She extricated a small plastic bag stuffed with curly white hair. "Is this right?"

Daisy's foot fell to the floor, and she stuck out a hand.

Monica stepped into the kitchen like the floor was lava and her hair was already on fire. As soon as the bag was in Daisy's hand, she retreated to the carpeted living/bedroom.

Inspecting the bag with her eyes narrowed, Daisy sniffed at it and held it up to the light. "Plenty of follicles. It'll do nicely, I think, if you ladies are sure you're ready for this."

They shook their heads in unison.

With a chuckle, Daisy waved them out. "We gotta prepare the spell. Alice might need some help in the morning. Go see her first thing."

Nodding, Monica hooked her hand around Grace's upper arm and tugged her from the room.

Grace's feet moved like she was trudging through molasses. What they were going to do, it was, well, it was necessary. They had to get the demon off guard.

But if what she'd said was true, she was just fighting for her freedom. Hers, and Grace's freedom from some demon named Raga, whose name she'd heard somewhere before. But Grace hadn't had time to find more out before Mon had come back from the bathroom. If only there were some way to be sure Karithexis told the truth.

Mon shuffled to the middle of the courtyard, the fire cold and dead tonight, and stared up at the stars. She hugged herself. "It's nice, being this far away from town. The view of the stars is almost as good as the convent."

Grace sat in a lawn chair, its thatched fabric seat creaking. "Monica."

"Yeah." Still looking up.

"Tell me."

Monica blew air out her nose. "I designed the spell." She glanced over her shoulder, and a tear tracked down her cheek. "It was my first big assignment, and I was supposed to officially join the Order after it worked."

Reaching out with numb hands, Grace grabbed the nearest chair and pulled it close to hers.

Monica sat, arms still wrapped around herself. "We tracked you down after you killed all those people in that convenience store. The one Daisy was talking about, where she saw you on the surveillance video."

Nodding seemed the thing to do, but Grace could barely breathe listening to this, much less move.

"It was Halloween, which in itself holds a lot of power. We tracked you down and trapped you. You seemed, in a way, happy to be caught."

"None of this means anything to me, Mon. I can't remember any of this."

Monica shook her head, one curly lock of hair flying loose from her bobby pins. "I know. If you could, you wouldn't be my friend anymore. I cursed you." She met her eyes, her pupil taking up most of her iris in the dark. "I bound you, and I cursed you. You resisted, and you ended up fighting with Mother Mary. You tried to kill her, she almost gutted you with her ancient sword, and someone dumped holy water on you both."

Grace's fingers rubbed an unconscious circle over the scar tissue on her face. The burn. "What was the spell for?"

"It's like Karithexis said. We wanted to use you. I turned you into a weapon, one that could help us hunt demons. I thought it was going to turn out different, but you resisted. You kept resisting after Mary tried to kill you." Monica stopped, tears seeping out from under the patch and rolling down both cheeks now, glistening in the starlight. "You escaped. You were more powerful than my binding."

A small wave of pride surged through Grace. Since waking in that hospital, she'd been weak almost all the time, like a scared rabbit. There were some standout exceptions, of course, but for the most part, she couldn't escape whatever was going on if she wanted to.

But if what Monica said was true, she'd escaped the Order. She'd overpowered them, even with all their tricks, and escaped. "So what then? How did I end up in the hospital?"

Mon's slender shoulder bobbed up and down. "We couldn't finish the spell; you ran away with it half-done, bleeding all over the place. We followed you to the hospital, and I sat by your bed until you woke up. Ready to kill you."

Bile burning her throat, Grace covered her mouth. "You were going to kill me? Why didn't you?" She stopped, swallowing. "Why didn't you do it while I slept?"

That slender shoulder rose and fell again. "I don't know. I watched you, recovering from the wounds we'd caused, and I...I couldn't."

Grace stood so fast the chair rocked and fell over with a clang.

She started, heart thumping her rib cage, and turned her back on Monica. "You couldn't, because you still wanted to use me." Her face tightened, blood rushing through her cheeks and forehead. The hair on her head stood up, and she spat out the next words before they ran away. "You're still using me. You're only here because you want to spy on me. To get me back to the Order when it's convenient. That's why you're here, isn't it?"

Twisting her fingers together, Monica shook her head. "No." Her voice almost broke a whisper. "No, Grace. That's not why I came with you."

"Bullshit."

Monica jumped from her chair. She grabbed her again, her fingers, like always, squeezing tight enough but not too tight. "That's not why I left with you."

"Why, then?" Grace tried to look up at the stars, but they were all blurry.

Monica stepped in front of her, her hand still on her arm. Her other hand snuck up the side of Grace's neck and cupped her cheek. "I'm sorry. I fell in love with you."

Grace blinked the tears out of her eyes. They coursed down each cheek, leaving cold tracks behind them. "You did what?"

"I left my family because they hated what I am and joined the Order because they didn't care."

"What you are?"

Monica swallowed. "I wasn't always a nun. I had boyfriends. And girlfriends. And when my family found out about the girlfriends"—she cast her eyes down—"they treated me like a monster. I went to church to see if God hated me like my family said, and instead I found Mother Mary." She dropped the hand from Grace's cheek. "And I'm sorry. I didn't mean to tell you that way."

The feelings from the morning crashed into Grace again, almost knocking her over but for Monica's hand still on her bicep, steadying her. Her stomach glowed, and she didn't care if it was Natalie or not. Before Mon apologized again, Grace did what she'd thought about doing that morning and slid her hand along Monica's waist, underneath her jacket. The skin beneath her shifting shirt warmed Grace's cold fingers. Without thinking any more about it, she leaned into her warmth and closed her lips over Monica's.

Her silky smooth lips melted into Grace's, slightly parted and softer than Grace imagined. She pulled her closer with the arm around her waist and leaned into her, a low moan escaping her throat.

Mon inhaled through her nose and pulled a bit away, breaking the spell that'd descended over them. "I didn't mean to tell you that way. I didn't mean to tell you at all."

"It's okay." Grace sighed, long and low, through her lips. "This morning, I saw you lying there, half-dressed, and I wanted to slide into the bed with you. I didn't know if it was Natalie, because she likes women, or if it was because—"

"Wait. What?" Monica stepped back.

"I know, I shouldn't stare at people while they're sleeping. Although you did the same thing to me, so I guess it was kind of like returning the favor."

Teeth digging into her lip, Monica stepped back again. "You're right. It's probably Natalie and not you, and I'm taking advantage of a woman trapped inside her body by a demon." She covered her mouth. "I'm so sorry, Grace."

She turned and disappeared into the dark before Grace spoke another word.

*

After Monica ran off, Grace sat in the courtyard, coat wrapped around her, tears drying on her cheeks.

Was Monica right? Was it all Natalie?

Though the cold night seeped into her bones, up through the soles of her feet and down from the top of her head, through her ears and stiffening fingers, she leaned back in the chair and took in the stars.

After she accepted Monica wasn't going to return and continue their conversation, she closed her eyes and did what Karithexis said. She called Natalie to come talk.

The cold night disappeared from around her. It opened up onto a black, empty room, a single spotlight illuminating a microphone atop its skinny stand. A small round table held one framed picture in the middle of it— the one with Natalie, Shanna, and the boys.

Grace entered the spotlight and tapped the mic.

It echoed and whined with feedback.

She spoke into it. "Natalie? Natalie Bauman, I know you're here. We need to talk."

A voice came from outside the circle of light. "This isn't what you promised. None of it."

A weird doubling sensation hit her, listening to what she'd come to think of as her own voice come from outside her.

"I know. I can't remember what I promised you. I can't remember anything."

Natalie scoffed and stepped into the light. Her curly brown hair fell past her shoulders, with a few streaks of gray here and there.

Grace ran her hand across her own head. The hair there was still short, only now starting to touch the tops of her ears. She stared into eyes she'd never see in a mirror, deep brown eyes that matched the hair.

Frowning, Nat drew a rickety metal stool into the light with her and sat. "Convenient."

Grace spun a circle, looking for her own chair or stool, but there was nothing but the spotlight, the microphone and table, and Natalie. She stepped toward her. "How? How is that convenient in any way? I've been getting my ass kicked, everyone hates me, I don't even know what I am. Not really."

"Ha. Well. We have a few things in common, like when I signed up for this trip. Nobody likes me either." The smile that touched her lips rueful, it curled one side of her mouth and looked for all the world like the kind of grin a clown wore. Painted on.

Grace knelt in front of her. "That's not true. Shanna still loves you. Did you see any of that?"

"Sort of. I don't choose what I see, although I can choose to run away from it, sometimes. I'm getting better at controlling it, I think."

Grace chuckled. "I wish I was. You come along at some really inappropriate times, you know."

Natalie twisted a strand of hair with her index finger. "I knew that deal was too good to be true."

Sitting on the scuffed black floor with her legs crossed, Grace gazed up at the bottom of Natalie's chin. "Tell me about the deal."

"Right. You don't remember it. Do you ever get tired of that?"

"What?"

"Forgetting everything."

Grace rolled her eyes so hard she could see next week. "Of course I do. I feel like I'm stumbling around blind, and the floor is made of grease and I can't even get my feet under me. I have no idea where I'm going, no map to get there, and I can't keep a single relationship steady long enough to figure it out."

Nat chuckled. "Now you know how it feels to be an alcoholic, and why I'd do something as desperate as make a deal with a demon to get away from it."

With a sigh and a tight chest, Grace repeated her request to hear about the deal.

Something squeaked in the dark once, twice, then over and over again, faster and faster. It approached them, and Grace clenched her teeth, waiting for whatever it was to appear.

A television on a stand rolled into the light. It popped on, the picture fuzzy.

Natalie adjusted the antenna on top. "I know it's old-fashioned, but so are you. Here. Look." She pointed at the clearer picture.

Grace leaned closer to the blurry black-and-white picture, the people in it in sharp contrast to the background. They sat at a bar together, and as the camera approached their backs, it panned up to the mirror behind the bar.

Through all sorts of liquor bottles, Grace caught Natalie's reflection. Her hair was still long and curly, her eyes bloodshot but normal.

Next to her sat a lithe white man in a suit nice enough to have a pocket square. He glanced into the mirror, and Grace followed his gaze.

His eyes were black holes, sucking all the light into them. Darker than black, they ate up half his face. Dimples framed his mouth, deep in his cheeks as he grinned and sucked on a piece of ice.

They murmured together.

Natalie spun the volume button, and their words came into focus.

"There's a lot of reasons why I'm offering you such a good deal," he said.

I shook my head. "Let me get this straight. You inhabit my body, you use me to free some demons, and you fix my life? What's the downside?"

He sucked the ice cube. "There has to be a downside?"

His cavalier attitude grated on my last nerve. "You're a demon. Don't take this the wrong way, but history says this is pretty much my one-way ticket to hell."

"History." He chuckled. "A book written by men. Fallible, to the last word. Now, I won't lie. This deal isn't without its downsides. I can make no guarantees you'll see your family again. I can make no guarantees you won't end up an eternal slave to someone worse than me. What I can guarantee you is your family will be taken care of. Your business will be saved."

"My charity."

"Yes. Your charity you so lovingly ran into the ground will rise from the ashes like a phoenix. If we survive my mission, you'll be returned to your life."

I swigged the beer. "And my alcoholism?"

"I can't take it away from you; that's one of those things you have to do on your own. Sorry."

With a sigh, I sat the bottle down. I'd emptied it so fast beads of condensation still stuck to the outside. Though I'd called him and not the other way around, it didn't mean I wasn't skeptical of his deal. It'd be reckless not to be.

"Listen," he said, leaning over. His cold finger traced its way up my arm. "You're the perfect vessel for what I need. You have an inherent spell-crafting ability, and most of your kind have already been snatched up by hunters or those damned nuns, hangings, or burnings at the stake."

My gut curled in on itself. What he was talking about was absurd. Never mind he was an actual demon from hell, his eyes in the mirror said so. But me, a witch? Fucking nuts. I spoke under my breath. "What was I thinking?" I dropped a few dollars on the bar and slung my bag over my shoulder. The leftover ingredients for the spell I'd used to call him clanked inside.

His hand snaked across the bar so fast he knocked over the beer bottle. He caught my arm as the bottle rolled to a stop on its side, sweat still beaded on the label. "Fine. I'll take away the alcoholism. Are we gonna do this or what?"

The picture on the TV grew fuzzy again, and Natalie slapped the off button. It faded to nothing more than a dot in the middle of the screen, and a low murmur of static remained until the dot disappeared with a small pop. "You're a smooth talker; I'll give you that, Grace."

Grace shook her head. "I saw that beer bottle. That was you."

Nat smiled. "That was me. I was trying to show you the mirror, but I didn't have a handle on what I was doing yet."

"And you do now?"

"It's better. What is this you're getting us into?"

Heat crawled up Grace's cheeks. "With um. With Monica?"

Nat waved her hand. "Not that. With your friend, the other demon, the one possessing my mom. What's her name? Karthex?"

"Karithexis. I wouldn't call her a friend."

"You promised me my family would be safe, but that's not what this looks like at all. It looks like the exact opposite." Her fingers dug into her hair, and she swiped a swath of it away from her face. "What happens if a demon breaks a deal?"

Grace pinched her lips together. "I hope we don't have to find out."

*

Grace didn't know where Monica ended up sleeping, but they met in the morning at Alice's apartment. Alice showed them what she needed and how to get it, and they split up to gather materials. They didn't speak otherwise, and Grace didn't see her again until the evening, when everyone piled into the cars and drove further away from the city and deep into what the road signs said was a national park.

Grace and Monica sat in the backseat of Gareth's car, Alice between them, Daisy at the wheel, Gareth in the passenger seat. It wasn't any use to try talking to Mon; there was nothing she wanted to say that could be said in front of four other people. Hunters, no less. She fidgeted with the seat belt.

Daisy, her arm draped over the wheel, spoke without turning from the road. "You sure you want to be part of this? Gonna be dangerous."

Alice patted Grace on the back. "Danger is her middle name, boss."

Gareth scoffed. "Somehow, I don't think that's true." He twisted in his seat and looked over his shoulder, blue eyes twinkling at Grace. "But I owe you, you know. I don't think I thanked you yet." He winked.

Mouth flopping open and closed, Grace couldn't think of a single comeback. She glanced around a grinning Alice and eyed Monica.

Her elbow rested on the door handle, her hand under her chin. She stared toward the window, but raised her eye in the reflection and met Grace's.

Stomach flip-flopping, Grace leaned back into the seat. Filling all the space for thought was the desire to tell Mon she was sure all the feelings were hers, though what she should be thinking of was the coming night and the danger they were all about to be in.

But that was too much to look at head-on.

Daisy stopped the car in a gravel parking lot and got out. In silence, she removed bag after bag of supplies from the trunk and doled them out. Spell materials, weapons, a wild assortment of all kinds of things. Some people chopped dead wood from nearby trees, presumably for a fire. None of them talked much; they'd gathered in the courtyard before leaving the complex and gone over their roles, the plan, all of it.

Now was a time for action.

They built a twenty-foot circle out of rocks, poured some of that "fancy salt," as Gareth put it, around the entire circumference, and chopped, ground, and mixed all the spell ingredients. Daisy brought out the book with the strange writing. In the car, Daisy mentioned going into debt over the salt, but after what had happened last time, she didn't want to take chances.

Grace and Monica stood off to the side, watching the hunters ring the circle.

By the fire at the circle's head, Alice held the book for Daisy with one hand and offered the other to her.

Daisy produced a long silver dagger and, taking her hand, pierced the tip of Alice's pinky finger. Grace counted seven drops of blood as they fell into the bowl of spell ingredients.

It was funny how much Daisy talked about the sisters and their witchcraft but used spells as much as they did. Why she declared herself a hunter and not a witch was a question Grace might ask if they lived through the night.

The flames jumped when Daisy started reading in a

guttural voice.

Eyes narrowed against the smoke floating into her face and up her nose, Grace listened to the incantation. The language vibrated deep in her bones, words she almost recognized. And in her head, beyond the smoky wood scent burying itself in her sinuses, deeper than the words Daisy grunted, was a peculiar sense of being in two places at once.

In front of her, the back of Daisy's head bobbed up and down in time with her strange words. But also, before her, Daisy's face rippled in the heat of the fire. Pain coursed through her, joined by the feeling of being stripped down naked before this group, in the midst of the circle between them.

Monica clutched her arm. "Stop," she whispered, her lips almost touching Grace's ear. She tugged.

Grace's feet hit the dirt. Cold realization washed over her, starting at the crown of her head and covering her in a sheet of sweat and fear. She turned to Monica and whispered, almost against her lips, "I was floating toward her, wasn't I?"

Mon licked her lips and grimaced, firelight flickering in her eye. "I didn't bring you any earplugs. Goddamn it, what was I thinking?"

Grace clutched her arm. "It's too late now. We're here. We have to do this. Karithexis has Natalie's family in the palm of her hand because of me. It's my responsibility."

Wrapping her other arm around her, Monica shook her head. "It's not. It's not your fault; it's not your responsibility. You don't have to die here tonight." She pulled Grace close and shivered against her.

Daisy continued with the spell, all her concentration on the circle before her. Still chanting, she held out her hand.

Alice dropped the hair in it. Hair Monica had taken from Karithexis's pillow, hairbrush, and even the shower drain. Assuming she was the only one in the house with white hair, they'd made sure to collect only those, even though Daisy assured them the spell would summon one thing and one thing only.

The fire crackled, burning the hair.

The stench of burning hair was one of the least pleasant things that had ever crawled up Grace's sinus cavity and died. She wrinkled her nose and hugged Monica back, shaking as much as she was.

A memory tickled the back of her mind, an important one. It was something to do with curly, white hair.

Daisy punctuated the spell with the scream of a banshee, a sepulchral shout that ripped from her toes and out into the still night, echoing off the stars themselves.

The fire blazed, twenty feet high.

A groan came from the midst of it and resolved into a deep laugh. The shadows pulled in.

Grace's head split open. She gasped, unable to feel anything but the pain.

The pressure of Monica's grip on her arm disappeared. Not all at once, but in stages, like her fingers were slowly dissolving or turning to dust.

She cracked her eyes to look down at Mon's hand.

It was still there, wrapped around her arm, but

Grace's arm faded out of existence like some kind of hologram at an alarming rate.

And yet it was as solid as ever, only it wasn't where she'd left it.

She looked to her left, her head screaming and mouth hanging open. The heat from the fire dried all her spit.

Next to her, in the center of the circle, the shadows solidified into a shape she'd become familiar with over the last few days.

Karithexis smiled, her dentures orange in the firelight. "Guess the cat's out of the bag now, huh, Grace?"

*

All the hunters around the circle shifted on their feet.

Monica rushed to the edge of it, arms wrapped around herself, and cursed aloud.

And Grace's head, her head still throbbed, absolutely throbbed, the pain so great her eyes watered uncontrollably. She squinted through the tears, staring into Daisy's wide eyes.

Silence descended over all of them, and the spell book dropped to the dirt with a thump and a puff of dust.

The fire crackled and popped, sending hot ash spiraling into the air.

Karithexis sat in the center of the circle. She drew in the dirt with a finger and chuckled. "I had hoped I'd be around when they found out. Maybe not like this, trapped in a circle, but at least we're trapped together, huh?" She tugged Grace's pant leg. "Sit. And follow my lead."

Grace raised her hands to either side of her head and pressed, trying to close the invisible fissure that'd opened in it. It worked, at least enough for her to see straight.

And what she saw was shock on all of their faces, like they'd never considered something like her could infiltrate their home. She wanted to apologize. To explain. To do something.

The gun.

She pulled it from her pocket, the sight catching before she fully extricated it. Aiming it at Karithexis's head, she glanced at Daisy.

Three things happened at once.

Karithexis continued to draw in the dirt, sucking air through her teeth and ignoring the gun.

Daisy leaned over and picked the book up out of the dirt like a woman in a trance.

And Natalie screamed. She flat-out screamed in Grace's head.

Grace's knees buckled, and the gun fell to the dirt, hitting the ground at the same time Grace did. She gasped, holding her head again.

"You're never going to get out of this behaving like that, my friend," Karithexis said. Her finger swirled the dirt into shapes Grace swore she'd seen before.

"Neither of you are getting out of this alive," Daisy said, dusting the book and turning to a new page. "I can't believe you. I should have known. You can't trust those fucking nuns." She jerked her head.

Jim and Lindsey appeared on either side of Monica and grabbed her arms, Lindsey's usual smile pulled into a deep grimace. Gareth stood behind Mon, his sawed-off aimed at her back.

On her knees, Grace sobbed. "Do what you will with me, but leave Monica out of this. It isn't her fault."

Daisy stopped reading. "You're fucking kidding me. She's as guilty as you, demon. She hid this from us, and I know she knew. I *know it*." She glared at Monica. "I can't believe I let either of you touch him." Her eyes flicked to Gareth. "I guess I'm lucky you didn't kill him, and if I wasn't so pissed I couldn't see straight, I'd make you tell me how you did that."

Monica sniffed, struggling against Jim and Lindsey's grips. "Demons have so much power, Daisy. And they don't just have power to do evil. I've seen it; I've watched Grace. She's performed miracles right before my eyes. Healing Gareth was the biggest, but there's others I never believed a demon capable of. Please. Please don't hurt her."

Scowling, mouth pulled into a frown so severe it would have cut glass, Daisy jerked her head again, long hair and necklaces flying.

Gareth pushed Monica with his gun, and Jim and Lindsey tossed her into the circle.

Her feet tangled on the ring of rocks, and she fell on her face without getting her hands in front of her. She grunted.

Grace crawled to her, one eye on Daisy.

She spat, her face twisted with disgust. "A fucking demon." She squatted on the other side of the circle, her face less than a foot away from Grace's as she knelt next to Monica. "In that surveillance video, what were you doing, you evil bitch?"

Although fear rode down Grace's backbone in a violent shiver, the core of her warmed when she wrapped her arms around Monica. The touch centered her.

She met Daisy's eyes. "I was killing them."

The memory—of the warmth coursing through her when she controlled the killer, made him murder each of them and then himself—came back full force, almost knocking her on her ass again. She remembered how she'd tingled with joy controlling him. How giddy she'd been, watching them die at her command.

With everything she had, she reflected that feeling toward Daisy.

Daisy's hair blew, her necklaces rattling. She grinned, orange firelight making her teeth look like fangs. "You can't hurt me. Not from inside that circle." She picked up the book and read aloud, spitting the words.

The words ripped at Grace's intestines—the ones she'd almost lost not so long ago, the ones that still twinged with pain sometimes when she sat wrong. They twisted inside her gut.

Someone tossed a bucketful of holy water into the circle.

It drenched both demons. The scent of spent matches and the sickly-sweet stench of burning skin filled the air along with their screams.

Grace couldn't catch her breath. Her insides on fire, her outsides matching, she fell to the ground and writhed. The headache returned with such force she lifted her hundred-pound hands to her head to make sure it hadn't caved in.

Monica shouted from somewhere far away. "Stop! You're killing her!"

Sweet little Alice answered, "That's the point, bitch."

From where Grace lay on the ground, twitching, curled into a ball, she glared through slits as Monica leapt and landed on the circle of rocks.

In one movement, she wiped away a swath of the circle.

A breeze blew through Grace's center. A cool, refreshing breeze swept into her like mint burning her tongue.

She breathed deep, sitting up.

Behind her, something like thunder crashed. Karithexis shouted her name.

Grace spun.

The symbols Karithexis had drawn in the dirt glowed, and a black gash, outlined in shimmering red light, wavered in the air next to her. "Grace, we have to go! Come on!"

Gareth gripped Monica and lifted her off her feet. He shouted in her face. "What the fuck are you doing?"

She twisted away from him. "Grace, go!"

Daisy picked up the sawed-off from where Gareth had dropped it when he grabbed Monica. She cocked and aimed. "You're not going anywhere."

She fired.

Karithexis grabbed Grace and tossed her toward the black gash, sticking her hand up between them and the buckshot.

Pain peppered Grace's left arm, dozens of red flashes of heat. She stumbled over her own feet and screamed for Monica.

"Fuck's sake, just get in there," Karithexis said. Her glasses hung half off her face, broken where the holy water had hit her, searing a swath across her nose and forehead. Still, she gripped Grace's arm and shoved her through the rip.

The last thing Grace caught before the dark swallowed her was Monica, struggling against Gareth's grip, and Daisy, taking aim again.

She took one last shot as the rip closed behind them.

THE REALM

Chapter Eleven

All Grace wanted to do was scream for Monica.

Scratch that.

All she wanted to do was scream. And scream. And never stop.

The things in front of her, what'd been on the other side of that rip in the air, she couldn't process any of it. It was all a convoluted mess of blood, gore, fire, and pain that made little sense.

"You get used to it," Karithexis said. Hand still gripping Grace's arm with claws that dug into her skin, she pulled Grace along some kind of earthen hallway lined with people in varying states of pain.

Some looked up, their faces blank, and held up their own insides in their bloody palms for Grace to inspect as she passed.

Some never made anything close to eye contact. Either their eyes were too wild to even try, or they simply didn't care to.

"I don't think they know where they are, if it helps," Karithexis said, dragging her past them. "Here. In here." She shoved her at a door made of steel and kicked one of the people lining the hall in the face. "Piss off, vulture."

The man—or filthy woman, who could tell—backed off, stuffing the viscera he'd been shoving at Karithexis into his own mouth.

She closed the door behind herself and Grace, and sighed. "Not that you would, but if you take any of what they're offering, you're stuck with them until you can guide them out of this godforsaken hallway."

Grace glanced around the room, if it could be called that. Also earthen, it stank of mold and rotten vegetables. The walls dripped, water hopefully, and one single light bulb hung from the center of the rounded ceiling.

In its dusty light, Grace tried to forget about her aching head. She squeezed it down like the other times and found it got easier and easier to contain as long as she concentrated.

She swallowed. "How long is the hallway?"

Karithexis stood under the light, the tips of her white hair shining. "It's eternal, Grace." She rolled her eyes. "There has got to be some way to get you to remember this shit. Do you remember any of this at all?" She stepped out of the light, and something clicked.

A bank of lights came on behind her. They shone down another hallway, this one gleaming, clean and white.

Grace took a few steps into the new hall. She fingered a miniature statue of a horse that sat on a long table along the wall and picked up a worn doll carved from a single piece of wood. Her hair was made from cloth, features crudely painted on, and half her mouth smiled at Grace. The other half had rubbed off.

"What about this?" Karithexis walked deeper into the room, pointing at another table.

Grace put the doll down and approached the table, almost tripping over her own feet. Neither of them wanted to move. The table stood on spindly legs and leaned to one side. Grace felt a strange kinship with the wonky thing.

She gripped the listing table and held both it and herself up.

It was what was on it that truly sent her sideways, more than the crooked table and the crooked painting on the wall behind it.

A charred piece of wood sat alone in the center.

Grace's fingers trailed over the burnt wood, following the dips and cracks. Tiny bits of ash rested between some of the breaks in the log. She laid her whole palm on it, and the warmth of the fire it came from touched her hand. Rough bark scratched along the pads of her fingers when she gripped it and turned it over to inspect the underside.

It was flecked with what may have been rust but wasn't. After all she'd seen, it could only be blood—burgundy, dried, portentous. She whispered with her teeth clenched, "What is this?"

"Well, fuck. I thought for sure you'd remember this. You really don't remember shit, do you?"

Eyes round, Grace turned to the demon dressed as an old woman. "What am I supposed to remember? Why do you want my memory to come back so bad? So I won't keep trying to kill you?"

"That's one reason," Karithexis said, walking down the gleaming, white hallway. As she passed under the lights, her hair glowed almost blue. "But like I said, we had a plan. I'd rather not talk about it down here."

Leaving the warm, charred wood on the spindly table, Grace caught up to her.

Karithexis leaned close. "The walls listen. So does the floor and ceiling."

Grace considered the people she'd seen in the hall. Their despair. The fact the hallway was infinite. "Karithexis, where are we?"

"Where do you think we are?"

"Is this hell?"

With a snort, Karithexis started walking again. "Don't be so damned trite. There's no such thing as 'hell.'" She hooked her fingers around the word and lifted one curled lip. "It's not Earth; we call it the Realm, but there's no judgment from on high when a person leaves Earth." She poked Grace in the abdomen with a gnarled finger. "We get stuck here all on our own, thank you." Digging her nails into Grace's arm, she yanked her down the hall. A door appeared from the gloom ahead.

"So you want out of here? Or something? Why do you need my help to do that?"

The door opened before they got there, squealing on hinges that hadn't seen oil since it was invented. It literally groaned as it opened, a creature in the dark crying about its own fate.

A thin woman stood in the door, her golden-brown skin gleaming, her high cheekbones sharp enough to cut the air. Her perfectly tailored suit hugged each and every curve and angle of her. One small black stone glittered in the middle of her forehead.

Grace swallowed. She hadn't expected the woman's slick grin in such a place, especially coming out of the dark the way it did. It put her off in a nonspecific way, like the squeaking of a cotton glove between your teeth when you bit the fingers to take it off. She stopped short of the doorway and stared up into her deep brown eyes.

The woman's smile lit her face and lifted her cheeks. She stuck out a long-fingered hand and waited for Grace to take it.

Grace took her cold fingertips. A chill crept up her own arm.

"So glad you have returned to us, Grace. It's good to meet you again. You can call me Raga."

*

Without knowledge of how they'd gotten there, Grace found herself following Raga through a field of flowers. Her deep black hair swung down the middle of her back, tied in several sections with golden string. She glided through the field of wildflowers, brushing against their petals with delicate *swish* sounds.

"You look as though you've seen a ghost, dear Grace. And Karithexis, how kind of you to bring her back to us."

"I live to serve, my lord."

"Oh shut up, demon. You may lie to the humans all you like, but you never could lie convincingly to me, so why don't we drop the charade." Her smooth, almost English accent lengthened the a's in "charade" so it didn't rhyme with "parade."

Grace swallowed, forehead tight. It hit her, where she'd heard the name Raga before. The demon who'd taken Monica's eye called out to her, called her a "child of Mara," and invited her to come eat the souls of the sisters. Or something.

Karithexis had mentioned her too. This was the very demon they were trying to escape. And yet here they were, within her clutches in a place Grace didn't know how to escape from.

Perfect planning.

Raga laughed from deep in her throat. "Last I heard, you'd been lost to us, dear Grace. Something about those nuns and a spell?" She cocked her eyebrow at Karithexis.

"That's right. The Order of Saint Raphael trapped her with an amnesia spell and turned her against her own kind. They hunted down Jalithesh. He tried to call you, lord."

Raga pursed her lips, hands clasped in front of her. She stopped and lowered her sculpted jaw. The perfect skin next to her mouth wrinkled. "I heard him, but what could I have done? Most of those witches have already denied me. They practice ridding themselves of desire each day, and where does that leave the goddess of passion?" She turned to Grace. "Could you give me a way in? If you could, my gratitude would be eternal." She smiled, her beautiful mouth twisting into an ugly scowl, for a moment turning her perfect face into a parody of beauty more like a wax figure, carved by clumsy hands and melting into a grotesque, dripping facsimile of a human.

Grace blinked, her throat closed. She wanted to raise her hands to her face, cover her eyes, forget she saw any of it.

But before she moved her heavy limbs, the demon's face rippled and returned to a human form. "Eternal gratitude from your master, that has to be worth something, doesn't it?"

Stuttering, Grace tried to answer, but Raga's face melting like a candle filled her mind.

"Oh, but that's right." Raga slipped her arm around Grace's shoulder and pulled her deep into the field of flowers. "You don't remember anything about your master. Allow me to enlighten you." She lifted her hand to Grace's forehead.

Karithexis caught her arm. "Please, my sweet lord. Her memory has been returning in small stages. I'm afraid if you give it all back to her at once, she'll lose her mind."

Raga chuckled and continued to lift her arm, dragging Karithexis's hand with it. "That is a gamble I'm willing to make. Do you think her mind will leak out the sides of her ears? Do you think it will smell of blood, and fertilize this lovely field?"

Grace dry-heaved, trying to pull away from Raga and failing. She whimpered, imagining the brains of a thousand souls that may have already done just that.

Karithexis raised her other hand and tugged with both, slowing Raga's reach. "Please. If we lose her, we lose our door into the Order. As it is now, they would give her whatever you desire."

Raga's rich lips lifted in a smile that showed all her teeth. "Is this true, Grace? Would you really do that for me?"

She couldn't escape the iron grip; all she could do was nod. Nod and hope she didn't throw up. "If I save Monica from the hunters, I think the nuns will take us both back. Tell me what you want."

The iron arm encircling her loosened. "What's this?"

"One of her friends is trapped with some hunters," Karithexis said. "I blasted her out of there, but her friend put her own life on the line to make it happen. She's one of the newest of the Order. I'm sure if you help us help her, then we can—"

A growl came from deep in Raga's throat, cutting through the rest of Karithexis's speech.

Karithexis's mouth snapped closed, the broken glasses bouncing off her chest as it heaved up and down, the burned gash on her face deep red. She bowed, her forehead almost touching her thighs. Her voice shook. "I am so sorry, my lord. How have I offended you?"

The growl grew and grew until Grace's ears ached from the inside out. She covered them, but it didn't do any good.

Eyes wild, she searched for an exit.

A wooden door sat in the middle of the field, with wide slats held together by a long piece of wood nailed across them. Surrounded by nothing, an orange glow emanated from between the slats. The growling coming from Raga invaded every thought she had; the only one left was that she had to escape and help Monica.

She approached the door. Something flashed in her memory, like half-eaten chocolate sundae and wasted wine, spilled and tacky on a table. She gripped the warm doorknob and yanked it open.

"No, wait. Grace!"

Ignoring Karithexis's high-pitched, wavering voice, she slipped through the door and into the orange light beyond.

Chapter Twelve

Before her, three people—a man and two women—sat in front of a fire, most likely the orange light she'd seen through the door. Grace shuffled closer.

Hello?

None of them turned. They didn't even react to Grace's voice.

Uh. Hi? Can someone tell me where I am?

Still nothing.

She spun back to the door and reached for the handle.

Her hand passed through it.

What the hell?

Wait.

Was she speaking aloud? She tried again, shouting this time.

What is this place?

Her head pounded. She approached the murmuring people by the fire. As she got closer, the fire lit more of the room on the other side of them.

The body of a man lay on a table, a candle at his head and foot, his lips blue and parted, his skin pallid. If Grace could touch him, he'd be cold. Frozen, like Maria had been.

She spun to the people sitting around the fire. They murmured, and something told Grace these were only the shape of the words. They spoke a language, something she didn't recognize, and Grace was certain she wouldn't understand it under normal circumstances.

Clearly these were anything other than normal circumstances.

With one hand over her throat, she tried once more. *Who are you?* Her throat didn't vibrate. She wasn't speaking, and they couldn't hear her. If her hand passing through the doorknob was any indication, they couldn't see her either.

How would she get out of here?

Her chest tightened. How would she get back to Monica? Hell, even Karithexis would be acceptable at this point. Anywhere other than this dusty, one-roomed wooden house with dirt floors and three people sitting around a fire with a dead body on a table beside them.

The woman in the middle, a baby suckling at her breast, glanced up.

For a wild moment, Grace held her breath and waited for the woman to see her.

Instead, she looked down at the baby and sniffled. "What are we going to do now? I have this baby to take care of and no husband to provide for us. The white plague has come into our house like a spirit. Like an agent of black magic. We're destitute. Broken. Spoiled."

The man grunted and rocked in his chair. "Find you another husband is what you'll do."

"Godwin," the other woman hissed. She rocked at a furious pace, the chair creaking and squealing. Her feet tapped the floor in a staccato.

"We can't afford it, Mother. And she can't inherit anything without a husband. All my land, all my work, for nothing? No." He shook his head, the firelight flicking over his severe frown. "I won't have it. You'll marry again, daughter. It's what you're going to do."

The other woman rocked faster. "You listen to your father." Her feet beat the staccato.

Coming off the breast with such force Grace heard the tiny pop when the baby's mouth broke the seal, the little thing started coughing. It was too tiny to cough so big. She didn't even know babies that small could cough. It couldn't be bigger than her forearm.

The girl whimpered. "Do you think we could take him to get the royal touch?"

Godwin shook his head again, the severe frown shadowed in the firelight, his forehead so wrinkled the shadows almost looked like horns. "Didn't I say we can't afford to feed you, girl? No way to afford a royal touch. No." He shook his head, the chair popping as he rocked.

Below the arm of the chair, the girl's mother gripped her leg. "Isn't the king coming next week?"

The girl gave such a fierce nod the baby popped off her breast again. "It's doesn't have to be long, Papa; he just needs to touch the baby to fight the black magic making him sick. Just a little touch." She stared down at the baby and settled him back on the breast.

"I won't be argued with." Godwin stood, staring into the fire. His chair rocked so hard it toppled sideways and hit the girl in the arm.

Tears streamed down her face, landing in her baby's eyes. The baby squirmed.

"You listen to your father, child."

Grace's eyes stung. She wanted to cry along with this desperate woman whose husband lay in death mere feet away from her, whose baby was obviously already sick. Her domineering father wouldn't listen to either of them, and her baby was going to die. Even if the touch of a royal hand wouldn't heal him, and Grace was sure it wouldn't, the poor girl's father wouldn't even give her a chance to try.

She wanted to punch him in the head to see how thick it really was.

Before she tried, the scene in front of her faded into fog. Like pea soup on a warm, humid morning, she couldn't even see to the end of her nose.

Fingers spread, she held her hands out and spun a circle. *Hello?*

The fog cleared in stages, like the sun burning it off. First, she made out shapes. Then some of the shapes coalesced into something large, like horses. Then a crowd of people surrounded her, holding their outstretched hands up.

And in front of Grace, the girl, holding her baby boy aloft, clutching his legs and neck in her hands, the skin on her face stretched tight over her grimace. Eyes wide, she pulled the corners of her mouth wider and stood on her tiptoes. "Please."

It wasn't even a whisper, but it was all she could say. All she could muster.

Around her, people moaned and begged, pled for relief.

Grace spun toward the center of their attention.

The horses she'd seen pulled an ornate open carriage. Someone's hand hung out the side, brushing over many of the outstretched hands in the crowd. As they touched, the people would wail, falling back into the ones behind them.

The pale hand was draped in rings, the skin fine and smooth.

They came closer.

Grace spun back to the girl and her baby. She'd defied her father to come here, and they had to get the touch. They had to. An unexpected urgency consumed Grace. She was so desperate for them to get the touch it ached in the back of her throat and tightened her chest, her windpipe a pinhole. If only she could push them forward, get them closer.

She moved through the throng, careful not to touch other people. She might have brushed through a doorknob with her hand, but she had no desire to whiff through a whole person.

But before she thought about it, she put her hands on the uplifted baby.

And they didn't pass through. She tugged the baby and the woman holding him forward. Higher. Closer.

The hand approached.

She followed its progress, sweat on her brow, her breath held tight in her chest. It had to work. It had to work.

The white, smooth hand came down on the baby's forehead, the fingertips brushing along his eyebrows.

And then it was gone, leaving only the smell of powder.

The girl inhaled sharply. She whispered, "What?"

Grace shouldn't have been able to hear her over the keening throng. But she did. It was all she heard. The girl's inhalation, and that one small word.

She spun and caught the girl's eyes. In that moment, she fell into the eyes and looked out of them, up at the baby, and she knew.

It was her.

This was her baby. And the girl, it was her.

Chapter Thirteen

"Fuck's sake. Wake up."

Grace opened her eyes.

Cold ground under her, low ceiling above her. Garish neon light glared down from it and into her eyes.

She squinted and turned toward the voice.

Karithexis sat on her heels, her broken glasses banging off her thin, drooping breasts, and frowned. "There you are. Thought I'd never get you out of that damned place."

"Where—" Grace started. She paused, sitting up on her elbows, linoleum slick underneath them. "Where was I? Where are we now? What happened?"

"Raga." Karithexis stood and hooked her hand under Grace's armpit. Before Grace could protest, she pulled her out of the floor and nearly tossed her into the air before setting her on her feet. "She sent you off to a pocket universe, for lack of a better word. What did she show you? What room was it?"

"My—" She gripped her forehead and gazed out at Karithexis from under her fingers. "My own memories. I think."

The demon rolled her eyes. "Of course she did. Did it help you remember anything?"

Eyes narrowed, Grace shook her head. When they passed the charred lump of wood and the wooden doll, she stopped. "I don't think so."

Arms crossed tight over her chest, Karithexis walked past the spot where they'd entered the hall and continued to stalk into the next hallway. Every few lights had gone out in here, some completely, some still flickering. "I suppose we're lucky she didn't turn your brain to mush. I thought she was going to kill us both for a minute there."

Grace stopped, gazing at the door they'd originally come from. "I need to get out of here, Karithexis. I have to help Monica. I need to find out why the nuns wanted to erase the only memories I had. And if they ever planned to give them back." She reached for the doorknob. "Maybe there's some spell, or—"

The demon stutter-stepped to her and leaned on the door. "You can't go out that way. Besides, what do you want with any of those nuns? Isn't it enough they tried to kill you? Tried to turn you against your own kind?"

A hot breath escaped Grace's nose. She flared her nostrils around it. "You're not my kind. I'm not like you."

Karithexis snorted. "Just because you can't remember all the fun we've had doesn't make you better than me."

"My lack of memory doesn't erase who I feel like inside, Kari. I'm a good person, no matter what 'fun'"— she hooked her fingers around the word—"we had together. That's not who I am anymore." She turned the knob.

Karithexis slapped her hand against the door and held it firm. She snorted. "Kari. You haven't called me that in about a hundred years, give or take. I thought you'd forgotten you ever gave me that nickname." She leaned on the door. "I told you, you cannot go out this way. You'll get pulled in by one of those awful specters and never get out."

Grace sighed, frown so tight across her lips and cheeks they stretched to their limit, burning a line across her face. "Fine. Where do I get out? I'm leaving. I don't know how many different ways you want me to say that."

With a huff between tight lips, the demon narrowed her eyes. "Fine. Fine. This way." She grabbed Grace's wrist with surprising strength and yanked her down the hall, back toward the way they'd met Raga.

Angling for the door, Grace set her mouth and considered what she'd do if they ran into the demonic lord on the other side of the door again.

But before they got there, a great black maw opened in the floor in front of them. Tiles broke apart, falling into the hole, and the ground developed a noticeable tilt.

Gravity pulled Grace's feet toward it.

She fought, scrambling onto her heels, but Karithexis yanked her forward, her glasses banging against her chest.

Head tilted up, the demon grimaced. "I don't like it either. It's abyss-adjacent. But it's the best way out of here that Raga doesn't watch. She hates this door, and she thinks we'll stay away from it too."

Grace dug her heels in. "I'd prefer to do that." She wrinkled her nose. "What is that stench? Smells like..."

She sniffed again and gagged. Between dry heaves, she tried to tell the demon it smelled like rotted fruit in the bottom of a fridge but mixed with sewer sludge and the sweat of a thousand bodies pressed together well-beyond shower time, but all that came out was a dry heave and a burp.

Karithexis shoved her into the hole and jumped in after.

*

The falling went on forever. Years, it felt like.

The utter dark tore at her hair, pulling her clothing, nipping at the tips of her fingers.

She opened her eyes wide, as wide as they'd go, and she couldn't make out even a shadow.

A scream bubbled up in her throat, but she couldn't let it loose. The fear it would come out silent, sucked from the air like the light had been, engulfed coherent thought.

When Karithexis snatched at her hand, her withered fingers gripping with that same surprising strength, Grace clutched her back with desperate abandon. The dark continued nipping at the fingertips of her other hand.

The changing air hit those same fingertips first. Instead of biting at them like small frozen teeth, the air flowed through them like water, at first. Then, like oil, it thickened and collected against the webbing between her fingers. As it grew warmer around her, it became almost like petroleum jelly, gooping around her fingers, collecting in her palm.

She shut her eyes tight and gripped Karithexis harder.

The demon yanked her close and wrapped her in her tiny arms. Her cheekbone pressed into Grace's jaw. "Hang on, Grace. We're about to—"

Around them, the air sucked close. It suffocated Grace from the inside out.

Were they in space? What the hell was this?

She opened her heavy eyes again, and though it was brighter, she couldn't focus. It was all a blur. Her limbs weighed two hundred pounds each, and she couldn't breathe.

Karithexis kneed her in the thigh.

Her thigh cramped and she gritted her teeth. Paralyzed with the pain, she wanted to scream but still couldn't.

The air popped, and her ears exploded with a tearing deep inside her ear canals, almost like it was inside her brain.

Taking in a lungful of hot, oily air, she ran her fingers along the side of her head. There wasn't any moisture, so probably she hadn't ruptured anything in her ears. Still, the rushing sound, any sound, disappeared, and the pain rolled down the sides of her throat.

With no preamble, they landed on the ground. The trees around them blew over like they would in a strong gale, the smaller ones bending almost double, their crowns nearly touching the ground. Every surface of Grace's body lit up in pain, her skin screaming as it fought itself to stay intact. Somewhere near her left armpit, warmth hit her, and she didn't know if her skin had split or if Natalie was having a heart attack.

She lay on her back in the crater they'd made, breathing what had to be Earth's air through sharp spikes of pain in her ribs and staring up at the sky. A couple clouds floated by. One of them looked like a nun's habit. Her thoughts drifted to Monica while she waited to see if Natalie's body was dying. What would she tell Mon if that happened? If Nat never got back to her family?

Coughing, she worked to sit up. The pain shot through her chest again, but as she wrapped herself in a ginger hug, it lessened and shrank to a pinpoint in her right side. Probably—maybe—just some broken ribs, then.

Lifting her left arm, she checked her armpit. Blood flowed down her side, caking into the seam of her shirt and pooling at her waistband.

With a grimace, she put her arm down and squeezed it tight against her body. Eyes closed, she focused on the injuries and sought the stream of her essence like the one she'd found inside Gareth.

When she found it, it was as though the picture had been filmed in the highest definition she'd ever seen. Healing took a fraction of the time. Before she truly formed a thought, the light emblazoned itself inside her eyelids.

Her side stopped hurting. In fact, she had energy enough to run a marathon.

With caution, she ran the pads of her fingers over her armpit. They slipped over blood still drying on her shirt, but the wound itself had knitted together as though it had never been there at all.

A rattling noise brought her out of her reverie.

Karithexis lay next to her, sprawled on her back, with her limbs at unusual angles. Her wide eyes all but popped from her skull as they rolled to Grace. Her mouth moved, but only blood came out of it.

Grace sat and stared at her, mouth curling in an unconscious snarl. Let the bitch die.

That's my mother! You can't let her die! She's in pain; you have to help her!

Fuck. Natalie was right.

Gripping one of the demon's wrists in her hand, she squeezed the way Karithexis had done her.

A whimper escaped from her open mouth.

Grace smiled. "Just a little payback, Kari. Hold still."

Karithexis grunted from deep in her throat and twitched when Grace laid her hand over her heart.

"Stop trying to escape. I'm not going to hurt you. Although this might hurt me more. Probably going to find a river of blood in there or something." Her lip curled further. "This is going to be uncomfortable for both of us, I think."

She closed her eyes.

The scene before her was so clear and beautiful it jarred her to her core. She almost opened her eyes in shock.

Energy from a demon had no right to be so breathtaking. For one thing, it was bigger than Gareth's. The river flooded, bulging and surging over the banks, pushing branches and twigs, in some cases whole trees, along with it. Heavy boulders crashed in the riverbed, far below the swollen surface.

As Grace marveled at the beauty and the absolute power of the river, she spotted something unusual, something that hadn't been there in Gareth's head.

A shape clung to a tree by the bank.

She moved closer.

It was a woman, old and frail, and she looked like Karithexis did on the outside. She'd lost her shawl, and there wasn't a surface of her clothing that didn't have a rip. Her shirt hung half off her shoulder, and she bled from at least a dozen slashes. Broken glasses hung sideways off one ear. She shivered.

Grace approached her. The tree shook, its roots being eroded by the deluge below.

"Are you Natalie's mom?"

The old woman nodded, watching the river. "She told me she'd take care of me and help me find my Nat." Her eyebrows drew together, and she shifted her gaze to Grace. "Are you the one that took her?"

"Don't I look like her?"

Nat's mom shook her head. "You look like light, like this one did when she came to take over me. She's a liar though. That river has been trying to kill me."

As if on cue, the tree shook again, listing dramatically to the right, hanging Nat's mom over the turbulent water.

Grace shook her head and closed in on the water, trying to figure out how to calm it long enough to infuse it with the light. "She's dying, I think." She chewed her lip. "I could let her. You'd go with her though."

She waited, listening for Natalie's protests, but it was as though Nat couldn't follow her here. She was alone.

"I want to save my daughter. I want you to heal this demon. Promise me something."

"Anything."

"Once my daughter is safe, kill this demon. I don't care if you take me with her, as long as my daughter is safe."

She shook her head. "Your daughter would never let me hurt you."

"Promise me."

Grace focused on the water again, and beams of light broke the surface. She spoke out of the side of her mouth. "I promise. I will kill the demon."

*

Karithexis limped down the sidewalk in one broken shoe. "How'd you learn to do that, anyway?"

"Do what?"

"Heal. I've never seen a demon do something like that."

A car whipped Grace's ripped shirtsleeve around her arm. "Sure you have. Hasn't anyone ever made a deal to make themselves not sick anymore? Or one of their kids or something?"

The demon snorted. "People are a lot stingier than you think. They don't generally deal eternity away for other people, even their own children." Her toe caught a crack, and she stumbled.

Without thinking about it, Grace caught her and held her arm. It trembled.

"They're liars, most of them. Just like us. I wouldn't trust any of them as far as I can throw them." Karithexis chuckled. "Deals don't work exactly that way anyway. I wish you remembered this; it'd be a lot easier than explaining it all to you. Again." Her now-unblemished brow curved down.

"Tell me about Raga." Grace checked traffic. Clear enough. Whether Karithexis knew it or not, she'd landed them in a familiar neighborhood.

Karithexis chuckled. "I hate using that door, now you know why, but she won't know we're gone for hours, days, maybe even a week. We might have some time before she sends her minions to look for us."

"Why would she do that?"

She tripped up the sidewalk. Stopping, she extricated her arm from Grace's, ripped off the broken shoe, and threw it in the road as a car passed. It bounced off the windshield, and the car laid on its horn, Doppler effect lessening the honk as it continued down the road. The demon chuckled again, clicking her teeth together. "Nasty humans. Anyway." She continued down the sidewalk, unwrapping the broken glasses and chucking them in the gutter. "We belong to her. We used to be human, and when we went to the Realm to punish ourselves for whatever, we ended up with her. I don't know about you, but she talked me into serving her with a promise of—" She stopped. "You don't want to hear that. Suffice it to say, we belong to her until the end of time. Then we'll be free."

"The end of time? When will that be?"

"The heat death of the universe."

"Of the universe? Wouldn't that include us?"

"Now you're getting it."

Grace stopped, staring down the row of townhouses. "So you and I had a plan to escape her. What was I going to do?"

Karithexis stopped with her and folded her hands together. The pouches around her eyes drooped. The body might have been healed, but it was still tired. Nat's mom was barely hanging on in there. "I don't know, Grace. That's the problem. That's why we need your memory back. The last you told me, you were going to meet this girl." Her eyes crawled over Grace's body with a greasy up and down motion.

Grace shuddered and dropped her eyes.

"I know you made the deal, because you sent me the signal, but then you dropped off the goddamned map. I don't know what you were doing, but we have to find out what you did after you made the deal with this Natalie girl, and we need to find out what you planned to do with her." Karithexis started walking again, approaching the blue townhouse with the sparkling white trim. "I know you had a plan, and you didn't choose her at random. You're going to have to talk to her. Did you do it already? Did you talk to her like I told you to?"

"You didn't tell me to," Grace said, jogging to catch up. "You told me how. That's not the same thing."

"Whatever." Karithexis mounted the porch stairs, stomping on them as hard as her tiny feet would allow. The boards creaked.

Grace stopped at the bottom of the stairs and glared at the house. "Kari, wait. Why are we here?"

"Besides the whole summoning thing, this is the safest place we can be right now. We can't go to your hunter friends—"

"They're not my friends anymore," Grace interrupted.

"And we can't go to the nuns," Karithexis finished. "We don't have too many options, and Shanna can't help it. She'll take us in. Both of us." She raised her hand to knock.

The laughter of children playing came through the open window in the front room.

Grace cringed.

So did Natalie.

But Nat did one other thing. She caught the demon's hand. "Let me."

Karithexis stepped back. "Be my guest."

And as Grace knocked on the door, almost hard enough to be heard and at the same time almost too light to be noticed, Natalie disappeared. She left a gaping hole inside Grace.

With her guts quaking, Grace almost spun and ran off the porch. Before she even twitched, the door opened at the same time she knew, without a doubt, they had nowhere else to go.

The look of utter shock mixed with love, disappointment, and Shanna's immediately watery eyes told her she'd take them in.

Just like the demon said.

*

Once Grace and Karithexis got changed out of the bloody clothes Shanna hardly commented on, Grace ended up sequestered in the kitchen with Shanna and listening to the boys playing with their "grandmama" in the other room. It was all she could do not to scream Shanna had chosen the wrong demon to trust.

Instead, she crossed her legs and leaned on the table. "Can I at least see them?"

Shanna shook her head, reddish bangs falling into her eyes. "I can't believe you'd come here like this again. Unannounced. Why?"

Grace made something up off the top of her head. "Mom insisted. What was I supposed to do?"

"Not listen to her, like you spent thirty-eight years doing anyway."

She blew out her nose. "Is that how old I am?"

Leaning on the creaking chair across from Grace, Shanna frowned. "You really don't remember anything. I keep forgetting that. Sometimes, I think—" She stopped. "Never mind."

Grace swallowed around the lump in her throat and tried to wish Natalie back. She was still all alone here, with no guidance from Nat and not even her presence to keep her company. "You think I'm lying."

Shanna's cheeks turned an alarming shade of red, her green eyes popping out of her face. "That's not what I said."

"It's okay," Grace said, unsure if it was or not, "you're not the first one. You probably won't be the last. Kar... Mom pretty much interrogated me the whole time we were gone. It took her forever to believe me." She leaned onto her elbows and lowered her voice. "I still think she thinks I'm lying."

Sitting with a sigh, the chair legs squeaking against the hardwood floor, Shanna met her eyes. "I don't think you're lying. I think you forgot me on purpose."

Grace tried to think of something to say. She searched Shanna's pale face, noticing, maybe for the first time, the delicate half circles of blue under her eyes and the way the thick makeup on her lids couldn't hide how red-rimmed her eyes were. The nervous way she swallowed and tucked a short strand of hair behind her ear without looking up.

Grace reached across the table and laid her hand over Shanna's. Conjuring up the feelings she'd had when Natalie saw Shanna last, she spoke from deep down and tried to say what Nat would. "No one could ever even think of forgetting you on purpose. I love you more than I love myself, babe. You have to know that."

Shanna sniffled. "Not more than alcohol."

Grace balled her fist. "More than anything. I might not remember myself, my life, the details, but I know for a fact I love you more than I can express."

But the words rang hollow, like she'd read them from a script.

Shanna knew it. She backed up from the table, eyes cast at the floor.

In her mind's eye, Grace conjured a picture of Monica. Well, she tried for one. Instead, once she opened the gates, images flashed through so quick it took her breath away.

Monica sleeping half under the covers, her long leg stuck out, the short shorts exposing her upper thigh.

Monica in her novice headscarf, pinning back a loose curly hair that'd escaped.

Kneeling in the sanctuary, her perfect lips moving in time with the prayer Father Moscone led with listless abandon.

Laughing over a joke Grace made.

Poring over a dusty old book.

Lying facedown on the porch of that cabin, bleeding from her eye.

Clutching Grace's head to her breast, protecting her from the exorcism.

"I couldn't imagine loving anyone as much as I love you," Grace whispered. Her voice wavered. "You saved me when I couldn't save myself. You gave me everything without asking anything in return, and I love you more than breathing."

Tears sprang up in her eyes, and her vision trebled. She blinked, trying to clear them. Hot tears tracked down her cheeks and didn't stop. She wanted them to stop. She wanted to say all that to Monica.

Shanna leapt up so fast the chair clattered to the floor. The boys pounded down the hall as she rounded the table and knelt in front of Grace. "Oh my god, Nat. If you remember at least that much, I think we can try and work through the rest." She grabbed her hand.

The footsteps stopped in the doorway. "You okay, Mom?"

Shanna nodded, bangs falling in her eyes. Her tears fell too, through her waterproof mascara. She stood on her knees, clutching Grace's hand in both of hers, and leaned into her. "I love you too, Natalie."

But the moment her lips hit Grace's, warm and soft and thin, Grace backed away. The tears would not stop, nor would the words, now running constant through her head. *"I fell in love with you."*

She stood, pushing the chair back and away from the woman kneeling in the floor. Hands covering her mouth, she glanced at the boys in the door.

Before she spoke, Natalie came screaming back from the depths and crying out for her children as they stood there, mouths open, arms out for her.

Grace shoved her away too. "I can't. I'm sorry. I have to go."

The back door banged into the fridge, and she was out before it had time to swing the other way.

Chapter Fourteen

Before she reached the back gate, the kitchen door banged again. She didn't stop to see who was following her, but she had a pretty good idea anyway.

"Grace!"

Tearing open the gate, she stopped before stepping into the alley. "Karithexis, I can't stay here." Arms crossed, she leaned on the gate and cut her eyes at the demon.

Panting, she stopped a few feet away. She'd found a new pair of glasses, and they hung half off her nose. "You shouldn't go out there. Raga can't find us here. The barrier is strong; it'll protect us until we figure this out."

Grace blew a breath out through her nose. "It didn't protect you from the summoning Daisy did."

Fist balled, Karithexis shoved it into her elbow. "Fuck those hunters. They didn't catch me, just delayed me a little. Is that where you're going? To get your precious nun back?"

"First of all, she has a name. It's Monica. Second—" She sighed. "—yes. She's mine, and I'm going to get her back. She risked her life to save me, and I have to make sure she's okay." She stepped away from the gate and shoved a finger in Karithexis's face. "You don't dictate what I do; I don't care what plan we had together. You're not my boss."

Eyes flashing, Karithexis took a step toward her and leaned into her pointed finger. "What are you going to do, huh, Grace? You're not going anywhere unless I say you are." She grabbed Grace's arm, hooked fingers digging into the soft flesh of her underarm.

And that was it. She'd had enough of being ordered around by one person or another. More than enough. Plenty.

The heat built inside her like a campfire with kerosene poured in it.

She grabbed the demon's hand and twisted, focusing the heat on her own palm.

Mouth open so wide her jaw unhinged, Karithexis screamed and dropped to her knees. She kept screaming, writhing and trying to jerk her hand free.

That same warmth Grace had experienced when she'd controlled those people flowed through her, but more, so much more. She wondered how using the power to kill this demon would feel. She might even be able to touch God with such a power, transcend this awful earthen place and reach the heavens.

Before that feeling swept her off her feet, the image of Monica holding her to her breast leapt into her mind again.

Reeling, she let the demon go and backed away. She bounced off the fence and opened the gate again. "Are you going to show me how to do that thing where you appear places, or am I going to have to figure it out on my own?"

Karithexis groaned. Wobbling to her feet, she leaned on a knee. "You're a real bitch, you know? Some things never change."

"Fine." Grace stormed through the gate.

Catching it before it slammed home, Karithexis followed her to the alley. "Wait. It's easier if I show you." She grabbed Grace's wrist.

Grace jerked it back. "No tricks or I really will kill you."

"No tricks," Karithexis said, crossing her heart. "Scout's honor." She held up a peace sign.

Grace sighed. She slipped her hand inside the demon's. "You know where the compound is?"

"No, but you can show me. You think of it, and I'll get us there."

Before they popped out of existence, Grace considered the wisdom in taking Karithexis to this place—in showing her where it was.

But it was too late to think about. No sooner had the thought coalesced in her mind, they'd arrived.

In the frigid air, not many people moved around outside. Grace's breath fogged in front of her face, the tip of her nose already numb from standing in Shanna's yard for so long. But that didn't mean there was no one, and as they stood watching, a car pulled into the small lot.

Karithexis, still holding Grace's hand, pulled Grace behind the closest tree. "Make yourself hard to see," she hissed.

"Do what now?"

"Come on. You heal people, you tried to kill me, you kill people with that mind control trick you're so good at.

You certainly know how to make yourself hard to see. Thin."

She started to shake her head, but her thoughts drifted to Raga. That jewel on her forehead, for some reason, made her think of being hard to see.

Instead of trying to catch the memory head-on, she let it slide to her peripheral and pretended she wasn't interested.

It floated close enough to catch.

She grabbed on.

Oh, of course. The statue outside Mother Mary's study—the one Grace had believed was a nun but wasn't—she had a spot like that in her forehead too.

The empty air next to Grace spoke. "Hurry up."

Grace kept concentrating on the day she'd hid in that corner and eavesdropped on Monica and Mary as they talked about lying to her, and the way Mon had walked down the hall, eyes sliding over Grace like—

Like she couldn't see her.

She focused on that feeling, the feeling of sinking into the background, of trying so, so hard to not be seen.

"Good job. Are you sure you don't remember anything?"

She glanced down. Her body had disappeared. Taking her hand from Karithexis, she laid it on her face. It was still there, but she couldn't see the arm in front of her. She'd become effectively invisible. "I really don't remember."

Why wouldn't anyone besides Monica believe that?

"Where do we find Mon?"

"This way, sweetcheeks." Karithexis's voice floated from about ten feet ahead. She'd already started walking around the back of the compound.

Grace followed, trying to track the demon's silent footsteps in the dirt. It being dusk, orange washed everything out and shadows laid over all of it, so she almost lost her more than once. As they approached the compound and Grace spotted a few hunters gathered around the campfire, she bit her tongue and didn't call out. She couldn't risk them hearing her, so she just did the best she could in the half shadows.

Karithexis led her around the corner of the complex, where windows lined each side of the U-shaped building. There were two windows per room and at least eight rooms per side, and each window was ringed in bars— probably warded against demons too.

"Is she in a room?"

The footsteps in front of her stopped. "I can't tell. It's impossible to read anything inside this place. Their warding is excellent. As good as your nuns, I'd say."

Grace wanted to tell her they weren't her nuns, but after the week she'd had, that seemed a foolish thing to say. Living with them had been heavenly compared to the last few days.

"How are we going to find her?"

"I'm looking for the one with the best warding."

"Why?"

"Because they want to keep her in and you out." Karithexis kept walking, letting her silhouette shimmer in the twilight so Grace could follow.

They rounded the next corner, and even though Grace didn't know what they were looking for, she found it anyway.

Karithexis clicked her teeth. "There she is."

It was the same room Alice had given them. They must have locked Monica in and doctored it with spells and sigils.

Throat tight, Grace rushed to the window. She balled her fist to knock.

The demon caught her hand. Grace's balled fist floated in midair. When she'd lost her own invisibility was anybody's guess.

"I wouldn't touch that window. It's warded. It's likely to hurt you, maybe even trap you."

Teeth grinding, Grace tried to peer through the curtains. A shadow crossed them, back and forth, back and forth. Her throat hurt, and she spoke through sudden tears. "I have to get her out of there."

Letting her go, the demon lifted her glasses and their chain over her head and handed them to her. "Use this to tap on the window. Try not to touch the bars."

Grace did.

The curtain slid aside a millimeter.

Monica's deep brown eye stared out the slit. It widened in surprise, and she pulled back from the window.

Hopping from foot to foot, Grace waited to see if they'd be discovered.

Instead, the apartment door opened and closed.

Footsteps rushed to the window.

Monica flung it open. "Grace! Oh my god." She crossed herself. Sticking her hands through the screenless window, she grabbed the bars. "I was so afraid you were dead. They said you were dead." Her breath came in sharp bursts, like she'd run a marathon, and tears ran down both cheeks. "I couldn't believe them. If you were dead, why would they keep me? I can't believe you're not dead." She leaned out the window and touched her forehead to the bars.

Grace wrapped one hand around hers and leaned into the bars. The skin burned on her face and her hands, like Karithexis had said, but she didn't pull away. It was worth the pain to touch her.

"It's hurting you," Mon said, not backing away.

Grace shook her head. "It's fine. It's fine. I've got to get you out of there." Lifting her head, she searched for a sigil she might recognize. She found one, something she'd seen at the convent. She pointed. "Mon, if I get rid of that, could I get in?"

"I think so. They didn't put down any salt in here. They don't trust me." She lifted half her mouth in a grin. "Can't imagine why."

Grace kissed Monica's fingers where they wrapped around the bar, her lips on fire, and let her go. Reaching through the bars with the glasses, she scratched at the sigil until its outer ring split.

Her hands stopped burning.

The door to the apartment opened.

And someone screamed from the courtyard.

*

A man's voice came from the door. "What are you doing at that window?"

Monica whispered, "Run, Grace. Get out of here."

Grace stepped back, making herself thin. She wrapped a hand around the bars again. This time, it didn't burn.

Monica stumbled away from the window with a shout. Jim leaned out, checking the yard with his nose wrinkled. He inhaled. "You trying to escape? You know Daisy wants to see you one more time before she lets you go."

Shouting continued from the courtyard. Why couldn't this fool go see what was wrong?

Grace glanced behind her.

Karithexis had fully disappeared again. She may have even run away.

The door to the apartment rattled against the wall. "Jim! We need you. It's bad."

Alice.

Swallowing around the lump in her throat, Grace stepped closer to the window and peeked into the apartment, watching Monica.

She sat on the bed, massaging her shoulder.

Jim cursed. "Get out here with me. I'm not supposed to let you out of my sight. Can't believe you talked me into getting you coffee. What the fuck?" He jerked her off the bed by an arm and dragged her from the room.

"This is what I should have fucking done in the first place," Grace said. Hands wrapped around two bars, she gritted her teeth and pulled.

Nothing happened.

Without instruction on how to use the power inside her, she wasn't sure she could pull it off, but she'd seen Karithexis reach straight through someone's breastbone and into their rib cage. She ought to have strength for this in her own arms, and it was just a matter of finding it and putting it to work.

She thought of fire and of the heat she used to threaten Karithexis. Of ripping something to pieces from the inside out.

Destruction.

The bars sheared off with such force they flew over her head and landed in the empty field fifty feet behind the compound.

She hooked her invisible hands into the windowsill and crawled through. Empty cups and plates lay strewn about the room, making it clear Monica had been in this room for days and not the handful of hours it seemed like. Time was weird where Grace had gone.

A breeze blew through the room, knocking off a few plates and cups and blowing the ajar door all the way open.

Grace slipped through it before it swung the other way. It slammed home behind her, and she took in the scene in the courtyard.

Raga stood in the center of the fire, flames wrapping her arms, legs, and torso like armor. The black jewel in the center of her forehead shone and glittered orange in the firelight, and her hair whipped around her head seemingly of its own will.

She held a hunter in each hand, clawlike fingers wrapped around their necks. Samantha and Lindsey, at the mercy of the demon, struggled. Kicking their legs and scratching at her hands, they fought for their lives, but Raga smiled down at the others gathered in front of her.

Daisy and Gareth stood at the head of the group, almost flanking her, their guns out. Daisy took a shot.

The fire licked out and caught the bullet in a tiny mouth. The slug turned to liquid and dripped to the ground like copper tears. They splashed in the dirt, metal rain from an inferno.

Raga chuckled. "It's no use, hunter. You cannot escape the demon of desire. Now tell me what it is I want. Where are my children? I know they are here. I can smell them."

Daisy seethed through her teeth. "You have no children here. Leave, before we destroy you." She cocked her gun again.

The laugh exploded from Raga's mouth, deafening Grace. In fact, everyone in the courtyard covered their ears.

Except Daisy. She backed up a step, and her hair streamed away from her face in waves, as if she stood toe-to-toe with a hurricane. And really, was that so far from the truth?

With a scowl, she regained her footing and aimed at the demon again. "I'll ask nicely one more time. Leave. Don't come back."

Raga hissed, her beautiful smile turning into a rictus as her face froze. The growl from the back of her throat began as it had before she'd tossed Grace into the past. Something bad was coming, and it was coming quick.

Grace took off at a dead run.

Monica stood with her hands over her heart. Her mouth moved so fast her lips almost blurred. She was working a spell.

She wouldn't have made it. No sooner had Grace leapt in front of Daisy that Raga's curse, intended for Daisy, hit her.

Grace slumped to the ground, eyes stuck open.

She could see her own hand, caught half in and half out of the fire. It burned, but she couldn't move it.

Raga dropped the struggling hunters to the ground, and a grin spread across her face, a real grin. She shimmered once again, the beautiful goddess Grace had met in the Realm, and dropped to her knees in front of Grace. The fire ringing her lit them both in flickering orange light and covered them in the smell of thick smoke. "There you are," she whispered. "I knew I'd find you. You cannot resist me."

Daisy fired again.

The fire licked out, but too late. Raga screamed as the bullet tore through her shoulder. She stood, her eyes wide, the fire leaping through her hair and into the sky. "You dare? You dare!"

"I told you, that was the last time I was asking nice. Gareth?"

He spoke a few words, and air rushed over Grace's head. It crackled like lightning as it went past, creating swirls in the air she might have been able to see if she could move. Tiny thunderclaps followed it.

It hit Raga square in the chest. She screamed, her voice breaking at the top of its range.

Someone hit the dirt next to Grace. The cool hand touching her forehead told her exactly who it was. "You're cold, Grace. We've got to get you out of here."

Daisy knelt next to them. "Take this demon and go, Monica. And you." She poked Grace in the shoulder with the end of her gun. "You consider us even." She stepped over them, her necklaces tinkling in the wind. "I don't ever want to see either of you again."

Raga screamed again, a growl also building beneath it, and the flame leapt for Grace.

Daisy jumped in front of it, and it consumed her. A thousand hungry mouths ate her hair, her skin, her clothes, her necklaces.

Grace got her mouth to move. An inch. "Nnnnnnn....." Her fingers twitched.

Gareth shouted, "You heard the woman! Get out of here!"

Karithexis materialized in front of Grace. She grabbed her shoulder and reached over her for Monica. "Ready?"

Before Karithexis whisked them away on a breath and a shadow, Daisy's screams gurgled to nothing.

*

Light swirled around Grace, air coming into and going out of her lungs, but not on her command. She wasn't sure how she was breathing, or why, but only the searing burn in her hand got through to her brain. She looked around for Nat but couldn't find a trace of her. She might even be dead for all Grace knew, and the only thing now holding this vessel together was Grace's own demonic spirit.

Because who but a demon could let someone like Daisy sacrifice themselves for her? Who?

"Grace. Grace, breathe. Are you okay? Fuck. Fuck," Monica cursed, shaking Grace's shoulder and feeling her forehead. "She's so cold. Is she dying?"

"Probably." Karithexis had never sounded smaller than she did right this second.

"Fucking do something."

"What would you have me do? I can kill her, if that's what you want."

Grace tried to nod. Her body still paralyzed, she could only lie there and let the air seep in and out of her lungs.

"Heal her, you bitch."

Karithexis knelt, staring into Grace's open eyes. "Demons aren't made for healing, woman. I don't know how she pulled it off, at all, and I could never replicate it." She leaned so close a blast of minty breath hit Grace in the face. A small round candy circled her mouth as she spoke. "Nor would I ever want to."

"Fine. Get away from us then. Leave. I'll figure it out." Monica ran her hand across Grace's forehead again, speaking under her breath like she had all those times she'd changed Grace's bandages. For weeks, she'd muttered words like this, and it hit Grace all at once. Monica had been using healing magic on her, maybe even teaching it to her without realizing it.

Or maybe she had realized it and Grace was just a good study. Either way, she couldn't help this time. She couldn't even close her eyes, much less think about helping. The more she tried, the further she drifted, which was nice.

Drifting was nice.

Chapter Fifteen

The farmhouse. Again.

But this time, Grace looked out from the other Grace's eyes. Not that that was her actual name, but it's what she heard when the others spoke, overlaid atop the real name like a double exposure.

Through her eyes, she glared down at the rough wooden table where her mother kneaded bread, staring at her own clenched fists. Her eyes hurt, and so did her throat. Tears tracked down her cheeks.

The emptiness washed through her in waves. Despair.

Godwin, who she now knew was her father when she was alive, sat by the fire again. His chair squeaked and squealed, squeaked and squealed, as he rocked and stared into the flames. "Will of God, child."

Grace cried, and her other voice came out of her mouth. "He had the touch. He had the royal touch, and he was supposed to get better." She balled a fist and laid it on the table. "This black magic is strong, Papa. It's taken both my husband and my baby under the guise of the white plague."

He shook his head. "Black magic. No one has done anything to you but God. He's punished you, and that's all."

She pounded the table. "For what? I've done nothing wrong."

Mother clucked her tongue. "Hush, Grace."

"For not loving your husband enough. For disobeying your father and going to see that useless king instead of praying for God's mercy. For letting them both die. Pick one, nasty child." He grunted. "I bet you enjoyed the sex too."

Mother gasped. The dough stopped rolling. "Godwin. Please. Let's not talk like that."

"It's true, isn't it? That's what happened. You got down on your knees and you—"

Grace put everything she had into struggling to her feet. The despair made her so heavy. So heavy. "No, Papa. I did nothing wrong. I have been nothing but a woman of God, done nothing but his will for me. I married the man you told me to marry, the one to whom you paid the dowry. What have I done but obey you?"

He stared into the fire, his eyes red-rimmed, the frown crossing his face so tight it should have given him pain. He grunted and continued as if she hadn't spoken. "You're a wicked child. Wicked. You always have been." He narrowed his eyes. "You've brought this on us. All we can do now is pray for forgiveness. You," he said, pointing a gnarled finger at her, "you must pray the hardest. You will have one week of fasting and prayer. Hope that it is enough."

Grace wanted to scream at him to listen. They'd gotten sick. She'd lost her family so quickly she hadn't had time to collect herself. She hadn't loved her husband; she'd known him less than a year, but she'd come to like him already. And he was a good provider.

The baby she had loved with all her heart. All of it. She'd done everything right, and still, she'd lost him too.

The only reasonable explanation had to be a curse.

Her mother sat and kneaded bread, deaf to Grace's pleas, deferring only to her father.

He sat at the fire, muttering about God and sin, the flickering firelight turning his face into a play of shadows.

It was down to Grace to find out who was doing this to her before it happened again. And if Father wouldn't listen, and Mother wouldn't help...

"I'm leaving."

Father stood as she tried to pass and grabbed her arm with an iron grip. "You'll go nowhere. You'll stay here and pray like I've told you to do." He shook her, hard.

Her teeth rattled in her head, and on one of the shakes, her tongue got caught between them. With a horrendous crunch, the taste of hot blood filled her mouth.

He flung her to the floor. "You'll fast and pray, and hope God will bless us with another suitable man." With a well-aimed foot, he kicked her in the stomach.

Heat bloomed in her midsection. She lay in the floor, struggling to pull a breath, not knowing if her bones or her will were broken. Or both.

He spun and sat in his chair.

The only sounds in the room, besides Grace struggling for breath, were the *slap-slap-slap* of her mother kneading and the *creak-crack-creak* of Papa's chair. And he sat there, seemingly satisfied with himself.

But Grace knew. She knew it was a curse put on them.

She crawled to the door, her fingernails digging long furrows into the dirt floor, creeping silently. She held her breath as she crawled rather than drag air across her broken midsection. It had to have been a mile between her and the door, and as she approached it, her head swam. She needed air.

Gripping the handle, she hauled herself to her feet and finally pulled down that full breath. It hurt, it burned, it gouged her stomach like a hot poker, but she sucked it in and pushed it back out over her vocal cords.

"If you won't help me, I'll find someone who will."

Chapter Sixteen

Grace opened her eyes to darkness.

Hands creeping to her face, she pressed her eyes to make sure they were open and that it was Natalie's face under her fingertips, not her past self.

Heart skipping, she confirmed yes, her eyes were open, and yes, they were Nat's. As her eyes adjusted, she caught the outline of the drapes above her head where soft beams of moonlight fell into the room.

A light snore came from next to her.

She extended her fingers and found the edge of the bed. It ran into another, like two small beds had been pushed into one.

Pain shot up her arm and into her shoulder, all but flaying the skin.

She pulled cold air through her teeth with a whimper and cradled it.

"Grace?" Monica's whisper barely moved the air in the room.

Grace pitched her voice low. "Yeah. I'm here. Is that you?"

Bedsprings squeaked. The mattress next to Grace depressed as Mon slid over next to her, the side of her face outlined in silver light. "Are you okay? I didn't want to sleep in a different room in case you...in case you needed me."

"Where are we? It's cold in here."

"Shanna's house."

Grace rolled to her back, still hugging her arm, and let out a low laugh. "Why here?"

Monica shifted. "Karithexis said we'd be safe here, at least for a bit, so I could try to get you healed. How are you feeling?"

"I don't know. This hurts." Grace stretched out her arm and inched her fingers across the bed until they met with soft resistance.

Monica took her hand and held it. Her other hand rubbed up Grace's arm, brushing past the burn. "Raga put some kind of spell on you. I think it would have killed a human, but you withstood it. It's still affecting you, but—" She paused, and when she spoke again, Grace heard the smile in her voice. "You're strong. I think you'll be okay."

Grace forced an exhale out her nose and laced her fingers through Mon's even though it burned her left hand. "I had a vision. A memory, I guess. Of my past. My life."

"Did you? What was it like?"

"Sad." A tear rolled down her cheek and soaked into the pillow. "I was a sad, sad person, and I had a horrible life."

Mon's voice came out of the dark, just loud enough to break. "You didn't remember anything good?"

"I had a husband and a baby, and they both died. Some kind of sickness. I think it was called the white plague."

"Tuberculosis. There's a bunch of stuff in the library at the convent about it." She caressed Grace's burnt hand and took her other, kissing the tips of her fingers. "I'm sorry you were so sad."

Like a snap of her fingers, Grace's grief-stricken past faded into the distance, as did the pain of the burnt hand. Monica's kiss on her fingertips sent zings of electricity all through her, and she thought again about her bare leg hanging half out of the blanket. About her holding her head to her breast, protecting her from the exorcism. About their kiss in the courtyard.

She pulled one hand free and reached under the blanket, searching for Monica's leg. When she found it, she spread her fingers and gripped her thigh. She ran her hand up it, like she'd fantasized about doing, her skin as soft as she imagined.

Monica shivered. "Grace," she whispered, like she could hardly speak. "We talked about this. I can't take advantage of Natalie."

Sliding her arm behind Monica, she pulled her closer and shook her head. "It's not Nat, Monica. It's all me. I promise you, it's me. You've been on my mind since I left you. I don't ever want to be apart from you again. Not ever." She shifted and pulled her in until their hips touched.

Monica eased closer, pressing her belly into Grace's. Letting go of her hand, she lifted the cover and slipped her leg between Grace's. She slid her thigh up as high as it would go, setting off fireworks inside her.

Blood rushing to her face and between her thighs, Grace got as close as she could. So close their skin melted together. She ran her hand under Monica's shirt, fingertips sliding over her full hip, up her waist, and across her nipple. It hardened under her hand.

Monica's response, and the way her breath shortened, lifted Grace to a new level of desire. She'd never been so consumed by something that literally made her fingertips tingle.

Licking her lips, Grace wrapped her leg around her and ran her hand all the way up to Monica's face, where she sunk her hand into her hair and pulled her close.

Mon shivered again and gripped the back of Grace's neck. She squeezed even closer, like they occupied the space of one person instead of two, and pulled her into a kiss. Her tongue snuck into Grace's mouth, light as a bird in flight. Her other hand slid down Grace's stomach and fingered the elastic waistband of her pajama pants. She whispered into Grace's mouth, "You're sure?"

Biting her lip, Grace buried her face in Monica's neck, breathing in the scent of her skin like an aphrodisiac. With a nod, she took Monica's hand and pushed it under her waistband and into her underwear, guiding her where she wanted her to go.

Without hesitation, Monica's fingers found what they were looking for, slipping easily into her.

Grace moaned into her mouth, fighting the need to cry out. Monica helped by sealing her lips over Grace's again, kissing her so deep she forgot she even had a voice.

In all the time in this body, in all her memories of life and death, she couldn't remember a more pleasurable experience. Even using her powers to heal or kill, as all-encompassing as that feeling had been, held no comparison to Monica's gentle caress inside her. The sheer depth of feeling that overwhelmed her, how much she completely loved this woman, overtook her every sense.

All she wanted to do was tell Monica how she felt, but she couldn't even speak. The only thing she could do was lose everything she ever was, again, and give it all to her.

*

Sun streamed into the room through gossamer curtains. Eyes cracked, Grace lay there, staring at the shaft of sun and thinking about the dark room from last night.

Speaking of last night.

She turned her head, hair scratching across the pillow.

Monica gazed at her, her hands laced across her chest. She grinned, sun-tinted lashes following the curve of her smiling eye. "Morning, Grace."

Grace couldn't help but smile so wide it almost split her face. "Morning. Wow. I never thought—" She rolled into her, straightening her leg and laying flush against her side. "We can do that again, right?"

Mon giggled. "Anytime you want to."

Sitting up on an elbow, Grace hiked herself up in the bed a bit and lay half over her, planting her other elbow on Monica's other side. Her insides floated. They may as well have been the sun streaming in the window for how warm and bright they were. "How about right now?" Her burnt hand twinged when she leaned onto it, but the pain barely registered. What burned inside was far brighter.

Monica met her halfway, one hand on Grace's cheek.

The kiss was so deep, and she was so intensely entranced, Grace didn't register the knock on the door until it creaked open.

"Nat, did you and your friend want breakf—"

Monica's wide eye met Grace's.

Grace snapped her head to the left, to the door, but it took years to get there.

Shanna stood in the door, a pitcher of juice in one hand, her mouth hanging open. Her jaw clenched, eyes narrowing, as surprise faded into anger. Her raised eyebrows drew together.

One of the boys came down the hall. "Mom? Did you take the juice?"

Shanna's mouth snapped closed, and she shut the door in silence.

Grace turned back to Monica. She couldn't break a whisper. "Natalie is going to kill me."

*

Grace sat still at the kitchen table while everyone bustled around her. Shanna and Karithexis got the boys ready for school, and each of the boys took a turn in Grace's lap while they ate. They even tried to sit on her at once, but she couldn't handle hardly one of them in her lap. What did she know about kids?

Nat watched so closely Grace's eyeballs bulged. Once or twice, she begged Nat to come out and say hi or hug them or something, but Natalie was having none of it. This was the perfect family she'd always dreamed of having with her dream woman, and she'd fucked it all up with drinking. And now she'd made a deal with a demon, and Shanna thought she was cheating on her. What else could possibly go more sideways?

Karithexis brought the boys their backpacks and ushered them toward the door. "Say goodbye to your moms, boys." She peeked over her shoulder at Grace and winked.

The boys hugged her, and they were real and alive and warm, and Natalie cried softly from wherever she'd buried herself inside Grace's head.

The front door closed.

Shanna stood at the counter with her back to them, her hair up today, the nape of her neck exposed. "You said you were a nun."

Mon swallowed and eyed Grace. "I was. I'm not anymore. I wasn't when we met; it was a lie."

"So. You lie. And you fuck other people's wives. Yeah, you're not a very good nun."

Monica opened her mouth, but Grace beat her to it. "It's more complicated than that, Shan."

Shanna slapped the counter. "Amnesia. Don't give me that bullshit." She spun. "Yesterday, you said you remembered you love me. You haven't said such beautiful things to me in so long I thought you'd forgotten how much we used to love each other."

"Used to?"

"Yeah, Nat. Used to. Since you started drinking more, and you lost the org, you got worse and worse. I've been thinking about leaving you for a while. I'm surprised you didn't notice." She crossed her arms and pressed her lips together. "This seems like a good time."

Grace's stomach roiled, threatening to hurk up the few bites of bacon she'd taken. "No, Shanna, please don't leave Natalie. She doesn't want that. Everything she's done has been to make you happier."

"Oh cute. Now you're talking about yourself in third person."

Karithexis cleared her throat from the door to the hall. "You gonna tell her, Grace?"

Monica caught her eye.

Grace widened hers, asking the question in silence. *Should I?*

The way Mon's shoulders moved up and down told Grace what she needed to know. It was up to her.

She stood, swallowing past the dry click in her throat. "Shanna, I think you should sit down." She pulled out a chair.

"Fuck you." Shanna spat at her feet. Her eyes shot daggers at Monica. "And you, you lying bitch. You can have this cheating whore." Pushing her shoulder, she tried to slip past Grace.

Grace caught her hand. "Please. My name is not Natalie. It's Grace."

"Let me go."

She did. But she went on. "I might look like your wife, but that's because she's loaned me her body. She's still in here, and she made a deal with me to get your lives back on track."

Shanna blinked. "A deal?"

"I'm a demon."

Lucky for Shanna, Grace shoved the chair under her before she fell in the floor.

"You're a what? You're kidding. That's not real."

Grace sat again. "I'd show you, but 'Mom' here"—she hooked her fingers around the word—"put a spell around the house so we can't use our power here. It protects us from others who might want to hurt us—"

"And there are a lot of those," Karithexis supplied.

"—but it also keeps us from using any of our powers. I could heal this burn," she said, holding up her blistered hand, "if it weren't for my powers being stripped while I'm here."

Shanna's wide eyes moved over each of them. Her mouth flopped up and down, and she blinked lashes out of her eye. "You're delirious. All of you. You're demented people." The blood drained from her face, and she whispered, "Are you going to try and kill me? You can leave. I won't take anything from you in the divorce. Just please don't kill me."

Let me talk to her.

Grace swallowed. "She wants to talk to you."

"She?"

"Natalie."

"I don't—Um. What?"

Grace repeated herself. "I'm a demon using Natalie's body, but her consciousness or whatever is still inside me. She's part of me, and she wants to talk to you."

It was so quiet in the room Grace heard the click in Shanna's throat when she swallowed. Eyes wide as saucers, she nodded.

Grace closed her eyes.

*

The spotlight drilled into Grace's brain, blinding her.

Squinting, she raised a hand and tried to shield her eyes. "Natalie?"

"You're a real bitch, you know that?"

She swallowed. "I'm sorry. I shouldn't be using your body this way."

Nat scoffed and came out of the shadows, dragging a wooden chair like the ones around Shanna's kitchen table. She sat and pulled another from the shadows.

Grace sat. The light dimmed enough for her to see.

"I don't care about that. Remember the deal? I gave you permission to use my body; I knew what that might mean. You're a demon. It's not like you're an untouched virgin, nor did I expect you to stay that way."

"Then what's the problem?"

"In my house? In front of my wife? You're wearing my pajamas, for God's sake. You had to do that?"

Grace stammered. "It was—We didn't plan—I mean—" She exhaled. "I love her."

Natalie stared at her and spoke without moving her lips. It echoed all around them. *I'm in this mind with you, Grace. I know.*

Grace frowned. "Of course you do. I'm sorry, Nat. I really am. How can I make it up to you?"

"I wasn't going to do this, but I want to talk to her. She needs to hear, from my lips, what this whole thing is about. And that I do still love her."

Biting a nail, Grace shook her head. "You think she'll believe you?"

"Do we have a choice?" Nat stood. The TV sat where it had been before, and she turned it on, static playing across the screen. "You can watch from here. Let me finish, and then the body is all yours again." She paused, staring down at the TV. "She's cute. Seems a bit of a mess though."

With a chuckle, Grace turned the volume up. "You're one to talk."

Nat snorted, and without another word, she disappeared into the shadows.

The picture on the TV lightened and came into focus.

*

"Shanna."

She jumped, bangs falling in her eyes. "Natalie. It's you." She looked around.

Nat followed her gaze.

Monica stood by the door, on the opposite side from Karithexis, both with their arms crossed.

"Can you leave us alone for a minute?"

Mon shifted on her feet. "Are you sure, Grace?"

Grace's heart hurt. Could Monica not tell it was Natalie and not Grace herself? Maybe she didn't feel as deeply about Grace as Grace did about her.

But before Nat spoke, Monica did.

"Sorry, I meant Natalie. I can see you're not Grace. You hold your face different. And your posture." She looked her over. "That's kinda wild." She grabbed Karithexis by the arm. "Come on. Let's leave them."

Grace exhaled, her abs tight. She didn't know how much she needed that confirmation until she had it. Monica loved her for who was inside the body, not for the body itself.

Her eyes stung, and a tear dropped into her lap. She leaned into the TV again, face wet.

Natalie turned back to Shanna and took one of her hands.

"I know this is weird, and I'm sorry I got us into this mess."

Shanna didn't pull her hand away. "Nat. This is so— What are you doing?" She lowered her voice and leaned in. "Are these people really demons?"

Grace couldn't feel Shanna's hand holding hers, but she got some kind of residual feeling from Nat. Like the air softened when Shanna leaned in, and it smelled a bit of lavender.

"They really are. Well, not the one girl, Monica. She was a nun, but she decided to come with the demon instead of stay at the convent."

"She's not a very good nun. I caught her kissing you. Her. Whatever." She blinked, but the hair stayed in her lashes. "I think they're sleeping together."

"Shanna. Honey, it doesn't matter. I don't know how long I can stay with you."

"Is the demon trying to get out?"

"No. She's accommodating. More so than I even thought she would be. I think since I agreed to let her have my body, there's some kind of magic or something keeping her in charge. I don't know. It's strange."

It was strange, Grace agreed. Not that she could remember possessing people before, but she and Nat enjoyed a kind of symbiosis she wouldn't have expected. Karithexis and Nat's mom certainly didn't have that kind of relationship.

Leaning back, Shanna crossed her arms. "First of all, demons are real. Second of all, you made a deal with one. What the fuck?"

Nat leaned back in her own chair. "I know. I'm sorry. I was living in that halfway house, and I was trying. I went to some meetings, strung together about forty-five days sober, and went back out. I couldn't stop thinking about what kind of pain I was causing you guys. The boys. And the org, how I failed all the families who depend on our help. All the donations I sold so I could drink them away. Christmas presents for poor people. Jesus Christ, Shan." She hit her own knee with a fist and inhaled through her teeth. "I was a fucking wreck. I ruined everything."

"Nothing we couldn't have fixed together. Why'd you run away from me? Didn't we promise to be there for each other?"

Nat stood and paced. "You told this demon, sitting right here in this kitchen, you wanted to leave me. You never told me that."

Shanna tightened her crossed arms. "I saw you lying in bed, making out with someone else. Are you surprised I lashed out? Besides. You didn't come back to me. You made a deal with a fucking demon, for Christ's sake."

"I fucking started drinking again, and it felt awful. It didn't even make me feel good anymore. Those meetings ruined it for me. I kept fixating on how I'm powerless over this addiction and how it fucked up my life. They wanted me to believe in God or something, and the only thing that mattered was how much I owed you." She sniffed. She was crying. "How you didn't love me anymore, and I couldn't blame you."

When Shanna stood and put her arms around Nat, Grace didn't feel her arms, not exactly, but the warmth from the hug surrounded her, filling her insides and lifting her spirits.

Nat didn't look at Shanna. Instead, she pried her arms off and crossed the kitchen again, leaning by the sink.

The picture started to get fuzzy again. Grace adjusted the antenna to try for better reception.

"I snuck out to a bar after work. This lady approached me, redhead, loud for a dive like that. She told me how I could fix things. She whispered a spell in my ear. She told me all I had to do was make a little deal and all the shit I'd done wrong would be wiped clean. So I did the spell. And the demon came. And it told me everything I wanted to hear. I just had to help it do something." She chuckled. "It was a man when I met it. I think they don't care what kind of body they have. I don't know if that means anything."

Grace's skin went cold. She recognized that redhead; she'd bet her life on it. Karithexis, recruiting Natalie like she said she had.

"How is this fixing things?"

"I don't know. But it was part of the deal. The demon would take away my alcoholism, fix our lives, and I'd belong to it when I died. It seemed like a small price to be able to make it up to you. You deserve all the happiness I can give you. Not the mess you've had."

Shanna sat at the table again. "Nothing you've told me is anything the demon couldn't've. Why did you come out? Why not let the demon convince me all this is real?"

Grace leaned into the TV. She turned the volume all the way up, the words coming from it hard to hear. Goose bumps raced across her skin in the sudden cold. So cold.

"The bottom line, Shanna, my forever love, is I don't think I'm coming back from this. I don't know if the demon will fix our lives like she said, but I think I'm going to die doing whatever it is she wants to do. And I need you to know I love you, and I love our children, and I'm sorry I'm such a fuck-up."

A tug hit Grace in her midsection, a pull from the TV. She tried to fight, but it dragged her, inexorable, toward it. The tip of her nose entered the glass screen of the old TV.

Natalie stumbled. "Oh God, Shan. I don't know if I'll ever see you again. I love you, okay? Try to get on with life and forget me. It's going to be okay." She breathed shallow.

Shanna leapt across the room and took her in her arms. "Don't leave me, Nat. I don't hate you. I love you. I love you so much. I don't need all our problems fixed. I just need you."

Grace fell into the TV.

She opened her eyes in Shanna's kitchen, cradled in Shanna's arms.

She stiffened. "She's gone, Shanna."

Arms falling to her sides, Shanna backed up. "It's you again, isn't it, Grace?"

"So you believe me?" Grace flopped into a chair at the table, her body exhausted.

Shanna sat with her. "I guess I have to. Will you be able to give her back to me when you're done? Fix our lives like you promised?"

Grace flashed on the scene she'd watched in the bar, when she'd made this deal with Natalie. "I don't know. I think so. But something has happened to my memory. I didn't know I was a demon until a couple weeks ago. I can't remember what I was even doing, much less how."

Shanna gripped her arm, digging in with her fingernails. "I want you to figure it out, and I want you to bring her back to me. You fix this like you promised her, you hear me, demon?"

Grace nodded. It was all she could do.

Chapter Seventeen

Grace sat on the couch with Monica, fingers interlaced with hers. "What did the hunters do to you?"

Mon pressed her lips together. "Nothing really. They asked me a lot of questions about you. Daisy kept trying to recruit me, honestly. Said she liked my 'gumption.' They wouldn't let me leave, but they didn't hurt me. They wanted to find you." She pointed her forehead at Karithexis, who paced in front of them. "They especially wanted to find her."

Grace laid her head on the back of the couch. Still worn out from letting Natalie have so much time out front, she followed Karithexis's pacing with only her eyes.

Mon exhaled through her nose. "Would you sit down?"

Karithexis stopped and jabbed a finger in Grace's direction. "No. I will not. She had a plan, a plan she didn't share with me. She didn't share with Natalie. She didn't share with anyone. No one can tell us what the damn plan was."

Eyebrows drawn together, Grace stared at her. "I still can't believe you didn't know the whole thing. You just took it on faith I had a plan?"

A smile curved half Karithexis's mouth. "To be completely fair, a rarity with me, I didn't tell you all of my part of the plan either. I suppose we're equal." She lowered her brow. "I didn't expect these damned nuns to get in the way of it." She glanced at Monica. "You certainly came along at the worst possible time."

Mon leaned back. "I did what I was told. Mother Mary said we were looking for this demon, she told me we were turning it into a weapon, and we did the spell. If my binding worked better, we wouldn't be in this mess." Her eye found Grace's. "But here we are. Down one eye and one memory."

Grace faced Monica. "There's got to be some way to get my memory back. Are you sure you don't know any spells?"

She shook her head, curls waving around her face. "None of the spells I know will work. Mother Mary and I went through everything we could think of. Maria helped. There was nothing."

"What if you heal me, like I did to Gareth? Would that heal my mind?"

Mon grasped her hand in both of hers. "It's not your mind, Grace. It's your spirit."

Karithexis scoffed. "Jesus. And you say I'm evil. You cursed her spirit? That's not right."

Holding eye contact, Monica squeezed Grace's unburnt hand. "I'm sorry." She lifted a hand to Grace's face.

Grace leaned into it, her heart hammering her ribs. "It's okay. I forgive you."

Karithexis slammed the coffee table.

Grace and Monica both jumped, and the moment was gone.

"Can we get back to business, please? We need to know what the plan was. Grace, do you think you wrote it down anywhere?"

Grace shook her head. "No. I don't think I did. It was dangerous, I know that."

"Of course it is." Karithexis sat in the armchair next to the couch. "We're going to be taking on Raga. Any rebellion against her has always been squashed in the most gruesome of ways. No one has ever escaped her."

"Obviously I knew something that would help."

Karithexis leaned forward and curled a gnarled finger. She tapped her knuckle on Grace's forehead. "Use that noggin then. Figure us a way out. Otherwise, we'll be stuck in this house until she rips it from its foundations to get to us."

Still facing Monica, Grace leaned sideways into the couch and closed her eyes. "Nat let me watch her memory of the deal. I told her I needed a witch. I told Natalie she had natural talent. It must be some kind of spell." She opened her eyes and drilled Mon. "It has to be, right?"

Monica shrugged. "I don't know why else you'd want a witch. Yeah," she said, tapping her chin, "spell work must be involved somehow."

Karithexis shoved all the magazines and kids' books on the coffee table to the floor and sat in front of Grace. She grabbed her knee and dug her fingers in. "What was the spell? You have to remember the spell." She scowled. "We are so fucked."

Grace peeled the demon's fingers from her leg and tossed her hand back at her. "I think it's—"

Pain coursed up her arm and into her chest. If she weren't relatively positive it couldn't happen to demons, she'd think the searing pain in the center of her chest was a heart attack.

As it was, she clutched at her chest and fell, ever so slowly, face-first into the couch cushions.

Monica's shout came from miles away, like Grace had pillows in her ears, or those bright orange earplugs. A ringing wailed inside her ear canals. She couldn't hear Mon over it. She wanted to grasp her hand, let her know she was okay. Maybe she just needed a minute.

A few words broke through.

"Must be the spell Raga threw at her. I tried to heal her but..."

"If anyone knows curses, it's Raga. Can you fix..."

"...don't know..."

"...gotta get out..."

And that was it. That was all she heard. Rushing red pain surged through her in waves. Every muscle in her body cramped, her chest encircled in one hot, constricting band, and she faded out. Away from the pain. Away from it all.

*

She woke on the floor of an unfamiliar room.

She woke.

That was the important thing.

Opening her mouth, she pulled in a complete, pain-free, all-the-way-to-her-toes breath.

Oh, it had never felt so good to fill her lungs with air.

She sat up.

"No, Grace, lie back. We're almost done."

Monica. What a sweet voice.

She did as Monica asked, turning her head to watch her.

Monica leaned over her, her curls obscuring her face except for snippets here and there. Her eyes and teeth shone in the black light covering the room.

"Where are we?" Grace's voice didn't go above a whisper.

"Friend of Karithexis." Mon glanced at someone on the other side of Grace. "Great witch. Surprised I don't know her already."

A woman with a husky voice chuckled. "You nuns do tend to recruit pretty heavily. Mary still in charge over there?"

"You know her?"

She grunted. "You a novice?"

As they spoke to each other, the room and whatever Grace lay on warm, they rubbed Grace's skin. Because of the warmth, and what had to be a heated blanket under her, she almost missed the fact her chest was exposed. Bare.

She lifted her arms to cover.

Mon eased them back down and continued to rub her chest and arms with some kind of smelly oil. "It's okay, Grace. I'm sorry we had to do this without asking, but there wasn't much choice." Mouth pressed into a line, she glanced at the other woman again. "Not anymore I'm not. I've left the Order."

"Well, I'd ask why, but it's probably boring. I'd take you on if you wanted it, but you wouldn't be doing spell work most of the time. Mostly I get people in here who want their tarot done. Maybe their auras read. Star charts. You know."

With a smile, Monica ran her hands down one side of Grace's rib cage. "Grace. Can you feel that?"

Grace's toes tingled, and she wanted to tell Monica more than just yes. But there was a stranger here, and they were in a strange house, and she didn't want to out Monica in front of someone they didn't know. So she simply nodded. "Am I supposed to?"

The other woman spoke. "Yes. That means the counter is working." The black light was switched for a soft yellow light.

Sitting up on her elbows, Grace eyed the woman.

She had hair as short as Grace's, but it curled around the bottom of her ears and at her neckline. At least two cowlicks made the hair on her forehead uneven, and the rich blonde color of it nearly blended into pale skin that sported freckles on every exposed surface.

"Kay says your master did this?" She flipped the pages of a leather-bound book in her lap.

Grace nodded, but the woman wasn't looking up. "Yes. And who are you?"

"Name's Tracy. Any friend of Kay is not necessarily a friend of mine, but I'll let it slide this time. You were in bad shape when you got here."

"The curse comes and goes in waves, I think," Mon said. "I started the healing on her physical wounds, but it's hard to crack the shell on this curse. I could only get a little under it."

Tracy looked up, and stunning blue eyes peeped at Mon, brows raised. She lowered the corners of her mouth in something like a grin. "I'm pretty surprised you could get to it at all. You're good."

Mon's brown cheeks took on a slight pink tone. "Thanks." Her gaze drifted to Grace's bare chest. She handed her her shirt, laying it over her exposed breasts, but not before taking a bit of a long look. "I was afraid it was going to kill you."

"Why would Raga try to kill me?"

"She was trying to kill Daisy. You got in the way." Mon leaned on her hands and watched Grace tug the shirt over her head.

Grace sat up and folded her legs under her. "Not that that helped, in the end."

"Wait," Tracy said, one page half turned. "Are you saying Daisy Weatherby is dead? Because of you two?"

Guilt wormed into Grace's stomach, dumping black ink in from the top where it swirled around her entire midsection.

Monica spoke. "We didn't actually see her body."

"We know she's dead, Mon. I heard her die before Karithexis took us away."

"You don't know that." Mon sniffed. "Not for sure."

Tracy spoke under her breath and glanced at them, closing the heavy book with a bang.

Grace started. "I'm sorry. Did you know her?"

"No." A dimple formed next to one corner of her mouth. "She wasn't my friend, if that's what you're asking. But everyone knows who Daisy is. Guarantee they find out you're responsible for her death, they won't be very friendly." She stood and threw the book on a table. "Look. We've got most of the spell off you. But we haven't cured you, not by a fair piece. Come on out here."

She opened a door and stepped into the next room. Bright light flooded in.

Squinting, Grace clasped Monica's hand. "A friend of Karithexis? Desperate?"

She squeezed. "Yes." Her eyes flitted down to her chest and back. "Sorry we undressed you. We had to work the oil into your skin as much as we could."

"It wasn't entirely unpleasant." Grace stepped into her and slid one arm around her.

Karithexis called from the next room. "Grace! You coming out here? We've got planning to do."

Her impatience didn't stop Grace from nuzzling Monica's neck before letting her go. She kissed her under her ear and tugged her into the next room, floating a few inches off the ground.

The spell and the oil might have been temporary measures, but any moments she got with Monica were worth it, even if they were only a few at a time.

They walked into the second room, lit only by a fireplace.

Grace frowned. "You don't have to be so impatient, Kari."

"The hell I don't." Karithexis sat by a fire, feet, up, hand covering her forehead. She looked every bit of the eighty years her vessel had seen, and then some. "This is some mess you've gotten us in."

Tracy stood between them, firelight glinting off her light hair. "Okay, I found something in the book that'll help. You guys, sit together." She pointed between Grace and Karithexis. "Here." She pointed to the floor in front of the fire. "Kay. Move the chair out of the way."

The demon stood and cracked her back in at least six places. "I'm old. You do it."

Exhaling through her nose, Tracy moved the chair, her muscled biceps standing out.

Grace sat, eyes on the spellcaster.

Karithexis sat in front of her, fighting to get her legs crossed. She cursed and muttered too low for Grace to hear.

She spoke a few words in that ugly language Grace almost recognized, and her legs folded easily under her. "Mind over matter, eh, Grace?" She chuckled through her nose.

On the dark side of the room, Tracy cleared her throat. "Face each other, touch foreheads, and put your hands on each other's faces."

Grace recoiled, her gut twisting. It was fine to work with the demon if she had to, but get close? Touch her face? She shuddered.

"Come on. I don't want to touch you either," Karithexis said. "You and your do-good attitude nauseate me." She cut her eyes at her friend. "Why, Tee?"

Tracy blew the dust off the book she'd removed from the bookcase. "You're going to share power. I think that will heal our friend here, and maybe even restore her memory." Eyes narrowed, she cocked a brow at Karithexis. "That's what you want, right? Her memories?"

Karithexis leaned in. "Grace. Let's get this over with."

Monica spoke from a corner of the room, mostly obscured in shadow. "I have a bad feeling about this."

But the temptation of having her memory restored convinced Grace. She leaned into Karithexis, some kind of perfume overpowering this close.

She wrinkled her nose. "What is that you're wearing?"

"Whatever the old broad had lying around. You like?"

"No."

Karithexis chuckled, her breath hot on Grace's lip. "Here. Hands on my face." Her fingertips landed on Grace's cheeks.

Grace swallowed her gorge and did the same.

As Tracy read from the book, the firelight flared.

In the bright light, Grace couldn't focus on the demon against her face, so she closed her eyes.

The effect was immediate.

Chapter Eighteen

A wooden door opened in her face.

"Aunt Mary. You must help me."

In the door stood Mary. Not Mother Mary. The other one. The one from the vision.

"Oh, it's my favorite niece!" She swung the door wide. "Please come in, Grace."

Oh. What?

What.

She walked in, palms sweaty, and closed the door after her. "Sorry to come like this, Aunt Mary. I—" She clutched her stomach. The toe of her father's boot was imprinted on the skin there, and she slunk to a chair and collapsed into it. She swallowed, and the taste of bile and coppery blood ran down her throat. "I have no one else."

"Are you okay?" Her eyes jumped to Grace's stomach and raked over her face. "Let me get you some small beer to drink. That will give you strength."

Grace shook her head. "My husband and son are dead. Father blames me for being a sinner. But it was something else."

Mary poured the beer into two small cups. "The white plague. It's a terrible thing. I've lost a lot of good friends to it this year. I spoke to a doctor friend, and he thinks—"

"No. Black magic."

Mary sat next to her, her mouth set, and handed her a cup. "What makes you think that?"

"The baby got the royal touch. He got the touch, and he died anyway. Someone has cursed me, Aunt. Someone hates me and wants to see ill come to me."

"Or the royal touch is false magic and the white plague is a terrible virus that—"

"What's a virus? More black magic?"

As Mary shook her head, Grace narrowed her eyes.

During Mother Mary's vision, she'd been inside this woman's head. Her loyalty to the Order was fierce, but so was her loyalty to her family, to all those nieces and nephews she'd thought about. Had Grace's own name been inside that book, the one the evil bishop carried?

Mary grimaced. "I know something about black magic, dear niece. The white plague is beyond even that, and there is no amount of white magic that can stop it."

Grace snuffled again. "How can you be sure? You speak as if you are sure." She clutched Mary's hands. "You must help me, Aunt." Hot tears coursed down her face and lined her lips with salt. "Please. You must."

With a flinch, Mary gripped her back. She swallowed and cast her eyes about the room.

Releasing Grace, she stood. With slow, measured steps, she walked to the table and glanced at a few small barrels stacked along one wall. "A new batch of brew is ready. We should have some of that."

"No, I don't want to cut into your profits. It's all you have to feed yourself."

Mary flinched again. "Don't worry about me, child. I have means. I am not only an alewife, though it has given me a measure of comfort and prestige I would not have known otherwise, making my living apart from men." She drew two more cups and bought them back. "But there is more."

Grace stuck her nose in the cup. It was a much sharper scent than the beer, and tempered with gruit to give it the bitterness of ale.

She knocked half of it back in a go. It did help. A bit.

"Come over by the fire," Mary said, pulling up a chair. "There are things I need to tell you."

Stomach gurgling, Grace crept across the room. The way the firelight gleamed on Aunt Mary's face gave her an uneasy feeling, set her mind sideways.

Easing into the chair, Grace held out her cup for more ale.

Aunt Mary refilled it in silence.

When she sat again, firelight dancing in her eyes, she frowned. "I only tell you this because of how much I love you, my dear Grace." The corners of her mouth lifted, and she looked down into her own cup. "You're my favorite niece. Did you know?"

Grace shook her head. At least someone liked her.

Mary stood again and walked over to her bed. With her back to her, she spoke low.

Stomach knotted, Grace leaned forward to hear her.

"I haven't told anyone in our family about this. It seemed better that way. And I'm not telling you so I can help you. I am telling you so you will know there is no way to help you. Not even magic." She pushed a panel in the headboard, and a piece of wood sprang out. She pulled it loose.

Metal gleamed inside.

Grace's heart leapt to her throat as Aunt Mary pulled a long sword inscribed with writing from a secret compartment in the headboard.

Aunt Mary spun, sword in hand, and took a few steps toward Grace. She spoke a few words and the blade glowed. Its own light—light from inside the cold metal—added to the flickering fire.

Mesmerized, Grace stood, hand outstretched. "Can I touch it? What's it for?"

"I'm part of an order. We use magic, and sometimes swords, to hunt and destroy true evils that threaten this world."

"Like the white plague?"

"No. Like demons."

Grace recoiled, bumping the chair with her legs. "Demons? Those are real?"

"You have no idea. Myself and a number of other women fight to keep you and everyone else safe from them. We have for thousands of years."

She sat with a boneless thump, her tongue smashed between her teeth again. "Thousands of...and you're just telling me this now?"

"It's not something I advertise. Even though we practice what you would call white magic, not everyone looks at us favorably. Bishop Savaric would put us in his precious book, burn us at the stake, if he knew anything about us."

The Grand Inquisitor.

Someone had given him Mary and the Order's names. Someone had gotten them burned at the stake.

With a smile stretching her mouth, Grace stood. Hands out, she approached Aunt Mary. "So you'll help me? Can you bring them back?"

Mary slid the sword back into the bed and closed the compartment with a small snick. She took Grace's hand. "I don't know how else to tell you this. It doesn't work that way. I'm so sorry." She kissed the back of her hand. "If I could bring them back, I would. I would do it in a heartbeat."

As it washed over Grace that Mary wouldn't help her, cold came over her from the forehead down. She withdrew from her aunt and backed toward the door. "You can't? Or you won't? You won't even let me touch the sword. You won't share this power with me!" Her back hit the door.

And that's when it happened.

Aunt Mary herself began to glow. When she spoke, a multitude of voices spoke with her. "We love you, child. But there are some things even we can't do."

Tears coursing down her cheeks again, Grace shrank into the door. "You're just like my father. You won't help me. You threaten me with magic instead." She ripped the door open and dashed from the cottage before Mary said another word.

Breathless, Grace raced across the village. She ran even though her legs and lungs burned; she ran for miles.

A building appeared in the distance, towering over the smaller buildings flanking it. As she got closer, the image of a cross emblazoned on the building became clear.

And who should open the door of this massive building to the pounding of Grace's fist, his bushy eyebrows raised, black and white robes swishing?

"Bishop Savaric. You must help me."

THE ORDER

Chapter Nineteen

Sitting on Tracy's front steps, misty rain falling on her face, Grace closed her eyes and breathed in the night air, pulling the fresh scent of wet earth deep into her lungs. It wasn't a struggle to put it all together now. She'd been the one to betray the Order, the one to get so many of them burned at the stake, and the very reason why they joined the Catholic Church. And for what?

There was little doubt Mother Mary, at the least, knew.

The screen door squeaked and fell against the door frame with a soft rasp.

Grace didn't have to turn to know who it was.

Mon sat next to her on the step, holding a large umbrella over them both. "What happened?" The street lamps cast an orange glow over her face, her skin shining in the mist. Droplets of rain caught in her eyebrows and her loose curls.

"It was me, Monica." Grace buried her face in her hands. "Mother Mary showed me a vision before we left the convent, and in it, the Order had been betrayed. They were being burned as witches."

"I know the story. I had to copy it from Mary's journal."

Weight sank into Grace's gut. "Did you know?"

"Know what?"

"That it was me."

Mon switched hands with the umbrella and slid her arm between Grace's knees, cupping her shin. "That it was you what?"

Turning to face her, Grace twisted one of her wet curls with her index finger. "When I was human, I was Mary's niece. It was me. I betrayed the Order to the bishop. I got them burned at the stake. I watched them burn." She lowered her voice to a whisper. "I finally felt powerful."

The umbrella fell to the stairs.

Grace flinched and closed her eyes, still not raising her voice above a whisper. "I'm sorry."

"Of course you are," Mon said. But her voice had a soft edge to it. Light fingers tickled Grace's cheek. "You're not that person anymore. Whatever has happened to you with this spell and your memory loss has given you a whole new shot at this."

Eyes open to slits, Grace cocked her head and leaned into Monica's fingers. "How do you mean?"

"You've spent centuries blaming yourself for their deaths. Running from it for so long, you've hurt countless others. But now, only now, you're sorry. You have a chance to forgive yourself."

Grace nodded, swallowing tears. "You didn't answer my question. Did you know?"

Mon smiled. "I've told you everything. Shared everything with you. I didn't. I promise you, I had no idea. It just—" She stopped and stared off into the yard.

A car splashed by, the orange of the street light shining off the side of it.

"It just what?"

Mon's smile turned down at the corners. "It just doesn't surprise me. You can bet Mother Mary knows. I'd bet anything on it."

"That's why you can't go back there, Grace." Karithexis banged through the screen door. She picked up the umbrella and stood, holding it over herself. Smiling down her nose at them both, she laughed. "That Mary. Such a wily bitch. She's known this whole time. When you go back there, she's going to turn you over to her angel, and that's the last we'll see of you."

Grace's breath stuck. "Do you think that's true, Mon?"

Monica shook her head, curls bouncing. "It can't be denied the mother knew. Probably the whole time. She probably targeted you, specifically, but if she wanted you dead, she wouldn't have asked me to come up with a spell to trap you."

Karithexis laughed. "Sure. Because the Order is always so up-front about things." She glared. "If you go back there, she will kill you. Stay with me and we'll figure out the next move against Raga together. After that—" Breathing in, she paused and glared at Monica. "After that, we'll kill every one of those nuns if they won't leave you alone."

"They won't hurt you, Grace." Monica leaned against her. "Not only will I not let them, I don't believe they will."

Grace rubbed the scar on her head. Her hair covered it now, but the skin still buckled from in front of her hairline to behind her ear. Her stomach flipped.

"Yes, they will." Karithexis grunted, her withered hands tight around the handle of the umbrella. "They already tried to kill you once. Would you let them steal your memory a second time?"

A hole opened in the middle of Grace. Her head filled with the thought of losing her few memories, of losing this new person she'd become, not the scared, hateful person who'd betrayed the Order and ended up a demon. Of losing the love she had for Monica and their precious little time together. Of losing it all.

She stood, ready to proclaim she'd never return to the convent.

Natalie stepped up, her voice weak. What if they know more? What if they know your plan?

Grace sighed. "I'm going back."

With a growl, Karithexis chucked the umbrella into the yard. "Fine. You're going without me."

*

The dark convent loomed over them.

Grace laced her fingers between Monica's. "Are we sure this is the right thing to do?"

She stared up at the building. "When I left that hospital with you, I never intended to come back here. Now that we are..." She squeezed Grace's hand. "I love you."

Still staring up at the sanctuary building, Grace whispered, "I don't want to lose you."

"Me neither."

"Are you ready?"

Mon chuckled. "No."

With a laugh, Grace tugged her toward the giant wooden doors of the sanctuary. "Let's go." She laid her hand on the door handle.

It burned, steam coming up from her palm.

"Ah, dammit." She sucked air through her teeth and yanked her hand back.

Monica jumped. "Sorry. I forgot. Here." She opened the door and investigated the vestibule. "Nothing else in here. Come on in."

Grace hesitated. She'd been in this sanctuary maybe a hundred times over the six weeks she lived here. It'd never hurt her before, and it even made her happy in a way. She liked the big, echo-y room with its single stained-glass window of Uriel filtering light in yellows and pinks and blues. The creaky old pews smelled nice, like earthy wood.

Now that she knew what she was, would it be different? Now that she knew she'd been responsible for so many murdered sisters...

Would their God welcome her back?

Did he even exist?

She stepped in.

Nothing happened.

Trailing Monica, she walked into the sanctuary itself.

Mon paused to light a candle, whispering a prayer, a prayer Grace swore she heard her own name in.

After Mon crossed herself and dipped one knee, she grabbed Grace's hand and tugged. "It's late. They're all asleep. Do you want to—"

"Not all of us."

Grace might have jumped all the way out of her skin. As it was, her heart raced along, threatening to take off without her.

Moonlight streamed in past Uriel's head. That and the candles were the only light in the big room. A woman sat in the second pew from the front, her long white hair falling beyond her shoulders and disappearing behind her.

Monica and Grace crept forward, clutching each other's hands.

"I won't bite." Mother Mary turned, her profile visible.

The desire to leave and never look back engulfed Grace. She had questions for the mother, and the mother probably had answers Grace didn't want to hear, and it would probably be better for everyone if she ran instead. Her teeth clenched.

She couldn't run. There wasn't just Natalie and her life, her family; there was the fact that Grace had to own up to what she did if she wanted any chance of escaping the pain she'd caused.

Now that the moment had arrived, though, it sucked. She didn't want to.

She sat.

Monica sat with her, arm linked through hers. "Mother Mary. We need to speak with you."

"Raphael woke me about an hour ago," Mary said, staring up at the pulpit. "Very strange, to be woken by an archangel. Not the first time, but the first in many decades." She turned to them. "He must think it's important to see you." Her gray eyes turned to Grace, and the sleep in them, coupled with her loose hair, softened her usual stern gaze into something like contentment.

Grace couldn't breathe. What did she mean, Raphael thought it was important? Did she not know? "I know who I am," she blurted.

Mary frowned. "Do tell."

"It was. It was me, Mother. You remember the vision you showed me?"

"I remember Raphael showed you a vision of the Order becoming part of the Catholic Church to avoid the Inquisition. I found it interesting that is what he chose, and not something else, but angels can be unpredictable." She glanced at the stained glass of Uriel. "Tell me what that has to do with you."

Monica squeezed her hand.

Squeezing back, Grace steeled her stomach. "Someone betrayed the Order back then. It was me. I gave all your names to Bishop Savaric in a fit of rage."

Mary turned to her, a serene smile on her face. "I know."

Grace exhaled, and her abs hurt. She'd been holding them in, waiting for the anger, waiting for the archangel to come out and destroy her. She wanted to ask so many questions but couldn't force one out.

"If you knew," Monica said, leaning around her, "why didn't you tell any of us?"

"A story for a different time, my dear."

Mon leaned back, the pew creaking. "You see I'm with Grace."

Mary nodded, gaze drifting back to the pulpit.

"Are you mad?"

"No, child. Why on Earth would I be angry?"

She cleared her throat. "Well, I—I left the Order. Broke my vows."

Grace ached for her. She wanted to tell Monica nothing she had done made her a bad person, but she got the feeling it wasn't her lips those words needed to pass through.

Mother Mary continued to stare at the pulpit, head tilted. "You could not make a proper commitment to the Order without the element of choice. When you came to us, it was no choice. We were your only choice. But now." Her lips pointed down, and she turned to them, eyes drifting over them both. "Now, it is a choice. You've experienced the hunters. You've experienced love. Choose what you will commit to and continue to make that choice every day when you wake. That. That will lead you to contentment."

Monica sniffed. Tears rolled down both cheeks. Her voice barely broke a whisper. "I don't know what that choice will be, Mother."

Five minutes ago, Grace would have known without doubt that, if given a choice, Monica would choose her. But this wasn't five minutes ago, and everything Grace expected when she walked through the door had been smashed to bits. Her stomach jiggled like warm Jell-O.

Mother Mary stood. "We have many things to talk about in the morning, including a fight to plan." Without another word, she squeezed past them both, her shifting robes sliding over their knees as she did, and left the sanctuary. The door clanged behind her, echoing.

Once the echoes died, the only sound in the room was Grace's and Monica's breathing.

Grace lifted their clenched hands and kissed the back of Mon's.

Monica silently met her gaze.

"I love you, Monica." She glared at the crucifix looming over the pulpit. "I want you and your God, your archangels, and anyone who is listening to know." Turning back to her, she wiped a tear from her own cheek. With the same finger, she wiped Mon's face too, resting her fingers under Monica's jaw. "I don't care if I can't remember my life. It wouldn't matter if I could, because I love you more than any memories. I don't need any of the other memories because you—" She stopped and sniffed, another tear sneaking from her eye. Her cheeks hurt from trying to smile, and her chin trembled. "You fill every moment of life I've had, and I never want that to change."

A continuous stream of tears dripped from Mon's chin. "I don't think anything has ever felt this way. Maybe. But for the life of me, I can't remember it." She gripped Grace's hand and leaned into it. "So really, we're in this together."

Grace took both of her hands, and they leaned their heads together, sitting in silence.

*

Grace sat on Sister Maria's headstone, the sun beating down on her head and making it feel like ants crawled along the scar crossing her scalp. She remembered Maria's sweet face, her quick Spanish and quicker wit, the way her brown eyes would twinkle when she taught Grace a phrase Mother Mary might not approve of. She spoke at length about her childhood in Mexico, how one time her father brought home pieces of a cow the train hit because he and his friends watched it happen and couldn't imagine wasting the meat. How the vegetables she grew up on were so much fresher than the bland, colorless things they bought in the grocery stores here.

Grace rubbed the rough headstone. She didn't know why Karithexis chose Maria out of the gaggle of nuns in the doorway. Maybe something in the demon knew it would hurt her, but not as much as killing Monica would. Maybe it was a form of slow torture.

Grace had done nothing to save Maria. Nothing when Monica flew across the room and slammed into the wall.

Nothing when Gareth almost died.

Nothing when Raga attacked Daisy. She'd lain there like a useless lump and let her die.

When Natalie said goodbye to Shanna, Nat didn't have any hope of living through this. She had no faith in what she'd seen from Grace or the deal they'd made.

And really, how could Grace fulfill the deal if she couldn't remember what it even was? None of them had any hope of getting out of this alive. Raga would find her within days, and she'd attack them like the hunters. Mother Mary wanted to talk about a fight they all knew was coming, and Grace wanted to fight it, but it had nothing to do with escaping Raga and everything to do with keeping her from killing anyone else to get to her.

Maybe she should give in and let Raga win. Then no one else but she and Natalie would have to suffer for it.

She eyed the low cemetery wall, the boundary of the convent's grounds. All she had to do to leave was step over it.

"I hope you aren't thinking of leaving us, dear Grace."

"Mother. I wouldn't dream of it." She waited for her to make her way down the hill.

Moving like the old woman she was, Mother Mary took each step with care, eventually stopping at the headstone next to her. She leaned on it.

They sat in silence, the January day a little warmer than the one before it.

After a few minutes of listening to traffic on the far-away highway, a few birds chirping here and there, Mary leaned forward enough to read the headstone. "Sister Maria. I do miss her in the strangest ways. Sometimes she would wake up and make us a feast for no other reason than she wanted to see us happy. She was singular."

"I'm sorry." Grace sniffed, gripping the warm stone.

"It wasn't your fault. If anyone could be blamed, it was me. I should have told them what they were getting into."

"They helped attack me, all of them. Seems like they knew a lot more than me."

Mary crossed her arms and faced her. "What else did you discover while you were gone?"

Grace's stomach gurgled. She couldn't refuse that gaze. "I found out the woman whose body I'm in, Natalie, has a wife and two children. She's an alcoholic who ran a charity that failed, and she was living in a halfway house when she called me and asked for a deal."

Mary's eyebrows went up and down in time with Grace's inflection. "Do you know what you promised her?"

"To protect her family, to save her charity, and to take away her alcoholism. If she lived through what I had planned." Grace stared over the cemetery wall.

"What you had planned." It was a statement, not a question. Mary followed her gaze. "Do you know what that was?"

Grace shook her head. "I know I needed someone with some natural talent. A witch. I know I planned to escape Raga—a demon who says she's my master—and I had some kind of plan with Karithexis. But she didn't know the whole plan, and I didn't tell anyone else."

"I've heard of Raga." Mary smiled. "We have a chapter in India. Surely you've noticed the statue outside my office?"

The woman with the nose ring.

Grace nodded.

"Raga is a demon they are familiar with. A child of Mara, an old and powerful demon. The demon of desire and passion. Difficult to defeat." She met Grace's eyes. "In order to defeat her, we would need to rely on an ancient method. Something we can learn from our studies."

Grace stood, a line across the back of her thighs tingling from where she'd been sitting on the thin headstone. "What method?"

"Speak with Monica. Have her show you the section in the library from about 400 BCE. There will be information there. Once you've decided on a course of action, inform me." She stood. "There is little we can help you do to defeat Raga."

Heat flared across Grace's forehead. "You mean you're not going to help? You're not even going to offer?"

"I didn't say that. Look it up. Then we can speak further."

Chapter Twenty

"I don't get this," Grace said.

The library sighed around them, books and dust and low artificial light. An ancient book sat in front of Monica, what she said was a copy of a copy of a copy meticulously kept by sisters of the Order since long before they were nuns. This one, *The Life and History of Siddhartha Gautama*, smelled like old paper, the pen strokes faded and hard to see in places. It'd need to be copied again soon, by hand.

"Well," Monica said, pointing at the page, "here it talks about the children of Mara."

"Right." Grace sighed. "Mara was the demon who sent his children to tempt Buddha, who defeated all of them, but it doesn't say how."

"It does." Mon turned an old page, her light, gloved fingers gentle. "Just not each one specifically. But I think it's the same idea."

Grace sighed again. The pages rippled.

With a stern glance that rivaled the mother, Monica pressed her lips together. She closed the book. "Let's go outside. I think we've gotten what we need."

"If you say so." Grace cracked her back and stood. The Order had been around for so long and gathered information from so many places. If she'd taken the time before, she would have understood this library was a treasure trove.

And that there was probably more than one book in here that mentioned her. By name.

On the way out, Monica dropped the book with Sister Quinn, who Grace had never seen outside the library. Taking care of the books was all she ever did, and if Grace had had time, she would have asked Quinn about the books she herself must surely be in.

When they passed the stained glass of Raphael, Grace paused.

Once Monica realized she'd stopped, she backtracked to her and stood, gazing at the window, sunlight falling at her feet.

"Do you think he's going to help us with this?"

Mon took her hand. "Even if he doesn't, I'll be right there with you."

Grace swallowed over a dry throat. It hurt, and not only because of a lack of spit. When she opened her mouth to speak, she felt the quiver in her voice before it came out, so she closed her mouth again and left it at that.

With a squeeze of her fingers, Monica led her outside. They sat on the stoop, and Mon opened a notebook.

"What I got from the books was that the children of Mara illustrated the root of suffering to Buddha. Raga, in particular, represents desire. Attachment." She cleared her throat. "Passion."

Grace leaned into Monica's shoulder. "Great. How the hell do we defeat that?"

Mon shrugged, moving Grace's head up and down. She flipped a few pages. "It says something here about letting go."

Grace's stomach cramped. She clutched it, the ghost of her injuries riding the wave of pain, and sat up. She caught Monica's eye and tried to say what was on her heart. "I don't want to..." Her voice wavered. She stopped and swallowed. To have gone through all they had, to have been given the gift of each other, and now to have to let it go? Just the thought of it made her sick. "I don't want to lose you."

"Me neither, Grace." Mon sighed and ran her arm around Grace's shoulders. She pulled her in.

Staring into the yard, eyes unfocused, Grace considered what that meant for Monica's life. What it really, really meant. She'd have to leave the convent. She couldn't go back to her family. And for what? A dirty demon who barely did anything good in her entire existence.

But how to let go of her own feelings? There was no possible way. She couldn't; they were the only thing she had, the only thing in these months she remembered that truly belonged to her.

They were all that mattered.

She pried Monica's hand off her shoulder and stood. Stepping down the stairs with numb feet, she walked out into the yard, hugging herself. She turned and did something she'd never done—she looked at the window of Raphael from outside.

It was as though she saw it for the first time.

The peaceful scene she'd always loved to gaze on was gone. In its place, two people knelt in pain, almost writhing, before a glowing angel who scowled at them. Their tears of blood drained them of their lives as he towered over them, shuffling them to the next plane without compassion.

Grace clenched her teeth. That was what would happen to her once the nuns finished with her. Their angel would come to "release" her, send her off to God knew where, and steal every thought or feeling she'd had. Even if she regretted everything she'd been, all the betrayal and killing and duplicity, it didn't matter. She was a demon, and she needed to be "healed."

She tightened her arms around herself as Monica approached, one finger between the pages of her notebook. "I don't know if I can do all this, Mon. I don't know if I want to. It's all so complicated."

"I'll be right next to you. The whole way."

Grace's chin trembled, tears falling to the dirt. "I know, and I don't know if that makes me happy or not."

Mon's brow creased. "What do you mean?"

"I can't ask you to...to give up your whole life because of me. Look what I've done. What I'm capable of." She eyed the window. "I don't deserve any better than those demons." She turned back to Monica. "But how would I even let go of you?"

Still frowning, Monica took her hand. "Who says you have to?"

"Your ludicrous book." She ripped her hand free. "Your book said I have to let go of desire. Passion.

Attachment. I have to lose you." She spun a circle and turned her face to the sky. "I can't! I won't!" Her face hot, stomach churning acid up into her throat, she dropped to her knees. More tears hit the dirt, coating her face in either blood or water. She cried, rocking.

Monica sat next to her, silent.

"It's too hard," Grace whispered.

"Anything worth fighting for isn't easy. *You* are worth fighting for, Grace."

"Even with all the things I've done? I've killed people, Mon. I remember it. I remember how good it felt."

Mon scooted closer. "*Because* of what you've done. You want to fix it. You want to make up for it. I'm going to help you, I promise. I won't leave your side. I won't ever stop loving you, do you understand that?" She put two fingers under Grace's chin and lifted her head.

Grace met her eye. Her chin trembled looking at Mon's other eye. The patch had fallen a bit and exposed the healing scar slicing vertically over her eyelid and the sunken space behind it. Grace couldn't speak, so she nodded.

Monica wiped her cheeks and leaned her forehead into Grace's. "We can do this. We will do this. Together."

*

"Sisters, please." Mother Mary held her hand above her head, palm out. "If we could be seated and begin, we have a lot to go through."

Cloistered inside a small, half-earthen room in the basement, the sisters gathered around a white table.

Grace had never seen the room before, lit with candlelight and oil lamps, symbols all over the walls, but she wasn't surprised to discover its existence. An extra folding chair had been pulled up to the table for her, and the seven of them sat, waiting for Mother Mary.

Mary closed the heavy door behind them and latched it, grabbing a handful of glittering salt from a bag on a shelf next to it and sprinkling it across the line of the door.

Grace shuddered, reliving being trapped in that burning wall of salt. She wasn't leaving this room until someone let her out.

She considered hiding from Raga in here, forever. Just curling up in the corner and forgetting everything.

Monica grabbed her knee under the table and squeezed.

Face tight, Grace laid her hand over Mon's and laced their fingers together.

Mary sat at the round table and took off her habit.

It startled Grace, made her feel something was deeply unsettled, seeing her without it twice in two days.

Was the mother afraid?

Mary cleared her throat. "Sisters, we have a fight coming to us. When we took Grace in"—she inclined her head toward her—"we knew it would come with challenges. But there is more I haven't shared with you."

Before the mother prostrated herself before the sisters, Grace stood. "It was me. I'm the one who turned the Order over to the Inquisition. When I was alive, I was the niece of the Head of the Order. I didn't remember this on my own." She glanced around at them, their faces all showing varying degrees of surprise. Sister Eliana's brow arched so high it all but disappeared into her hairline. "And I wouldn't call what I have memories. More like I was watching a movie from the inside. But I'm sure it is the truth."

Mary nodded. "It is. Raphael has been looking for you for centuries." She cleared her throat. "Throughout the Order's history as part of the Catholic Church, the Head of the Order has had one goal above all: to find the one responsible for the burning of our sisters." She met Grace's eyes. "We've known for quite some time you were a demon. It's been a matter of tracking you."

Sister Joan growled at the table. "When did you plan to tell us this, Mother?"

Eyes flashing, Mary looked around at them all. The faint glow started at the crown of her head and worked its way down her face until it covered her head and part of her chest. When she spoke, the multitude of voices joined her. "Raphael instructed me to wait, until last night when Grace returned to us. I awaited his instruction, and his alone."

Sister Joan's jaw clenched, her face red.

Grace sat, averting her eyes from the light. It hurt, looking at it straight on.

"If you have something to say, Sister," Mary said, "Raphael is here with us now."

Sister Joan whispered at the table, "No, Mother."

Grace inhaled.

Monica squeezed her knee again. "I do."

Mary turned to her, the glow behind her head brightening. "I haven't liked anyone as much as you in a long time, Monica. Whatever you choose, I wish you nothing but prosperity."

Monica waved her hand. "That's not important right now. What I want you to tell us, *explain* to us, is why you never told anyone the truth. Least of all Grace. She deserved to know *why*. After everything we've put her through and the person she's turned out to be, she deserved to know why." Her voice rising, she pointed her finger at the mother. "You treated her like any other demon, when you knew, *you knew*, she was different. And you let us think she was just some random demon. Some kind of weapon." Her eye wet, she glanced at Grace and lowered her voice. "I'm sorry."

"I know."

Her chin trembled. Releasing Grace's hand, she stood and ripped off the eye patch.

The mother lowered her eyes. Actually lowered them.

"Look at me, Raphael!"

Heart in her throat, Grace leaned into Sister Alexandra, sitting next to her. The sister crossed them both.

The mother looked up, face aglow.

For the first time, Grace saw someone else's face sitting on top of the mother's features, embedded in her skin.

Thank God or whatever, the archangel didn't look angry. In fact, curled lips overlaid Mary's.

Through her teeth, Monica drew in a whistling breath. "I don't know how you've been running this Order before now, but the lies have to stop. They stop here. They stop"—she rammed her pointed finger into the table—"now."

The mother, Raphael, whoever it was, smiled. "I can fix your eye."

Monica's mouth dropped open. For a second, it flopped like a carp.

Grace's stomach jittered, and she reached for her, her fingertips grazing the hem of her shirt.

Without looking, Monica grabbed her hand. "Come on, Grace. We're better off without them." In two large steps, dragging a breathless Grace behind her, she reached the door and swept away the salt.

It opened before she turned the knob.

Father Moscone stood there, holding his side and bleeding from the mouth. "I'm sorry. He insisted."

From the darkened stairs, someone pushed him out of the way and leaned into the light.

Blue eyes narrowed, Gareth hulked in the doorway. "Ah. Just who I was looking for."

*

The sisters gathered around the doorway. Grace expected the mother to say something, or for Raphael to lash out at Monica for mouthing off. Truth was, she was stuck between fear about what Gareth wanted, terror that Raphael was going to strike them dead where they stood, and absolute adoration for Monica's sheer, bullheaded bravery.

"I drove all day. We need you."

Grace pointed at herself, even though Gareth's eyes rolled like a wild horse about to bolt. "Me?"

"Anyone. Where's the mother?"

"Here," she said.

Heart in her toes, Grace spun. Mother Mary's voice had never sounded so weak, so frail.

She sat at the table, head in her hands. Sweat coated her brow and stuck her hair to her forehead, and she breathed deep like she'd run a marathon. Like earlier in the day, when she'd picked her way down the hill like the old woman she was, she sat in her chair, frail and shrunken.

It frightened Grace to her core.

Shaking her head, she glanced up at Gareth, whose stricken face told Grace pretty much all she needed to know about why he was here. He oozed lack of sleep and sweat and tears.

"Please, Mother." He sank down to a knee next to her and took her hand like a man about to propose marriage. "She's hurt. She's dying. It was a curse, and the doctors can't do anything. Please."

Grace inhaled like she'd been punched in the gut, even though she was expecting it.

Daisy. She was still alive. She was here, and she needed help.

"I cannot do it." Mary squeezed his hand. "Not right now."

Gareth shook his head. "Isn't there a spell, or—or—or something?"

Monica tugged Grace's hand. "Come on, Grace."

"Where?"

She spoke over her head. "Gareth. Take us to her."

His eyes landed on them, and for the briefest moment, they flashed anger. But something happened behind them, a kind of glow, and Grace almost caught an aura of the healing she'd given him.

She swallowed. "I'll try."

He rushed to her, hugging her so tight he lifted her from the ground. "Come on," he said, tugging her.

She grabbed Monica, and the three of them rushed through the convent and out into the parking lot.

He hadn't parked his muscle car in a space so much as crooked across the lawn, giving him the quickest access to the sanctuary door. He'd almost parked on the stairs, and the driver's door stood ajar. Mouth covered with one hand, he released Grace and pointed into the car. "There," he said, his voice cracking.

She wanted to tell Gareth she couldn't do this. She wanted to let Monica do it for her, or show her how, or place her hands. Something.

But truthfully, if anyone could do it, it was her.

She leaned into the car, trying desperately to ignore the stench of burned flesh and hair, sweat, urine, and something a lot less pleasant than the mélange of all those. Death crept up on Daisy, and not slowly either.

Her lungs rattled where she lay in the back, surrounded in a cocoon of soft blankets and pillows. She hadn't been strapped in because, honestly, there was nowhere to put straps. Anything tight over her skin, including clothing, would have ripped what was left of it off.

Green eyes open yet unfocused, she breathed in and out. No snark. No grin. No usual cocky scowl, even in the scant unburnt skin. She was dead already, and she knew it. To say she was peaceful wouldn't be right, but Grace couldn't put her finger on any other word.

Still. Grace knelt behind the driver's seat, knees wedged into the tiny floorboard between it and the backseat, and laid both hands over Daisy's heart. Some of her charms had melted right into her skin.

Grace closed her eyes and searched for the stream.

*

The scene wasn't bright like Gareth's and Karithexis's had been. Not even close.

Here, the sun had set, the stars shimmering above the nighttime landscape.

No trees lined the river, and as Grace approached, she couldn't hear water running or bubbling between the banks.

She tried to grip her stomach but found it didn't have substance. She'd never stopped to look at herself when she did this.

She held her hands out in front of her.

They shone, a few red spots here and there, but were mostly made of translucent shifting, opalescent rainbow light. She glanced down at her chest and found some more of the red spots crawling around her midsection. There was the suggestion of a body, like a pencil sketch of a person, but no more.

She approached the bank, creeping toward the edge. Edging up to the side, watching her footing in case the dirt slipped from beneath her, she stared down into the bottom of the river.

It'd once been deep, deeper than Nat's mom's, even though Daisy had to be half her age. The sides were worn away in curlicues, the still-wet dirt forming shapes and circles. When put together, it reminded Grace of Daisy's husky laugh, the twinkle in her green eyes, her wavy hair tucked into her jacket.

In the bed, at the very bottom, sat Daisy as she was, not the withered body in the backseat of Gareth's car.

Startled to see a figure, Grace leaned too hard on the dirt.

As she'd feared, it slipped from under her, and she tumbled down the steep bank, knocking her head, the small of her back, and one knee. She landed sideways on her arm at the bottom.

Daisy laughed. "Didn't expect to see you again."

Grace struggled upright and walked over to her, feet sinking in the deep silt. "May I?"

"Be my guest."

Sitting next to her, Grace frowned. "Where's all the water gone?"

Daisy pointed between her bowed legs.

A small pool had formed between them, dug out of the clay there. She dipped her fingers in it, picking up a handful of watery silt and letting it drip, clumpy, back into the pool. "This is it, Grace. This is all I got left."

Tears sprung up in Grace's eyes so suddenly her throat burned, and they dripped into her lap before she could stop them. "No, Daisy."

Daisy grinned at her with one side of her mouth, corner of her eye crinkled. "I wouldn't normally tell you this, but it was worth it. Tell Gareth I'm sorry, but it was worth it."

Grace's head started shaking before Daisy was even finished. "No. No it wasn't. You did this to save me."

"I know." She picked up and dropped another handful of water. "Look at you, coming to heal me. You know Gareth would rather kill you soon as look at you right now. But you came anyway. You might be a demon, and a liar, but who doesn't have flaws? I know I do. In spades." She chuckled. "Kinda wish I'd met you sooner in life, but then again, I might not have made it so far if I had."

Sister Maria's story about the cow flitted through Grace's mind again, and tears flooded so fast she couldn't see. Against reason, she reached for the pool of water.

Daisy didn't stop her and instead threw one leg over the pool and crossed her ankles. She leaned on her hands and chuckled at the sky. "It's pretty here. Wish I'd come before, but I was always so busy with everyone else." Eyes on Grace's hands as she lowered them into the tiny pool, she smiled again, one small wrinkle next to her mouth. "That was worth it too. I helped a lot of people."

Grace's own tears dropped into the pool, splashing light where they hit the surface. "I know, and I want you to help more. You can't die because of me." She reached into the pool with her hands, the light from them brightening the water. Her fingers dug into the silt, slipping into the wet, silky mud. All of her heart focused on making the water light.

It brightened from the inside.

Warmed, Grace smiled and looked at Daisy.

She sat, ankles still crossed, rocking back and forth on her hands. A few less lines crossed her face, her skin a bit tighter, but she wasn't glowing. She was still just Daisy. She grinned. "Not gonna work, sweetie. But if it helps, I do feel a little better. I can die without pain now."

"Daisy. No."

"Listen," she said, leaning over the pool and tracing a line on the surface with her finger. "I'm not gonna tell you you're different from other demons. You're not. You're the same old, tired demon I've seen a hundred times if it's a dozen."

"I know. I know. I'm—"

"Let me finish."

Grace's mouth snapped shut.

"But you've made some choices I ain't never seen from a demon. Now I don't know if it's the memory loss or what it is. But whoever you were when you started this, that demon is gone. You know that, don't you?"

Grace swallowed. That feeling invaded again, the good one, the one she got when she controlled people—the warmth, the power.

The red spots grew, swirling faster over her body.

She yanked her hands from Daisy's pool of water and clutched them. "I don't know."

Daisy gripped her hand, water dripping from it. The water soaked into Grace's skin. "It all comes down to choices. I chose to jump in front of that curse for you because you chose to heal someone important to me." Her hand faded. "Your nature makes you a demon, but your choices make you who you are."

The tears fell from Grace's eyes again, a never-ending stream of them, and they shone where they landed on their joined hands.

Daisy's hand continued to fade. "Take care of him for me. Tell him." She paused, fading faster. "Ah fuck it. Tell him he can have my books."

She disappeared.

Grace tried to grab her, but her hand passed through empty space. She landed in the mud and glanced at the pool.

The water drained into the ground, the pool growing shallower, until only a drip remained.

She grabbed a handful of the wet silt and squeezed it in her fist.

And opened her eyes in the back of Gareth's car.

Her chest hurt. Her throat hurt so much she couldn't breathe. The tears stuck behind her lids and burned.

Opening her hand, she watched as a tiny flash of light disappeared, like a lightning bug flying into the night.

"Oh God, Daisy," she whispered.

Chapter Twenty-One

They gave Daisy the same kind of funeral they'd given Maria, what Daisy herself called a proper funeral. Right down in the same graveyard, they burned her body and sent her ashes into the heavens.

Naked face exposed, blue eyes red, Gareth cried the whole time.

So did Grace, holding hands with Monica, staring at the heat from the flames and thinking about what Daisy had said to her before she died. She didn't know Daisy had had it in her to be so kind, and she wished she'd gotten more time to know her better.

She couldn't let this go. Raga had to pay for it. There had to be a way to remember the plan.

After the last of the fire died and Grace told Gareth what Daisy had said, he left, giving Grace one last, long look before climbing in his car and peeling out of the parking lot.

Grace walked the convent alone. Arms crossed over her stomach, she shuffled through all the hallways, looking at the statues and pausing, once again, in front of the stained glass of Raphael.

Now that she'd seen the scene from outside, it'd never look the same again. There was no peace to be found here.

"I'm sorry about Daisy. She never agreed with our methods, but she could always be counted on in a fight. We should have had Gareth stay to help us with Raga."

Grace turned to the mother. "You honestly think he would have helped?"

She stared at the window. "We've always had an understanding with the hunters. Though our relationship is a bit—" She stopped, tasting the words. "—tepid, they're allies when we need them. We return the favor when possible. The work of protecting people and saving demons is tireless and has no boundaries."

Staring at the stained glass, Grace couldn't find words enough to express her anger. "Is there no way to give me my memory back? You took it, didn't you?"

"Yes."

Grace spoke before she had time to think about it. "I could turn the hands of the clock back to that moment, if I had the power, and I don't know if I'd take them back or not." She sighed. "I want to remember the plan, but I don't want to be the person who made it."

Hands clasped, Mary turned to face her. "Turn back the hands of the clock? Is that what you said?"

Brow furrowed, Grace tried to remember planning to say that. She hadn't; it'd come on its own like Natalie's voice did. But she nodded, staring at the mother from the side of her eye. "I did. I don't know why, but I did."

"Come to my office, Grace."

Grace fought to keep her mouth from falling open. She'd never stepped foot in the mother's office. Did she have a time machine in there? A Grace-shaped iron maiden? Could be either at this point, and Grace followed her anyway.

Before they went in, Grace stopped and gazed across the hall at the statue of the woman with the nose ring and a jewel where Raga had one, in the center of her forehead. Now that Mary had mentioned they were from India, Grace saw the robes weren't really robes at all. It was a sari, artfully draped over her body and baring the slightest bit of her stomach under her elbow.

"Grace."

Leaving the statue, she followed Mary into her office, her brow furrowed.

The mother closed the door with a solid thump. The whole office was made of leather and wood, with an old Oriental rug beneath a giant black walnut desk.

It smelled like old leather and older books, a lot like Grace had imagined. She joined Mary on the couch.

Mother Mary spoke a few words and lifted her hand to Grace's forehead.

Grace leaned away. "Are you about to give me my memories back? I don't know if I want them. That's what I just said."

"Turn back the hands of the clock. You yourself gave me that phrase and told me when I heard it, it would be time to reveal everything to you. I'm not sure how you did it, but the reason you wanted a vessel capable of containing magic was so you could set up this back door and let me know when it was time."

"What? What do you mean?"

"I mean, it's time." She touched Grace's forehead and spoke a spell, a few words in that same language Grace had heard in the Realm, before Grace drew the breath to stop her.

Chapter Twenty-Two

I lifted an apple from the pile of them and tossed it from hand to hand. It made a hollow thunk, its skin a deep green. Satisfied, I laid it in my basket and selected another.

"The apples are lovely in August, aren't they?"

Startled, I looked up.

The man came from nowhere, but he stood next to me now in his three-piece suit, a basket over his arm with the farmer's market symbol emblazoned on the outside of it, and an apple in his hand. He took a bite out of it, dimples in his cheeks, the juice dripping down his chin.

My first instinct was to scold him for not paying first; instead, I hesitated. "It is their season."

He smiled, showing a mouth full of teeth, the eye teeth especially sharp and pointed, bits of apple caught between them. "Baking a pie, Mother?"

"Yes, I..." How had he known my title? He was better dressed than most of the people I saw on Sundays, Wednesdays, and Fridays for Mass, but I could find no other question to ask. "I'm sorry. Are you a congregant?"

If it were possible, he grinned wider, and the corners of his mouth turned down. "Mary. I'm surprised at you. All this time you've been searching for one specific demon, and you don't recognize me?" He leaned forward, meeting and holding my eyes with a mischievous snicker. "Look closer."

Cold washed from my crown to my toes. Squeezing the apple in my hand hard enough to dig my nails into the crisp skin, I backed up a step and almost tripped over my robes. Juice ran down the backs of my fingers and my wrist, wet inside my sleeve. But I kept my composure, standing straight and facing him down. I was almost sure I knew him, but as a woman. Not that demons cared about little things like gender.

I didn't call Raphael. He wasn't that kind of angel. He came when he wanted and left when he wanted, and never told me when that would be. Granted, I wouldn't call him if the need wasn't imperative. The older I got, the harder it became to recover when he came and went like the powerful archangel he was.

I backed up into the rack of squash. Several rolled off and split open at my feet. "I command you from this place, demon."

He laughed and threw the apple over his shoulder. He picked up another, took a giant bite out of one side, pieces of apple and juice slick on his chin, and laid it back on the pile with the bite mark facing inward. "So, here's the thing. You've been looking for me. I've been watching you. It was only a matter of who got there first." One foot stepped out in front of the other, and he slid over to me, leaning close and purring into my ear. "I got here first."

Demons had no right to smell so good, especially not with my vows to the Order.

I cleared my throat. "What do you want?"

"Let's talk somewhere else. This tent is tiresome and hot. It's the middle of August, woman."

He put his hand on my arm, and the next thing I knew, we stood in the middle of a restaurant.

"Please," he said, hand held out.

I glanced at the basket still over my arm. What could I do but set it at my feet and sit with him?

I did. The crystal glasses on the table sparkled with water and red wine. "You're the demon who betrayed us," I said, "the one who gave our names to the Inquisition and wiped out almost two-thirds of the Order in one go."

He held up a finger. "I wasn't a demon then, you know that." Taking a sip of wine, he waved to the waiter. "Want anything? My treat."

Bile climbing up my throat, I crossed my arms. "You're right; we've been looking for you for a long time. You were Mary's niece?"

"You do know who I was. Good. That'll cut down on explanations. And though you Catholics love recycling names, you're the first Mary since my aunt. Poetic, yes?"

The waiter appeared.

The demon whispered to him, watching me with a smirk as he did.

Once the waiter vanished, the demon continued. "Anyway. The guilt of that action has been chasing me ever since. It was impulsive." His lips turned down, sour. "I was so angry. At first, it was almost cathartic, watching them burn. I finally had power over something in my life. I thought it would gain me happiness, but all it did was cause me to damn myself."

"Damn yourself?"

He sighed. "Do you even know where demons come from? The ones that were human, not the ones like my master."

I shook my head. Even in all the years I'd been chasing and healing demons, I'd never known what caused them to be. I knew only they were once human and, as such, deserved a chance at salvation.

Even the one sitting before me.

"Guilt. Guilt makes us what we are. We spend centuries, lifetimes upon lifetimes, turning that guilt inside out. Torturing everyone else with it, as though that would make it better. Have you, in your perfect life, ever tried to heal pain by causing more?"

I didn't know how to answer. Never had I heard this about demons. Not even Raphael had told me. Centuries' worth of research by the Order, and they didn't know this.

It ached.

"What can I do about that? Let me exorcise you. At least you'll get rest."

He slammed a curled fist into the table. The glasses jumped and so did I. "My master is powerful. She won't let me escape that easily. You think some spell will just poof me to heaven?"

"There's a heaven?"

"No. That's beside the point. My master won't let me go. You can't exorcise me. If you could, the Order would have killed me long, long ago for what I did to you."

A spell crept to the end of my tongue. "I think you'll find we know more than you imagine. We have a few tricks up our sleeves."

"In those voluminous robes, I would hope so. But it won't be that simple. What if I offered you—"

The waiter materialized with a tray full of food.

In front of the demon, he set at least twelve plates of desserts. One of them, he lit on fire after tucking the tray under his arm. "Anything else, sir?"

The demon waved his hand.

With a bow, the waiter disappeared again.

Picking up a fork, the demon offered me some of the dessert, his eyes on the flaming one. It had bananas and burning liqueur, sweet and intoxicating.

I declined.

He scoffed. "I brought you here because this place has the best dessert in five states. This is a Michelin star restaurant. You must try some."

"I want nothing you offer."

With a grin and a mouthful of ice cream, he leaned over the desserts. His tie fell in one, getting chocolate syrup all over it. "Ah, but you haven't heard my offer." He spread both arms wide, ice cream dripping off the fork and into the floor. "I offer you myself, in exchange for a little help."

It was my turn to scoff, and as much as I didn't want to, I had to try the apple pie. It's what I'd planned on making with my fresh apples, something I did for the sisters every late summer. Buying the ingredients and baking the pie was some of my only private time.

I dug my spoon into the pie and tipped it with vanilla ice cream. Licking at the bite, I frowned. "What would you want in return?"

"I need help, Mother. I need you to help me escape one demon and kill another."

"Kill? You know that normally goes against our beliefs."

"Blah, blah, blah, you heal demons, yadda, yadda." He flapped his hand open and closed like a mouth. "I'm not asking you to kill. I'll be the one doing that. If I fail, or die trying, you're welcome to try to deal with the demon your own way."

I rolled another piece of the flavorful pie in my mouth. It really was worth a Michelin star. "Who are the demons? What is your plan?"

He blew out the flaming one, topped it with a separate bowl of ice cream, and took a bite of ice cream and banana. "Raga, she's my master. You've heard of her?"

I nodded. "She is a child of Mara. She tempted Buddha, tried to distract him from reaching enlightenment with passion and desire. We cannot harm a demon so powerful. How do you plan to escape?"

Lowering his brow, he smiled. "Just like Buddha did. Purify myself."

I didn't mean to be so indecorous, but I laughed and spit ice cream with chunks of apple all over the table. Still chuckling, I wiped my mouth. "Purify? How do you propose to do that?"

"That's the beauty of it. Memory loss. Not only will I not remember my sins, covering my memory, or erasing it entirely, will hide me and my intentions from the other demon." His brow darkened, and he stared off into the restaurant. "The one who keeps me in check for Raga. Like her right hand. Karithexis makes sure I don't step out of line, makes sure I never forget who and what I am." He sniffed and scooped up some more banana. Dipping it in chocolate on the way to his mouth, he shrugged. "You have to let me kill that one. If Karithexis lives, I'll never be free, no matter what we do with Raga."

A drip of chocolate oozed from the side of his mouth. I'd never considered a demon would speak like this, and I doubted he spoke the whole truth. Still, the prospect of catching the demon responsible for the catastrophic burning during the Inquisition was too tempting. "We could exorcise the demon for you?"

He shook his head, a small, rueful smile lifting one side of his mouth. "I told you. You can't exorcise me or Karithexis. Raga's protection over the two of us is too powerful. Besides. This one has it coming. Look it up." Laying the fork on a plate, he removed a shining silver pen and pad of paper from his pocket. He scribbled on the paper and tore the piece off.

I took it, paper crinkling in my palm. No doubt it would lead me to information I already knew, but knowing we couldn't exorcise Karithexis was not something I was aware of until this moment. I tried to hide my shaking hand.

"Look that up in your library. You'll find ample reason to rid the world of this demon." He sighed. "She thinks we're both escaping Raga, but when I give you the phrase 'turn back the hands of the clock,' you'll show me this memory. Whether you obliterate who I am or not is up to you. I don't care what you do with my memories. I don't want them anymore."

I sat back in my chair. "And you think all this will work?"

"What have you got to lose?"

Chapter Twenty-Three

Grace's eyes opened, but she didn't move. She couldn't. Mary's hands still gripped her head. The mother leaned down until she met her eyes, face solemn.

"Do you see now, Grace? Do you see it all?"

"I—"

Mary's hands glowed. Her eyes widened, but she didn't pull her hands away.

Grace shut her eyes tight. Maybe Raphael was about to kill her. She started to struggle, to wrench her head from the angel's grasp, but she still couldn't move.

Light came up, red on her eyelids. She opened her eyes and stared up, up into the face of a young woman. Did she recognize her?

Her perspective shifted, and she saw a man in a rocking chair before a fire.

Sweat popped on her brow, and she struggled to get away. She cried out.

It was a baby's cry.

Raphael. No. Please.

The multitude of voices spoke, almost breaking her eardrums. "How can you possibly achieve the purification you seek if you have no other choice? Remember now, and know."

Kicking her arms and legs, tiny arms and legs, she tried to run. But she was just a baby; there was nothing she could do.

Through the flashes of light, one memory after another came until they overlaid one another in a great cacophony of noise. Grace tried to cover her ears only to find she had no hands. She had no other choice but to take in all the memories. The speed they assaulted her with was enough to make her lose her mind as she hopped from one memory to the next, over her whole life, to the burning of the Order to her own death to waking as a demon. Raga, Karithexis, and centuries of torture, deals, murders, and blood.

The river of her own spirit was dyed red with it.

And still the memories continued to race by. Not only blinding her but entrenching themselves in her consciousness, becoming, once again, a part of her. The pain of it, the absolute deafening chorus of horrible deeds pressed on her chest, on every part of her.

Her eyes flew open again, and she slipped from the couch, landing on her knees with a crack. She fell to her back, slamming her head into the floor. Stars bloomed in her head, the pain radiating outward from where she'd smacked it. At least the rug had been there.

Mary sat in the corner of the couch, breathing heavy, sweating, her eyes squeezed shut. She pressed her lips together so tightly they almost disappeared. One shaking hand covered her eyes.

Grace moaned. She had no words.

She wanted to believe the memories, like the gas station ones and the ones from her life on Earth, still belonged to someone else, and that the memories she'd built in the past three months were the only ones that were real. That her time with Monica was all that mattered, still.

But that would be a lie.

All the things Raphael had shown her were now embedded in her psyche again. It wasn't so much that Raphael had shown her the memories; rather, he'd unlocked the door to them all and allowed her access to them again, where she could pick and choose to live through all the horrible decisions, repulsive behavior, death and murders and lies.

She rolled to her side and threw up. The acid from her stomach burned her throat and sinuses, and pressure behind her eyes rolled through her forehead.

Someone pounded on the door. "Mother? Are you okay? The whole building was shaking. Mother?"

When Mary didn't answer, they opened the door. "Mother? I—" They paused, breath caught. "Grace!"

Monica ran in, dropping to her knees next to Grace. "Are you all right?" She laid her cool hand on Grace's forehead, the other gripping her shoulder, her knees in Grace's back. "You're burning up. My God. What happened?"

Grace moaned again. Eyes still closed, she let the feeling of being comforted in Monica's arms roll through her, tried to let it cocoon her and protect her from the memory hangover. It helped a little.

She rolled to her back, wiped her mouth, and opened her eyes. The light from the windows pierced her retinas.

With a gentle grasp around her upper arm and a hand behind her back, Monica sat her up and took in her face, brows drawn together. "What happened? It felt like an earthquake."

Grace's chin trembled as a memory of killing a nun a lot like Monica flitted through her mind. She didn't know when, or where, or who it was, but after days of torture, she'd put the cherry on top by ripping the woman's throat out with her teeth. She lifted her voice to a whisper. "Raphael gave me all my memories back." Tears obscured Monica's face as they filled Grace's eyes. Inhaling through her clenched teeth, she backed away from Mon, breaking her hold on her arm and sliding her ass through the vomit. "Stay away from me."

Mon glanced between Mary and Grace. "What? Why?"

Drawing her knees up to her chest, Grace buried her face between them and her body. "I'm dangerous. I'm terrible, and I'll hurt you. Stay away from me. Please." She wanted to keep hiding her face, but she peeked over her knees to watch Monica, because if she knew anything about Mon, she wasn't about to listen on the first try.

Lifting to her hands and knees, Monica crawled toward her. "What are you saying? Let me help you."

Grace backed into the desk. "Mon. Stop. Please. I can't." The words bound up in her thick throat, burning with the stomach acid. Her cheeks and chin trembled, the tears collecting in her eyes, but the thing she was, the deeds she'd done, those things couldn't be forgotten.

Not anymore.

She grabbed the desk and pulled herself to standing, towering over Monica.

The mother lowered her hand and stared at Grace through tired eyes, still pushed into the corner of the couch.

"All of you. Stay away."

Holding her stomach, Grace ran from the room.

＊

The stench of drying puke stuck firmly up her nose, Grace sat in the graveyard again, leaned against Maria's tombstone, tears long gone from her eyes. She stared into the sunset, the half circle of the sun sinking below the horizon stamping an imprint inside her eyes. When she closed her eyes, it flashed inside her eyelids much like the memories of her long life had.

The semicircular projection of the sun turned into a whole circle of light, centered on a dark floor.

It wasn't just the TV and two chairs from Shanna's kitchen table here now. There was a whole room of furniture. Most of it was from Shanna's house—the living room, the kitchen—and tucked in the corner the bed Grace and Monica shared. But Mother Mary's couch was there too, and it was where Natalie sat. Waiting.

Grace took her seat there but didn't look at Nat. She folded her hands in her lap and stared at her fingers. "Did you see any of that? Those memories?"

"Some of it."

Exhaling through tight lips, Grace glanced at her for a second. Just a second. "Is that why we're talking?"

Nat shrugged. "I didn't ask you to come. Did you come on purpose?"

"No."

Pulling her hair over her shoulder, Nat laughed. "So we're stuck here. Together. Fun."

Grace sighed. Nat was the one person she couldn't run away from. "I don't know what to do, Natalie."

"In regards to?"

"Everything."

Nat snorted. "You remember our deal now? You remember what you were going to do? Do you remember how to do it?"

Grace considered. Those memories had to be in there somewhere. She narrowed her eyes and tried to rifle through them.

Every corner she turned had blood waiting behind it. Dead, mangled bodies. Crying children. The stench of burned matches and copper. It was one long, never-ending string of pain and torment.

And yes, in her wake there were hundreds of people she'd hurt or killed, but most of all, the pain came from inside. She suffered every time she killed someone and did it more and more and more, hoping that this time, *this time*, it would be the one to make her feel better. Instead, it got worse and worse and worse.

In the midst of that, she found it, the one memory that stood out.

Natalie glowed white in the memory; the reasoning behind the deal shone like the sun. Grace stopped, her memories rolling through like pages flipping, to look at this one.

Sure, she'd made the deal because she was tired of the pain. Bone-weary. Soul-weary. She saw a way out and needed help doing it, help she could get from this human, Natalie. In the process, she could help Natalie heal her own life, and instead of causing pain like she'd been doing for so long, she could stop it. Grace could show this one person how to change.

"I watched you," Grace said. "I watched you go to meetings. I watched you fall off the wagon. I recruited you to help us both."

Nat chuckled. "Help me? That's what you've been doing? I've been stuck with a demon who couldn't even remember who it was, what it wanted with me, and you got my mom possessed, my wife almost left me, and I can't even count how many times we've almost died. How is any of that helping me?"

Grace sighed. "I promised you I'd take away your alcoholism."

"You did."

"That was a lie."

Sending a sharp exhale through her nose, Nat stood and crossed her arms. Pacing, she glared at Grace. "When did you plan to tell me that?"

"I just remembered."

"What now?"

Heat rolling through her, the shame of lying in order to make a deal rising like a blush to her cheeks, she stood and caught Nat's arm to stop her pacing. "Go to meetings. *Try.*"

Natalie yanked her arm from Grace's grasp. "I fucking did that! I did. I tried. I can't do it. I need help."

Grace smiled with one side of her mouth. "You need help. But you don't want it."

"You're kidding. I made a deal with a demon because I wanted help. Of course I want help."

She scoffed. "You want someone to do it *for* you. It doesn't work like that, Nat. It doesn't. You've got to accept it's on you, and you've got to let go of this idea that you're alone in the world and no one will help you."

Mouth open, Nat exhaled. Her brows drew together, and she shook her head. "I don't think that."

"Please. You're so convinced you're alone and the only thing you can cling to is alcohol and drugs, you called a literal demon to take you away from it so you could continue to be alone. You'll never get through this alone." Grace gripped her shoulder. "You don't have to."

Nat met her eyes, tears welling in her own, and shook her head. She dropped her voice. "I'm scared. What if it doesn't work?"

Grace laughed. "Hey. If I die taking on Raga and Karithexis, you won't have to worry about it."

"Well, Grace." She grabbed for her hand.

Letting her take it, she stepped closer to Nat. It was so weird, looking at herself like this. The same body she'd grown accustomed to, but with someone else inside. Still, the way Nat bit her lip told her they were both in there together. There was so little separation between them, in the end.

Nat smiled with her lips. A tight, small grin. "I'll help you however I can."

*

Grace opened her eyes. The sun had set.

She leaned against the headstone, fingers in the dirt.

The earth shook, hard enough for the bells atop the sanctuary to swing back and forth, clanging into the early evening chill.

She stood. It was time.

Chapter Twenty-Four

As Grace walked up the hill from the graveyard and came around the corner of the sanctuary, the sisters walked down the front steps, armed to the teeth. She'd never seen them so armed.

It was a good thing. Raga stood in the parking lot outside the sanctuary, her hands clasped in front of her, long hair tied with gold bands once again. The black jewel in her forehead glittered so bright it practically reflected all the light of the moon as it rose in the east.

There was no denying she was absolutely alluring, but Grace regarded her with mild revulsion, remembering the things Raga had done to her to keep her allegiance. From cajoling to seducing to torture, she'd done it all. In the end, Grace succumbed, over and over and over and over again.

But like most things, the allure wore off in time. Her desire to please Raga faded until one day, her only desire was escape. Of course, Karithexis followed her around like a dog, pretending they were friends and never letting her free.

As Grace stood, staring at Raga and considering her next move, the sisters surrounded the demon, speaking their low spell.

Monica shouted for Grace, stutter-stepping down the stairs and running to her. She gripped her arm and tugged.

Grace met her eyes. "I wish you were far away from here right now."

"I'd choose to be here even if I were anywhere else. Do you know what you're going to do?"

"Not die?"

Even though the demon in the midst of the nuns growled at them, the earth itself shaking every time she put a foot down to advance on them, Monica chuckled. "Yeah. Please don't." She squeezed her hand. "No matter what happens, don't forget I love you. That'll never change."

Grace ignored the demon for a bare moment and caught Monica's eye. "I remember everything, and in all that, there's still nothing as good as you." She leaned into her space, their foreheads touching. Inhaling, she pulled Monica's sweet scent deep into her lungs and held it. "I love you, too, Mon." She kissed her, a gentle, soft kiss, and let the world fade. For a second. An eternity.

Raga shouted.

With reluctance, Grace let Monica go and turned to face the demon. "I guess it's—"

A voice spoke from her other side. "Am I late to the party?"

The skin on Grace's face tightened, and she jumped so hard she might have torn her intestinal scar right open.

Gripping her stomach, she turned. "Kari. Good of you to join us before the fight was over."

Karithexis chuckled and tucked her glasses in her shirt pocket. "You're lucky you're still doing so well."

"Yeah, well. Fight just started."

"Hmph."

The sisters, still surrounding the demon, had done that iridescent thing again, the opaque screen of air between them that they'd used on Jalithesh. The difference here, though, was no one bothered with salt. Likely it didn't work on a demon like Raga.

Raga stood in the middle of the circle and beamed at the nuns. "My Grace did promise to get me close to you lovely women," she said, all her teeth showing. "I can't get to some of you, which is a shame." She leaned into Sister Joan's face. "You're too good for me." Hot breath blasted from her mouth, so hot the air wavered.

Joan's veil flew away from her head, flapping in the wind, and she closed her eyes and mouth.

The shield rippled.

Letting Monica go, Grace stepped toward the circle. "Raga, how about you leave them alone and take your fight up with me? I'm the one you want."

"I'd happily take some of them as well, dear Grace." Lifting up from the ground about four inches, Raga floated in the air and spun to face Grace. "But I will definitely take you. You're mine. That will not change."

"I beg to differ." She inched closer, careful to avoid the shimmering shield between the sisters.

Raga lifted her arm.

An invisible hand wrapped around Grace's midsection. Giant fingers clutched her waist and back, each one depressing her skin and squeezing her lungs. She struggled to inhale.

Karithexis cursed under her breath. She spoke her own spell or something, dragging her toes across the pavement as she flew toward the demon. "Raga," she called, "I think we need to talk about something."

Raga stopped squeezing Grace long enough to glance at her. "Karithexis. You should assure me whose side you're on. I'm beginning to suspect it is not mine, in which case, I will have to kill you along with your friend." She raised her other hand.

Coughing, Karithexis levitated to Grace's level. "Shit. Shit, shit, shit." She struggled, trying to push the invisible hand off her waist. The old woman's arms were no match for whatever ethereal power Raga held.

Grace leaned about an inch. "Thanks for the help, Kari. But I don't think it did anything."

Karithexis snorted. "Piss off."

The sisters continued their chant while Raga was distracted, tightening their circle. Raga's skin smoked. Like closing an umbrella over the handle, they closed the shield around the demon.

She panted, tightening her grip on Grace and Karithexis.

Grace choked again, trying to pull in a breath. No more came behind the last one. She couldn't move. Her arms went limp.

"No!" Monica shouted, somewhere far away, and rushed beneath Grace's feet. "Raphael, you've got to help them!"

Not that Grace heard the response, but she didn't need to. The answer would be no. There was no help coming. Their plan hadn't been good enough, Raga had come too soon, and she couldn't be escaped anyway. Forget desire? Forget passion? Forget love? She couldn't do that. She wouldn't. Not when her love for Monica was the only good thing she remembered in a lifetime of pain. She'd rather go back to the Realm with Raga than do that.

Raga laughed. "That's right. Give your power to me, my dear Grace. I've always loved your strong will. It has made you such a good demon. One of the best at your job."

While she was distracted, Monica broke through the circle of sisters and ran at Raga with a weapon raised above her head. "You let her go! You do it now before I destroy you!"

Raga's grip loosened enough for Grace to breathe.

Blood rushing to her face, air burning her throat, she looked down at Monica, who held a shimmering, bright instrument up to Raga. Shaped almost like an exploded clock, with wheels and gears floating free, it ticked backward. Where on Earth did they get all these wild toys?

Monica slashed at her.

Raga screamed, so deafening the trees ringing the convent bent sideways, and clutched her midsection.

The pressure on Grace's lungs released, and she fell to the ground in a heap, Karithexis landing next to her with a grunt.

"I really hope this wasn't your grand plan," she wheezed.

Pain constricting her abs, Grace gulped breaths and shook her head. "No. But I know what was." Wincing, still holding her stomach where she might have ripped open her intestines again, she worked her way to her feet. She opened her mouth, drawing air into her lungs until it hurt like a knife to the side. She found as much voice as she could muster, pushing it out with her damaged diaphragm. "Raga."

The demon lifted her huge brown eyes, and blood dripped from her crimson lips, steaming where it hit the ground. Before Grace took a step toward her, she lashed out with one hand and gripped Monica's neck with her very real fingers.

Monica choked, eyes wide, dropping the clocklike weapon and scratching at the hand clamping down on her windpipe.

Raga chuckled. "I see that violence is the only language you speak, Grace, so let me show you what I can do."

She squeezed Monica's neck, and Monica quit making those squeaking, gasping sounds. She quit making sounds altogether. Still scratching at Raga's hand, she kicked backward, but it was a weak kick and already her legs sagged. She couldn't hold herself up.

Grace's eyes stung. Here she had this whole plan, and it was falling apart right in front of her.

She was supposed to be the one facing Raga, not Monica. Monica wasn't supposed to be the one in that iron grip.

Rushing at the demon, she tried to plow through the shimmering shield between the sisters.

It didn't just rebuff her. It threw her twenty feet.

Karithexis skittered over and helped her up.

The smell of burnt matches invaded her nose, and she figured she was bleeding from the face or chest or something, but her chest didn't hurt from the hit or the fall alone. It hurt from failure. Monica was dying right in front of her, and her only option was to fling herself, headlong, at an impenetrable wall.

As Monica's slitted eye closed, Grace gripped Karithexis and sobbed.

*

The glow began somewhere around Monica's feet.

Scratch that. It began with Mother Mary, whose hands no longer helped form the shield. She had split off from the rest, moving in front of them, and knelt below Monica.

Her hands lit the soles of Monica's feet. The light traveled up her legs, brightening her skin from the inside out. When it reached her fingertips, it spread from each of them, shining on the faces of the surrounding sisters in ten pinpricks of iridescent light, kind of like a disco ball bouncing rainbows around the dance floor.

Some of the sisters crossed themselves. Some knelt. A couple wept.

Grace couldn't process what she was seeing at first. Raga's hand loosened, and she backed off a few steps, her wide brown eyes reflecting the light back at Grace. Her black jewel glittered, and her mouth twisted into an ugly scowl.

The light flowing into Monica from the mother flared. It covered all of her now, and the iridescent light even rushed from the ends of her hair. Everything about her shone.

Raga stumbled.

Monica stood in the air above her. She flashed a quick look at Grace, grin curling the side of her mouth and corner of her eye. She spun on a toe. "You have no power here, Raga. Leave." The light flashed with every word.

The multitude of voices spoke with her.

Grace covered her mouth. Monica had chosen.

Chosen to let Grace go and fully become who she was meant to be.

And God, she was beautiful—and so strong, and so full of joy. Grace had never loved her more than in this moment, watching her realize her true potential. Watching her make the choice she was meant to make.

"I think they've got this handled, don't you?"

Grace jumped. "Fuck's sake, Kari. Forgot you were there. What are you saying?" She glanced at the demon.

Karithexis tried to smile, her withered mouth turned up at the corners. "I think we should make like a tree." She stepped back.

A tree.

She stared at the woman in front of her, the vision doubling.

"Once my daughter is safe, kill this demon. I don't care if you take me with her, as long as my daughter is safe."

She couldn't leave it at this.

Raga still stood behind the sisters, her eyes on Grace and Karithexis, her face still twisted into a scowl. She lifted one hand and beckoned.

Karithexis sidled that way. "You know, I think if we go with Raga now, the sisters won't kill each and every one of us." Grasping Grace's arm, she started to drag her with her.

Although she gripped with extraordinary strength as always, Grace resisted. She was never going anywhere with these two. Ever again. No matter the cost.

She ripped her arm free and stepped closer to the sisters and Monica, still floating in the air about four feet above them. She repeated Monica's words. "You have no more power here, Raga."

It hurt her heart to say it, but at the same time, as Monica looked down at her with her one eye aglow, she knew it was right. It was right that she should love Monica so fiercely but still let her do this, still let her be who she was. Not who Grace wanted her to be, not who she thought it was she loved, but who she *was.*

Grace shifted her eyes to Monica instead of Raga. "You're so beautiful. You're perfect; you always have been."

"Grace," Karithexis hissed, "what the fuck are you doing?"

A smile lifted Grace's cheeks, tightening her lips against her teeth. Her heart slammed into her ribs. "I have to let you do this. I happily let you do this."

Raga grinned. "You're joking. If she becomes one of these nuns, especially the one with the archangel inside, you'll never get to love her again. She will be untouchable. Out of reach. Not yours." She stepped closer and licked her lips, her mouth and eyebrows raised in a lascivious curl. "The one night of sex will be the only sex. Is that what you want?"

It threatened to overtake her, what she was losing. A whole future she'd envisioned with Monica where they stayed up late reading to each other and traveled the world, leaving both of their pasts behind as they made love whenever and wherever they wanted.

Her insides crumpled. She had to give all that up. All of it. Raga was right.

Raga leered. "That's better, my dear. I can see it in you. You know your master is always right."

Holding her stomach, Grace lifted her eyes to Monica again.

"I can't help you, Grace," she said, her eye glowing from within. "I can't do this for you. But you remember what I told you?"

"No matter what happens, don't forget I love you. That'll never change."

Tears standing in her eyes, Grace reached for her. "I love you, too, Mon. You're perfect, just like this."

Monica leaned down and took her hand.

Grace didn't know what she expected. For Raphael to burn her, maybe. For her skin to be instantly flayed from her bones.

None of that happened. Monica's cool hand took hers, their fingers twining together.

Mon tugged, and without moving, Grace stood at eye level with her.

Stomach in free fall, she glanced at her feet.

She floated next to Monica, several feet in the air. The light from Monica's hand engulfed her own.

Peace descended over Grace. It would be okay if she loved Mon like this. The circumstances didn't change the love they had. It changed the way they expressed it, but what in life didn't change?

Raga snarled. "Fools. All of you. What have you done? She's mine. Mine." Her long fingers gripped Grace's ankle. She tugged.

Grace didn't move, didn't budge an inch, even though she floated in thin air.

"You can't!" The demon grew in size, doubled, tripled, in the space of a blink, until she stood face-to-face with Grace. "You can't do this, Grace. You cannot refuse me, demon. You cannot forget what you are."

Curling her fingers around the back of Monica's hand, Grace smiled. "I know what I am, Raga. And I choose to let go."

She released Monica's hand.

Mon leaned forward, arms outstretched like she wanted a hug from Raga. "Cover your eyes, Grace."

She did. Her fingers and eyelids dampened the blinding light, but nothing protected her ears from a scream ripping out of Raga with such violence it shattered the windows in the convent.

Eyes popping open, Grace fell to the ground and looked back at the building in time to watch the stained glass of Raphael shatter.

*

Silence descended. The sisters all lay on the ground in a semicircle around Monica and Grace.

Mon floated down, her toes touching the dried grass with a light crackling. The glow around her faded.

Mouth open, Grace sat up. "Did we win?"

With a smile large enough to split her face, Mon leaned down to help her up. "You did, Grace. You did." She threw her arms around her neck.

Grace hugged her back with everything she had.

One of the sisters shouted. "Mother!"

Oh fuck, Mary.

Grace released Mon and spun, looking for the Mother Superior.

She lay on the ground about fifteen feet away, one leg stuck behind her at an odd angle.

Heart in her throat, adrenaline dumping into her so fast her nose got stuffy, Grace ran to her and fell to her knees, sliding the last three feet or so. "Mary. Mary are you okay?"

Her chest rattled. "M'ok." Blood crusted around the edges of her nostrils, and streaks of it came from both eyes and one corner of her mouth. "Doesn't hurt." Her hand floated up into the air.

Grace grabbed it and held it close to her chest, her eyes frantically searching the mother's face. "What can I do?"

Mary gripped her hand with waning strength. "Nothing." She stared past her, eyes unfocused.

Glancing behind her, Grace saw Monica standing. But it wasn't only Mon.

For the first time, she saw the archangel. Not his picture in the stained glass. Not the glow around Monica like a full-body halo.

The outline of a being overlaid Monica's body, and their energy stretched far beyond the boundaries of Monica's form. It didn't have wings like Grace had come to expect from all the pictures she'd seen of angels, but now she understood how a human's mind might translate what it was seeing into wings.

The energy stretched all around it like tendrils, wispy at the edges. It reached the sky and folded back down on itself, moving in a constant circle of iridescent light.

In that moment, Grace understood the sheen between the sisters had been Raphael's energy, stretched between them all, a riotous rainbow of color and air.

The angel spoke, voice like a chorus of wind. "Sleep, Mother. I will see you again."

Tears bound in her throat, Grace turned back to Mary.

She was already too late. The mother had stopped breathing, her eyes closed, a smile crossing her lips.

As Grace sat, wondering if she had tears for the mother and realizing she had so many she couldn't let them go, gravel crunched.

Karithexis grinned. "Uh. Yeah. So. Sorry about your mother, ladies. I'll go, then?" She hobbled backward a few feet, removing her glasses from her pocket and sliding them on. Her fake teeth clacked together.

Grace worked to her feet. "Think we need to have a talk, Kari. I got my memory back, you know?"

"Ha-ha. I mean. About that. You know I was as much Raga's prisoner as you. I had to—"

"Had to keep me trapped? Had to make sure I never got ideas above my station? Had to make sure I tortured my quota of people each month?" As Karithexis retreated, Grace advanced. "Who told Raga I was here anyway?"

"You're misunderstanding," she said, nervous laugh squeaking through her lips. She eyed the sisters falling in behind Grace. "I didn't have a choice, okay?"

"I remember each and every one you made me kill. Some of them I even enjoyed. You're right. It wasn't all just you, killing and torturing for sport. And if you had it your way, you'd pull me right back in."

"No, that's—I—" Another nervous chuckle found its way out. She clutched her shawl around herself. "Stay back! I know what you're planning, Grace, you tricky fucker, and I won't let you kill me too. Not after I finally got free of that demonic bitch."

"You know what I'm planning? How?"

Clutching the shawl, she continued to back up. "Yeah. Tracy. She let me in your mind while we were 'transferring power.' I knew what your plan was before even you did. I came here to watch you, and I thought maybe you'd change your mind. But I see you're as much the duplicitous bitch as ever."

Without stopping her slow walk toward the demon, Grace smirked. The fact Karithexis had read her mind should shock her, but at this point, what even could anymore? "You want to talk about it?"

Eyes rolling like a wild horse, Karithexis scowled. "I still have leverage!" Her ankle buckled, and she fell on her ass.

Grace laughed. "Leverage? What could you—"

With that grin that curled her lips like a paper blower, Karithexis disappeared with a pop.

Stopping, Grace stared at the empty air, hands on her hips. She spun to Monica, who was just Mon again now, and lifted her shoulders. "Where..."

It dawned in Monica's eye at the same time it hit Grace.

Grace's heart started pumping so fast she thought she might have a heart attack. She and Monica spoke at the same time.

"Shanna."

Chapter Twenty-Five

They appeared across the street from the dark townhouse, Grace staggering into Monica. "Jesus Christ, Mon. Don't do that to me again."

Monica chuckled. "That was all you. I didn't know you could do that."

Grace raised a shaking hand to eye level. "Me neither. Holy shit. Where are we?"

Clutching her arm, Mon pointed across the street. "Shanna."

The front door hung off its hinges.

Grace glanced around them. Looked like the only one she'd grabbed before coming was Monica. Although, even before Mon's change into—what? Was she Mother Superior now?—they made a pretty formidable team. Mostly.

Checking traffic, they crossed the street, ducking out of the circles of light cast by the streetlamps. The one directly in front of Shanna's house blinked in and out, and they skirted it like the others, cozying right up next to the hedges in front of the porch. The ones Grace fell into, so long ago, the first time she stood on this porch and realized how much trouble they were really in.

She whispered in Monica's ear, "Do you think the kids are home?"

Mon nodded in silence.

Of course they were. This could only be as bad as possible, not one iota less.

Swallowing the stomach bile surging up her throat, Grace crept toward the stairs. "Let's go in."

"Wait." Mon tugged her arm. "What if she's waiting behind the door?"

Grace took another step, dragging Monica with her. "Of course she is. But she's waiting with her finger on the trigger. We have to go in." She stopped. "Is your friend with us?"

Monica shook her head. "I don't know how to work this." Her smile crooked to one side. "I think he does what he wants."

"Well, I wish he wanted to help us." Grace held up her fingertips and rubbed the air between them. Closing her eyes, she tongued the roof of her mouth. "The protective bubble is still in place. She's scared of me."

Monica chuckled. "Who wouldn't be? Did you see what you just did?"

"You did that, Mon. Or Raphael. Or whatever. Both."

"Not without your help. I couldn't have done any of it if you didn't let go."

Grace stopped creeping forward and put her hand over Monica's. "I still love you."

"Of course. I still love you. You know that." Monica angled her forehead at the house. "Let's get this done."

Relief washed over Grace's chest and unbound the breath there. A day ago, she would have been a mess, thinking she couldn't kiss Monica again, but if she hadn't meant it when she released her, Raga would have known. They never would have won that fight.

Bolstered, she pushed the listing door aside and stepped into the doorway.

Nothing but pitch black stretched down the hallway before them.

A glow came up from Monica's hand.

Mon grinned. "Guess he's helping after all." She reached into the house. "Seems like the spell Karithexis put on the house doesn't work on Raph."

"Lead the way then, glowy hands."

Sliding past her, Mon slipped into the hallway, her glowing hand outstretched. "I feel so warm. This is wild."

"I spent some time in the other Mary's head. It feels pretty damn good, I know that. I remember that."

Mon crept deeper into the hall. She whispered over her shoulder, "Where do you think they are?"

In answer, a child cried out from the kitchen.

A lump formed in Grace's throat, and Natalie pressed against her eyeballs. She was in there, watching intently, her face right up against the TV.

Before Monica rounded the corner, Grace grabbed her. *Let me,* she mouthed.

With a bow, Mon stepped back.

"Karithexis. Let's talk about this." Grace stepped into the doorway.

Shanna's voice shook. "Grace, is that you?"

"Shut up." Skin hit skin.

Someone thumped to the floor, groaning. The kids whimpered.

"Not any closer, Grace. Keep your archangel friend back too." A match flared to life and illuminated about six inches around it. The dark was so inky in this kitchen it was as if it had never known what light was.

Karithexis touched the match to a candle, reintroducing light to the room, and the candle's flame spread about another five feet.

The boys flanked her, tears wetting their faces, Conor's cheeks flushed a deep shade of brick red. The demon dug a long-fingered hand into each of their arms, snarling as Grace and Monica sidled into the room.

"That's far enough," she growled.

Grace stopped, eyes on Shanna, who lay on the ground holding her bleeding mouth. A goose egg sat over her eye, and blood dripped from it, caked in her eyebrow and caught in her lashes. Clearly, she'd been about to go to bed or even in bed when Karithexis showed up because her face was, for once, bare of makeup. Her vulnerability sat on her face like it was the paint, not the other way around.

Her lip trembled, and she looked at the boys.

Karithexis whipped them both around, shaking them so hard their teeth clacked.

They cried, especially the youngest one, Deandre. With one hand, he clutched his crotch, where a wet stain spread between his legs.

Heat crept up Grace's chest, starting in her stomach. Her breath hot enough to be literal fire, she opened her mouth and tried to spit it at the demon. "Let those children go. They've got nothing to do with us."

Shanna sat up and leaned against the cabinet, her head tilted back. She pinched the bridge of her nose, presumably to stop the steady flow of blood from her nostril. "Please," she said, her voice nasal, "please give them to me."

Karithexis handed off the youngest one. He clutched Shanna and stared over his shoulder at Grace. He was silent, round brown eyes peeping out from his face.

But Karithexis clutched the other boy, pulling him against her chest. "I'm only here to make you promise to let me go. I'm doing what I have to do. How do I know you won't kill me as soon as I hand him over?"

Bile crawling up her throat again, Natalie leaning so hard on her eyes she could hardly keep them open without pain, Grace shrugged. "We're both powerless here. How could I hurt you when I have no weapons?" She lifted both arms in the air in an attempt to prove she was unarmed.

Which was so thoughtless. Why hadn't they brought weapons?

But the demon nodded. "You're right; how could you?" She clacked her false teeth together. "How, indeed? I can't believe you would turn on me, after all this. You said you got your memories back. You don't remember, none of this was my fault?"

Flashes of memory assaulted Grace at the mention.

Karithexis handing her a knife she used to eviscerate some poor man.

Karithexis knotting a noose so Grace could tie it around the neck of another man, throwing it over the sturdy limb of a tree and kicking over a stool beneath him to make it look like suicide, while his wife and kids sat inside, having dinner.

Karithexis plotting against Raga with her, while at the same time jabbing the dirty end of a needle full of heroin into a woman's arm as she lay on the filthy floor.

Grace's face hardened. "You don't deserve to live."

The demon snarled. "Neither do you, my dear." She lifted Conor's hand above his head, gripping his fingers in hers. She waved the other hand.

The bubble Karithexis had laid over the house disappeared in a sigh of breeze.

Meaning Grace was at full power again.

But so was Karithexis.

She snapped one of Conor's fingers like a twig.

The poor baby screamed, his entire face red, and Shanna screamed with him.

In fact, someone else was screaming, and it didn't surprise Grace to realize it was her own vocal cords vibrating. Natalie screamed from inside, too, and the chorus of them was like a symphony of the damned.

The demon threw the screaming boy at Grace.

She smacked into the table and sent it onto its side as she dove to catch him, to heal him, to fix what this demon was putting so wrong.

She started to find his river, what would surely be a babbling brook at his age, but a glowing hand landed on her shoulder.

"We can take care of him," the multitude of voices said. "You must pursue the demon."

Grace's head snapped up. "What do you mean, pursue?" She glanced across the kitchen, expecting to see the back door flung wide, the white hair of the demon bouncing across the backyard as she made her exit.

Instead of something as pedestrian as an open door, the crimson-lined rip in the air filled the kitchen.

Without thinking of how she'd get back, she sprinted through the door to the Realm.

*

The dark swirled around her, nipping at her hair and the tips of her fingers. A lot like when they escaped the Realm, the air was almost goopy like petroleum jelly.

Grace held her breath and walked toward the only light, a red light roughly the same shape as the rip she'd come through. Her footsteps echoed in the gelatinous air like they would through water.

Cloing, cloing, bloing.

The hole got smaller.

Picking up her feet faster, Grace tried to rush toward it, but it was like running through molasses, or like she was in a dream, and her feet were covered in cement and she was trying to swim. She used her hands to grip the air and propel herself forward.

Still, the hole inched closed.

If she didn't get to it before it sealed itself, would she stay stuck in whatever this limbo was?

Her lungs burned for a breath. Just one breath.

The closing hole created an optical illusion that she never got any closer, but she kept clawing at the air, shoving her feet against a ground she couldn't see.

Eventually, she reached it. It was barely bigger than her if she lay down.

Lungs still burning, she stuck her hands out as though she were diving and leapt.

She came through the hole, the dry air of this place hitting her as soon as she cleared it and landed on her shoulder. Rolling, she tried to minimize the blow, but her shoulder popped like a shotgun going off. She was at least a little surprised when she sat up, looked at it, and found it still in place.

She took in her surroundings.

It wasn't the hallway full of desperate people, eating their own intestines, begging for a way out. It wasn't the hallway with the wooden doll and the burned hunk of wood—the piece of wood Grace now knew must have come from one of the many stake burnings she'd witnessed with glee.

It wasn't the field of flowers where she'd spoken with Raga for the first time.

But this was a garden, filled with growing trees and shrubs. Statues spread about a place that had once been manicured and cared for but had now fallen to overgrowth and ruin.

She stood and inspected the nearest tree.

The peaches growing on it rotted on their stems. Maggots crawled around in one of them.

Lip curled, she backed up and glanced at another tree.

This one, apple, its fruit rotted like the peach tree. Funny thing was, it didn't litter the ground under the tree like rotted fruit should. No, it was still on the stem, ready to be picked and eaten.

Like this was the kind of place where rotted fruit was the harvest.

Gut rolling, she wandered until she came to the center of the garden.

Two statues stood in a circular area surrounded with a low marble wall. The statues themselves were of a man and a woman, each perfectly carved from marble and shining with something like their own inner light. The man was broad-chested, bearded, with curly hair that touched his shoulders. Half a mischievous grin played on his delicate marble lips.

The woman was beautiful almost beyond compare. Her hair fell in ringlets all around her face and shoulders, down almost to the breasts, which rested freely beneath her robes. Her tiny nose upturned, she gazed skyward with one hand uplifted. She had gorgeous full, wide hips Grace imagined would sway when she walked.

Between them grew another tree or large bush. On it hung dozens of red, round fruits, ripe and shining pomegranates.

She plucked one from the vine, the only fruit in this whole garden that hadn't rotted from the inside still hanging on the tree.

With one fingernail, she tore it open.

The inside glittered with seeds, ruby red and shining. She'd dug into one with her thumbnail, and the juice ran down her hand, staining her skin. She licked it off.

It hit her tongue like what ruby red should taste like, dark and sweet, with a hint of sour.

She wanted to peel a seed from the inside; in fact, she stuck a nail under one and lifted it from the bed of white membrane.

Stone grated over stone, like the sound of boulders scraping down a mountain on their way to crush the landscape below.

Grace looked up, pausing in her struggle with the seed.

The statue of the woman had moved. She no longer stared skyward, and her features twisted. Her brows drew together, wrinkles in her perfect marble forehead, her mouth open as if to shout.

One hand was now outstretched toward Grace.

The juice still fresh in her mouth, she glanced down at the fruit in her hand.

Maggots crawled down her wrist, wriggling away from the rotted fruit in her palm.

With a shout, she dropped it. The rest of the fruit on the tree was now rotted. Moldy clumps hung from the branches.

Unsure where the exit was but willing to run anyway, Grace dashed away from the two statues and their tricky tree. She ran between rows and rows of rotted figs and berries, olive trees and grape vines with curled and blackened leaves.

A stone wall appeared in front of her, and she followed it. The garden stank of rot, of old, moldy fruit so far past its expiration date it had mostly liquidized by now. Her hands flew across the rough wall as she ran, the stench almost unbearable, tears standing in her eyes, and she searched for the way out.

She found an old wooden gate, scratchy and weather-worn. Wrapping her fingers around the rusty handle, she flipped the latch.

"Leaving the garden so soon, Grace?"

*

Grace's insides froze, eyes popping out of her head. She turned, fingers still wrapped around the burred and rusted gate handle, feeling for all the world like that statue turning around, like stone scraping against stone.

Karithexis smiled at her, false teeth clacking, glasses chain swaying. "Clever of you to follow me. How'd you get through without the ferryman, anyway?" She glanced over her shoulder.

Stammering, Grace stepped sideways. "Why did you hurt that child? He didn't do anything to you."

Karithexis curled her lip. "I thought you'd gotten your memory back. You know why."

And as much as she wanted to deny it, she did. She knew. Giving pain to others made hers a little less, for a blissful moment. It was the only joy she'd had in life before she lost her memory, before she met the Order, before Monica. Any excuse to cause pain was enough to do it. Over. And over. And over and over and over.

Grace shook her head. "That's not me anymore."

The demon snarled. "Don't give me that shit." She took a step and stood right up against Grace, face to chest.

Fighting the urge to bend down, Grace struggled against her own feet. She wasn't about to take a step back and lose ground.

Karithexis gripped her shoulder with iron fingers. "You might not want to tell me what your plan was, but I know you want to kill me. I won't let you do it." She dug her thumb into Grace's shoulder, pushing her down. "Why do you think I called Raga?" She seethed.

Grace's knees buckled. She sank down, the garden surrounding her with the stench of rotted fruit, Karithexis herself wafting off waves of that burnt match smell.

"You're not stronger than me, Grace. You want to be. But you're not." She scowled. "All this love and forgiveness, all this 'letting go' bullshit. It doesn't make you stronger than me. It makes you weak." Her clawed fingers dug deeper.

Grace moaned under the strain, her shoulder creaking, the tendons popping. If she couldn't get the demon to let go soon, she was likely to tear her arm completely from her body.

Through the pain, she couldn't think what to do.

It doesn't make you weak, Grace. It makes you strong.

Nat, coming to her rescue. She'd never done that. Grace felt her in there, almost like a hug from the inside. Warmth spread from her head down.

Grace put one foot under her and pushed up. Though the claw in her shoulder seemed to grow talons, digging deeper and deeper, breaking the skin, she stood against it.

The scowl on Karithexis's face deepened, her dentures pressed together so hard they cracked. "You can't beat me. You never could." As she spoke, pieces of the false teeth flew from her mouth, mixed with spit and blood. Some of them landed on Grace's shirt.

Grace gripped Karithexis's wrist and twisted, digging her fingers in next to the tendon there.

Karithexis shouted and let her go. But Karithexis wasn't done yet.

She seethed through her teeth, bubbling spit foaming, still mixed with blood and bits of dentures, and growled in that language Grace almost recognized.

She recognized it now, though, the meaning of those words. Her returned memory gave her that.

It was an ancient spell, as old as the idea of demons themselves, as old as humanity, maybe more. And it was aimed at Grace, with the intent to rip what she was from the body of Natalie, to send her spiraling away from this corporeal form, so Karithexis could tear Nat limb from limb and then drink whatever was left of Grace, dumping her essence into her own frothing river of rage.

Without thinking about it, Grace charged her and gripped both shoulders, staring into her eyes and trying to find the river in the center of her, trying to enter that space and do whatever it took to stop her. Poison the river, maybe, drain it dry like Daisy's, or turn up the sun and cause every last drop to evaporate until Karithexis was nothing.

She almost succeeded. She forced her way into her head, or wherever the river was, looking down on the scene as she had before. The white river foamed at its banks, angry water rushing toward the crushing cacophony of a waterfall around the next bend.

Nat's mom clung to her tree, the whole thing drenched and hanging just above the roiling surface.

She cried, gripping the tree, her shaking arms and legs wrapped around it. Her wild eyes met Grace's.

She shouted over the raging river, "Kill her! I don't care what happens to me!"

Before Grace spoke, to ask her if there was any way out of this that didn't include her murder, the demon fought back.

"Get out!" Her screaming voice boomed in the grove, and an invisible rope tied itself around Grace's neck, yanking her from the scene and back into the garden, where the walls shook so hard pieces of them broke off and slammed into the soft dirt below.

Karithexis knelt on top of her, her knees in Grace's chest. She pressed down with all her weight.

She might have been ninety-eight pounds soaking wet, but as she knelt on Grace's chest and dug her knees in, she must have weighed two tons.

Grace struggled to escape, to move, to breathe. Red bars lined the sides of her vision, and she stared up at the deep gray sky of this underworld, with rolling black clouds, their white swirls and edges almost invisible in the storm.

Let me help, Grace. Bring her to me.

Better than nothing.

Staring into the demon's eyes, Grace reached out of her own chest with a giant, incorporeal hand much like what Raga had used to grab them both. She'd never known it was there, but as it surged out of her, it hit her that it'd been there all along; she just didn't know how to use it.

Grin crossing her lips, she grabbed the demon with that hand and tugged.

As they both tumbled backward into the dark, Karithexis screamed, sounding more like a lion than an old woman.

*

The spotlight was a few feet away. Grace crawled toward it, gripping a hand in her own. Arms reached into the dark and grabbed her, helping her that last two feet or so to the spotlight.

"Here, I'll pull you. You bring her."

Nat.

Grace did, yanking and cursing, the demon nothing but dead weight.

Finally, the three of them were surrounded by the spotlight and all the things Natalie had decorated with to make it comfortable. Now there were three walls, and it was almost a complete house.

The demon stirred.

Her body looked like Grace's, when she'd looked down at herself inside Daisy's head. She glowed opalescent, but the red spots that'd been so sparse on Grace literally covered Karithexis. If Grace stared at them too long, she made out shapes swirling inside, not unlike the sky over the garden in the Realm.

"Quick." Nat pushed her hair out of her face and grabbed at Grace, helping her sit up. "Do something."

Grace climbed to her feet, clutching Nat. She shook her head, no idea what she'd do now that she'd brought the demon here.

Karithexis chuckled. Her voice sounded different. Younger. But also deeper, more threatening. "Oh good. Thank you, Grace. Now when I kill you, I'll get Natalie. If I'm being honest, I would have preferred her body to begin with. She's much younger, obviously, but her gift is even greater than her mother's." She stood, smiling at Nat, and the shaky outline of her face solidified for a moment.

It was like looking into the face of pure spite. Folded eyebrows, deep frown lines, the expression of malice greater than any Grace imagined possible on a being. It was worse than Raga at her angriest. It was worse than staring down the mother. She broke out in a cold sweat.

The demon laughed again. "We'll make a good team, Natalie."

"Bitch, I don't think so." Nat picked up the nearest object, a giant crystal ashtray, and, with a grunt, flung it at Karithexis.

She didn't duck. She let it hit her square in the face.

It bounced off and rolled away.

Nat backed up and whispered under her breath, "Your turn, Grace."

Shoving the fear aside, Grace lunged at the demon, hands out. What she planned to do she didn't know, but it made no difference.

Karithexis grabbed her, those shifting hands wrapped around her wrist and neck, and lowered her head. A set of pointed teeth materialized where a mouth would be.

Grace brought up her other hand, getting it in the way of those teeth before they took a chunk out of her neck.

Red pain seared her palm, and she screamed, kicking at the demon.

They spun in a circle, bound to each other. Blood flew as the demon gnawed on Grace's hand, laughing through it and spraying it into her face.

It stung her eyes. She tried to rip her hand from the fangs, but the pain flattened her.

Nat screamed and came out of nowhere with a fireplace poker.

Grace threw her hips sideways and exposed the demon's midsection.

Ramming the poker through Karithexis with a shout, Nat broke the connection between the demon and Grace.

Grace stumbled, holding her bleeding hand to her chest. It throbbed with every quick heartbeat.

The demon snarled again, hand on the poker. It'd gone all the way through her and stuck out the back. She laughed, exposing each and every bloody tooth. "You think this'll hurt me? That's your plan?" She closed the distance between them and smiled. "It's going to be fun eating your heart."

Her heart.

Grace lunged for her.

Karithexis danced away. "It was a good try, my old friend. I'll remember you when—"

Nat grabbed her shoulders from behind and pulled the demon close. The poker rammed into her gut, and blood splattered the black floor and the leather couch. She moaned, peeking over the shifting demon's shoulder, and coughed blood. "Do it now, Grace."

And not that Grace had a clear idea of what Nat wanted her to do, but it was now, or it was never.

She grabbed the poker and stepped into the demon. "Say hi to Raga for me."

Plunging her hand between two red spots and into the shifting opalescence, right in the center of the demon's body, she gripped the first solid thing she found and pulled with everything she had.

Her whole forearm came out covered in dripping black viscera, the edges of it red, and in her fist, she held a beating heart.

The demon's eyes wide, she stared at it as it beat slower and slower. "I can't believe you figured out how to do that."

The heart stopped.

Karithexis dropped to the ground.

*

Grace opened her eyes and looked around the garden.

Nat's mom lay several feet away, half in and half out of a planter.

Clutching her middle, the scar from her intestinal wound open and bleeding again, Grace crawled to her and stuck two bloody fingers on her neck.

The heart inside beat. Weak, but it beat.

She hugged the woman and pulled her out of the planter, laying her head in her lap. She scooted until she could lean against the nearest low marble wall, what turned out to be the wall surrounding the two mysterious statues. Struggling with the pain of the freshly opened wound, she stared up into the dark sky and considered how she might escape. Maybe they were all stuck here.

At least both Raga and Karithexis had been defeated. There was that. Nat's family would be safe.

Grace had kept her end of the deal.

The fruit in this garden might be rotted, but otherwise, it wasn't so terrible here.

She closed her eyes.

Floating into unconsciousness, maybe bleeding to death, the peace that washed over her lay like a warm blanket, fluffy and just from the dryer. She snuggled into the feeling, drifting and trying not to think of seeing Monica one last time.

Footsteps in the garden.

Grace cracked her eyes and watched as a shadowy figure approached, someone she felt she should recognize.

As they got closer, they resolved into a woman.

She wore a simple dress, cut from one piece of cloth and fitted at the waist before it draped down to her feet. A piece of cloth also draped over her head and tied under her chin, not like the nuns and their veil or even Monica's headscarf, but simply a piece of cloth made to cover her head. Smiling as she approached, her lips red and eyes brown like Nat's, she knelt next to Grace. Thick lashes framed her almond-shaped eyes. "Hi, Grace."

Grace fought to keep her heavy eyes open. "Hi. Have we met? I feel like I should know you."

The woman smiled wider and sat cross-legged on the ground in front of her, pooling her skirt around her. "We haven't been formally introduced, I guess." She stuck out a pale hand.

With her red and bloody hand, Grace took it and shook.

And it hit her, much like it had when she'd looked into her eyes the first time.

It was her. This was her, as she had been in life.

She gripped the woman's hand. "I don't understand. How are you there and not here?"

The other Grace frowned, laying her free hand over their clasped ones. "The things I did, they were awful. I've torn myself apart over it. For eons. Over and over, we've torn ourselves apart, self-imposed punishment for what we did."

"I still don't understand. How can we be separate?"

"We were stuck in the illusion of separation. Stuck." Her face faded. "We're not stuck anymore, Grace. And I'm going to help you get these women home."

Fading still, she leaned over Grace, and whatever substance she was made of, more than light but less than flesh, rained onto Grace's face like a soft mist.

If that feeling of beating Karithexis lay over her like a warm blanket, the feeling of being whole again was beyond description. The power, the intensity of the healing was the most peaceful thing that had ever happened to her. She couldn't even measure it.

Her eyes slipped closed again.

Chapter Twenty-Six

The sanctuary loomed over her.

Behind her, the sun had barely crested the horizon, golden beams of light cascading onto the top of the building. They lit the bell tower, the bell inside shimmering in the soft dawn.

Nat's mom hung on her hip. She still hadn't opened her eyes.

Clutching her own bleeding abdomen, Grace dragged her to the door. Before laying her palm on the giant handle, she paused. Would it burn her again?

But it didn't.

She gripped the handle and pulled the door open, dragging the elderly woman inside with her.

Holding her breath, she laid her down on the carpet in the foyer, grabbed a forgotten jacket off a hook, and balled it up to put under Nat's mom's head. Funny how she'd never learned the woman's name.

Staggering back to her feet, she glanced down at her stomach wound.

Still open, still bleeding. It didn't burn; in fact, she almost didn't feel it at all.

She stumbled into the sanctuary, expecting it to be empty. She'd have to go find the sisters and hope they were home. There was no telling if this was the same night or if a week had passed or what.

Someone knelt in front, under the giant crucifix in the center of the sanctuary. Someone with a headscarf.

Grace limped down the center aisle, leaning on every other pew, passing the one where she'd met Daisy with a glance. Her bloody hand left prints on every bench she touched.

As Monica turned around from her prayer, Grace stumbled again and went to her knees. The stone floor rushed to meet them, the audible crack bouncing off the high ceiling.

Mon ran down the aisle as Grace's head lolled.

The stained glass of Uriel had remained intact. Grace guessed he wouldn't look anything like the stern angel in the glass with wings of feathers and gossamer light. He might not even look like a he. Who knew?

Monica knelt next to her and took her hand. "What happened?"

Grace's eyes rolled, trying to catch Mon's. "Are Shanna and the kids okay?"

"They're fine. Raphael took care of them. They're here, if you want to see them."

Grace closed her eyes, squeezing Monica's hand, and lay back on the smooth stone. "No. You're enough. Can you help them with Nat's charity?"

With a chuckle, Mon squeezed her back. "If that's what you want, I will. The church will help."

Grace nodded, her head scraping along the floor. She breathed deep, wondering what would happen to her if Nat's body died.

Monica whispered her name. "Can you heal yourself?"

Grace shook her head. "I don't think so. The wound came from inside me. It's not the right shape. I can't get my fingers around it." A thought hit her like a bolt of lightning. She sat up, pain ripping through her center. "Oh! Nat's mom. She's in the foyer. She's alive. Natalie helped me save her. She helped me kill Karithexis. That's how this happened." She gestured at her bleeding body.

"Okay, okay, Grace. Lay down." She pushed her shoulder. "Let me look at you."

She did.

Fabric rustled.

Grace looked over.

Mon had taken out her sacrament pouch and laid it open. She picked through the contents, shaking her head with her lips pressed together.

Reaching for her, Grace cleared her throat. "I think if you—" She stopped, blood collecting in her throat. "I don't know, but I think if you get me out of here, you can save Natalie."

Mon's face twisted. "No. That's—"

"Come on, Monica. We both know I can't stay. I never could." Tears collected with the blood in her throat. She struggled to breathe around them. "Your turn to let me go."

Tears dripping from her eye, Mon grabbed a communion wafer and the small vial of wine from the open sacrament pouch. Chin trembling, she turned back to Grace. "Have communion with me?"

Grace let go of her bleeding abdomen and gripped Monica's other hand. Unable to speak through the tears, she nodded.

Mon broke the wafer in half, murmured about the body of Christ, and stuck half on her tongue. She lowered the other half to Grace's mouth.

That burned. Yeah, it did.

But Grace closed her lips around it and let it dissolve on her tongue, sizzling as it did.

"Wine," Mon said, tipping the vial into her own mouth. She sipped half the vial and leaned over Grace.

The light came up behind Monica, around her.

It trebled in Grace's eyes, swirling like a prism around Monica's head. Grace sipped the wine and swallowed it and the wafer.

The vial clinked on the stone floor.

Hands glowing, Monica leaned over her. "Ready?"

Grace shook her head. "Do it anyway."

Monica reached for the sides of her head with her glowing hands.

Grace's bloody ones caught them, and she swallowed around the tears again, thick in her throat. "Not Raphael. Just you, Mon. Just you."

Tears dripping from her chin into her robes, Monica sat back and closed her eye. The glow faded.

"Do it in English, so I know what you're saying for once. Will that be okay?"

"It'll be fine, Grace." Monica opened her deep brown eye, thick lashes wet, and tried to smile. "It'll be fine."

With no voice left, Grace mouthed, *I love you.*

Mon did the same, wiping her cheeks. *I love you back.*

And then she spoke.

Demon, be free.

Forgiven are you, your mistakes.

Lifted from you, your anger.

Away from you the sadness,

And no more despair.

Give us your fear,

We give you love.

We free you from this life.

Leave this vessel as you found it.

Released from your burdens,

Free of your guilt,

Demon, you are free.

Epilogue

In the End

Against all reason, Grace opened her eyes.

Probably. She was like that shifting ball of light that hung over Jalithesh and disappeared. And so, she didn't have real eyes to open.

But she wasn't hanging over Nat's body, or her own, or anything. She was just here, wherever here was. It was no more solid than cloudy gray mist.

Emotion, and feeling, and all of it, had left her. She had no pain, physical or emotional.

She'd been healed. And freed. But where was she? Was this heaven? Was there even a heaven?

The cloudy mist around her brightened.

She turned around, trying to find the source of the light, but it came from everywhere.

If she had a heart, if she was corporeal at all, her heart would be beating a thousand miles a minute. As it was, she waited as the light brightened, shimmering with iridescence.

A shape materialized out of it, vaguely human-shaped, vaguely smiling. There was no way to assign gender, which wasn't necessary anyway. Given its shifting glow, she knew what it was.

An archangel.

The vague suggestion of a face lifted in a grin. "Dear Grace. In all my years of overseeing the Realm and the creatures in it, I have seen less than a dozen like you. I have come to offer you a rare opportunity."

Though she had no mouth, or vocal cords, or anything to help, she spoke. "Like me? Who are you?"

The smile went on. "Where are my manners? You can call me Uriel, if it would help you to name me." The shape floated closer, the iridescence increasing in its circling vibration. "I've overseen the Realm since the beginning of time. Only a few of your kind find their way out on their own, free of their torment. Only a few."

Its smile, its feeling of joy, enveloped her. If she had a mouth to smile, she would. "So what does this mean? Where do I go? Is this heaven?"

Laughter surrounded her. "No, dear, it's not. Not in the way you understand it. Regardless." The suggestion of a face materialized a bit more, cheekbones high and shining with rainbow light. "I have a favor to ask you. If you say yes, many years more will you have to experience the wonders you've come to love. To be among humans once again, to take advantage of all the things you wish you'd done." It moved closer, almost looming. "Many more years to make up for the pain you've caused in others."

Something shifted against her.

She looked down. Her own arms took shape, marks up and down them, wrapped around the inside and out like swirling tattoos, each a collection of twisted lines.

"These marks represent the pain you've caused over your life and throughout your time as a demon. If you choose to return to Earth, I'll remove one of them for every time you do its opposite."

She tried to swallow, even without a throat. "If I refuse?"

"If you say no," Uriel said, the iridescent shape growing darker, more solid, "you will end up back on Earth, but with no memory of your past life. You will have to learn, all over again, what you have already learned. No matter what, you must repay the pain you've caused."

Even with the fear creeping over her like a cloak, what could be construed as a threat looming over her, Grace couldn't refuse this being. "Is that all you want me to do? Help people?"

"Not exactly. Take what you've learned back to Earth. Use it to help others, stuck as you were. Use it to save people bent on a path that would lead them down your own. Free those who would remain in the Realm before they arrive. Or"—the smile widened—"those on Earth, wreaking havoc as you were."

"You want me to hunt demons?"

"For starters. Are you in?"

Acknowledgements

My family, as always, are my very favorite people and saints for putting up with me. I couldn't thank you enough for being awesome. My friends, especially those of you who beta read for me regularly, what would I do without you? You're the best!

Thanks to the team at NineStar Press for making my little demon book a reality!

About Bethany A. Perry

Bethany writes sci-fi, horror, and fantasy, and she is dabbling in romance under a pen name. After *Supernatural* ended, she took some time off. Grief is a thing she knows well, and writing is always something deeply personal to her. She shares stories with the hope others will be able to use them to heal, as she does.

Look for her other novels wherever books are sold: *Reclamation*, its sequel, *Reclamation 2: Revolution*, and *Reclamation 3: Reconstruction* available summer 2021.

Visit her website at bperrywrites.com to find out more and sign up for the mailing list, where you will be alerted to new releases.

Email
bperrywrites@yahoo.com

Facebook
www.facebook.com/bperrywrites

Twitter
@bperry_writes

Website
www.bperrywrites.com

Also from NineStar Press

Gretel on Her Own by Elna Holst

Once upon a time, a brother and sister were led away into the depths of the forest. It was only to protect them, their mother explained and the brother concurred; yet he insisted on pebbles, bread crumbs. He insisted on looking back for cats and pigeons and whatnots, brightened by the touch of the sun.

Twenty years later, Gretel Kindermann is on her own: her father has taken himself off to Dortmund, her mother is a fixture at the local mental healthcare institution, and her brother Hänsel, oh—

At the heart of the matter, like a thorny-rooted weed, is Frau Heckscher, the purveyor of all things sweet in the little village at the lip of the forest. And now, perhaps, also a niece that no one has heard of before, lately arrived from Vienna to wreak havoc on poor Gretel's nerves and heart.

In *Gretel on Her Own*, Elna Holst offers a contemporary sapphic twist to your favourite Germanic fairy tale of homicidal arsonists and houses built out of baked goods, trickster witches, and parenting skills that leave a lot to be desired.

Buried by Lizzie Strong

Quinn's mistake wasn't killing Leo Ashwood; it was bringing him back. Now in a cat and mouse game with a monster she created, Quinn learns what her powers are truly capable of.

Brought together by a vision, Cecelia and Quinn are entangled in the chase for Leo Ashwood. Cecelia, a seer who is known for sticking her nose into other's business for their better good, is now sent into a world unknown to her with no defense against the monster, her own powers, and the budding feelings for Quinn. Maggie, however, was merely at the wrong place at the wrong time and left with no other choice but to join forces. An up and coming

YouTube superstar struck down by sickness, her voice is both her magical survival and death wrapped in one.

These three young, untrained witches will have to lean on each other if they want to survive. Navigating the world of humans, the new reality of witches, and the horror of magic, they might just make it... if they can keep their secrets to themselves.

Witch, Cat, and Cobb by J.K. Pendragon

Destined for an arranged marriage she wants nothing to do with, Princess Breanwynne decides her only option for escape is to run away. After announcing this plan to her trusted cat, Fen, she's shocked when he asks that she take him along.

Following his suggestion to venture into the lair of the Swamp Witch begins a life-altering adventure and reveals shocking information that will lead to more than one happily ever after—if she and Fen survive.

Connect with NineStar Press

www.ninestarpress.com

www.facebook.com/ninestarpress

www.facebook.com/groups/NineStarNiche

www.twitter.com/ninestarpress

www.instagram.com/ninestarpress